slee

R.A.Sharpe

Sparkleberry Books
www.sparkleberry-books.co.uk

Sparkleberry Books
Stanton
Ashbourne
Derbyshire DE6 2DA
www.sparkleberry-books.co.uk

ISBN 0-9548185-0-4

First Edition – limited print run 2004-06-20

First Published in Great Britain by Sparkleberry Books

Copyright © R. A. Sharpe

Printed and bound in Great Britain by
TJ International Ltd, Padstow, Cornwall

Introduction

"…and with one stroke that thou givest him, he shall no longer live. And if he ask thee to give him another, give it not, how much soever he may entreat thee, for when I did so, he fought with me next day as well as ever before."
Extract from The Mabinogion, translated by Lady Charlotte Guest (1812 – 1895)

The Mabinogion exists, only it's nature is in dispute.

Chapter 1

Etta lay where she had fallen, soon she would be as cold as the worn slates of the kitchen floor. Above her, a calm hand wrapped two small pieces of magnetic ironstone in oak leaves and began to bind the wrapping with a thin leafless strip of ivy.

The sun blazed through the large rotten windows to the man's right, but no one was likely to be on the moor today and if they were, all they would see would be a figure at the window of a farmhouse.

He crouched down and placed the stones into the top pocket of Etta's overalls. He had watched her heart stop pumping and vividly seen her body fall, as a boulder into a pond whose surface had been calm for too many years. Placing one hand over the secreted stones he spoke in Welsh, "Deliver unto me my enemies."

The barren house held no more interest for now and he left by the front door.

* * * *

A few months after Etta's death, her closest neighbours, the Becks, were seated for lunch around the large oak table that vied with the Aga to be their kitchen's focal point. The tension that George Beck had become used to at meal times filled the spaces between the four family members at the table.

George and his wife were archetypal in their appearance, both well built and ruddy complexioned. George's large frame kept the spare tractor tyre around his waist from making him look obese. But it was at personal appearance that the stereotypical nature of the Becks ended.

The house was the opposite of Etta's; the units were all fitted and of solid oak, whilst the appliances shouted out their brand names. It was untidy, but only in the way that seems fashionable amongst the well-off country dweller with gun dogs and children.

The unpleasant atmosphere at the table was brought, as it always was, by Muriel, the Beck's youngest daughter. George had produced one daughter that he was proud of, Hazel. But an identical upbringing had produced Muriel, a seventeen-year-old rebel who held her family at the top of her "most despised" list.

Today, as always, Muriel was dressed entirely in black. There was black eyeliner, applied in mimicry of an ancient Egyptian style, black lipstick, black nail varnish and dyed black hair, which seemed to be master of its own destiny and was at present trying to get as far away from Muriel's head as it could.

Muriel's appearance was not a fashion statement; it certainly was not what her friends wore, for the only people who approached being friendly with her these days were the boys who paid her more than enough attention. But they had only one thing on their minds, her well deserved reputation, the foundations of which had first come to George's attention two years ago when he happened upon her having sex in one of his hay barns. The young lad had managed to outrun Mr Beck and lived to tell the tale. When George returned to the barn to chastise his daughter, he found her unrepentant.

"You like farming," she had said whilst buttoning her shirt. "I like fucking."

Today as then, hate was in Muriel's eyes as she watched the family eat, every one of their actions grating upon her mind. How did her sister manage to crunch peas? The muck under her father's nails, the smell of sheep dung that hung about the retrievers and the loathsome whistling that accompanied her mother's breathing.

"I see they've found an heir for next door," George said conversationally, referring to Etta's old place. "Very strange chap he is."

"Strange because he's not like you do you mean?" spat Muriel.

George rode the comment and continued, "He said he was Etta's nephew and that they'd had a bit of difficulty finding him because he's been living rough. Looks like a bleeding gypsy as well."

"He's moved in then?" Muriel asked.

"Yes," replied her father suspiciously. "He moved in last night."

That jogged Mrs. Beck's memory. "Talking of last night, something took a hen from the shed again."

"Fox?" enquired her husband.

"You know as well as I do that foxes can't get at our hens," she replied.   The conversation meandered into the tedious territory of hen husbandry. Muriel gave her half-full plate to one of the dogs and left the house, grinning at the beckoning of a new adventure.

As she walked along the long tarmaced road leading from her home, she skipped over the potholes and laughed aloud in expectation of a conquest and in reminiscence of past victories. Any time away from her family was bliss and this early evening had a perfect quality to it.

A clear blue sky allowed the sun's rays to heat up Muriel's body through the absorbent black that she wore. She thought of herself as a black cat, soaking up the heat, using it as a mild tranquilliser that would not allow her mind to concentrate upon what she would say or how she would react to the man she was about to meet.

The land in the area was mainly moor, and it was this barren aspect to it that she loved, often casting herself as a Kathy, yet to find her Heathcliffe.

The farmhouse that Muriel eventually reached was smaller and in far worse a state of repair than her house, but it did look like a home, cold but inviting, a refuge that had stood against the wind of centuries.

Muriel rapped the simple doorknocker, despite the fact that the door was hanging on by one hinge and leaning at such an angle that it had worn a groove into the slate floor and was now only partially closed.

Muriel expected to hear the sound of shoes walking towards the door, but she received no such warning. Instead she saw the door move, at first upwards, square with the doorframe and then inwards to reveal Etta's nephew.

Muriel received the briefest of overall first impressions before the man spoke and her attention was drawn to his eyes, bright blue, set against dark skin and black stubble gave them a life unconnected to the body, like predatory eyes standing out from the undergrowth in which the rest of the beast was hidden.

"Hello?" he said, a question not an answer. A fleeting smile giving a slight hint of nervousness.

His fresh eyes were not matched by the rest of his appearance. Unkempt black hair, which came to rest upon his shoulders, complemented his torn clothes, whilst a long, red, baggy jumper only hinted at an average build distorted a little by a slightly hung head.

Muriel replied, "Hello, I'm from the farm across the road. I just thought I'd call round and say hi. That's what neighbours are meant to do isn't it?" Her voice was confident but the accompanying bobbing motion of her body gave her a vulnerable appearance that, combined with an almost embarrassed smile, gave Muriel the look that always worked.

"Well, I'm pleased to meet you, neighbour. I'm Kerry Taliesin." Kerry was poor at guessing ages and Muriel's make-up was not helping.

"Muriel," she replied. Kerry's bare feet on the cold slate distracted her attention away from his face. She almost didn't want to look up again, she would certainly end up in those eyes and their stare was so intense as to be unnerving, regardless of the attraction that Muriel was sure she had spied in them. Muriel did look up again, she couldn't contemplate those feet forever. "Another thing neighbours are meant to do is to offer a new arrival a drink, but it was a little far to carry one from our farm."

Kerry's smile widened, he had appreciated Muriel's cheeky request. "Come in then. I'll sort some drinks out and you can tell me what I've let myself in for." His voice was strongly accented with a rough vernacular but it flowed smoothly from his lips and, like a hand, reached out and touched Muriel's most delicate parts.

She smiled. "And you can give me the gossip on yourself." Kerry's eyes didn't move but easily conveyed a light-hearted threat; his gossip was not a subject for discussion. He turned and walked into the house, she followed.

A musty smell was laminated with a hint of dog. Bare dusty stairs led up from the dirty red tiles and a small window kept the room in a dusk-like state.

Muriel was taken into what had been a large sitting room. Now it was too poorly furnished to give it such a name: one rocking chair, a pile of rugs just managing to form a bed, one tea chest full of books topped off by a fiddle, and beside that an open chest revealing a jumble of clothes and more books.

In spite of its empty appearance, Muriel liked the room. It was as a fairy tale witch would have it, except that where she would have had her black cat, in front of the fireplace, lay a huge grey dog.

The dog, a wolfhound Muriel presumed, was asleep when they entered the room. She sat down in the rocking chair without being asked, trying to appear more confident than she actually was. The chair squeaked a little as Muriel settled into it, and the dog opened one eye to look at her for a short moment before closing it again, arrogant, Muriel felt, in its ignorance of her.

Kerry spoke. "I found some homemade wine in the cellar. Would you like to see what it's like?"

Muriel agreed and was left on her own with the dog as Kerry sauntered off, his departure from the room somehow lifting a veil from the house. It no longer seemed welcoming, nor did it seem wise even to be there. Muriel felt a flush of panic. The silence gave her an exaggeration of the feeling she got from watching submarine films on the television, just before the depth charges started exploding. She strained to hear Kerry's footsteps in order to reduce the depth of the silence.

Standing up to calm her stomach, Muriel crossed the room to the box of books. With his front legs, the dog wearily raised his body into a sitting position, his eyes attentively following Muriel's movements as if she were a sparrow and he a lazy cat, temporarily too tired to put effort into chasing her but open to the possibility that she might stray a little too close to his jaws. Muriel picked up one of the top books; the corner of her mouth rose into a smile at the subject matter: witchcraft.

Another book was entitled "Exploring Books of the Dead" and a third "Mabinogi and the Triads".

She had always found occult and new age material interesting, fancying herself as a modern day witch, but the discovery that this man shared her interest was not entirely comforting and goose bumps erupted across her body. Spells and demons were fine in the safety of her own imagination but for them to be the passion of a stranger unnerved her.

A glossy hardback on demonology dropped from her paper white hands as Kerry returned, holding a dusty unmarked bottle and two coffee mugs.

"You're very into this stuff, aren't you?" Muriel said as she picked up the book.

"Some of it's interesting," Kerry replied, sounding blasé.

"What about witchcraft?"

Kerry gave Muriel a roguish smile, his lips appearing like food to the starving Muriel. "You look a bit of a witch yourself," answered Kerry.

"Oh." Muriel tried to look offended but clearly wasn't.

"Not that that's a bad thing," said Kerry. "Some people like that kind of a look." He poured out some wine and handed her a full mug.

"Do you like it?" she asked brazenly.

"The wine?" asked Kerry.

"The look."

That smile again, this time accompanied by a gentle nodding of his head, "Mmm."

Muriel sipped at the wine, her face contorting as her taste buds revolted. She took a large swig in spite of them. "This'll knock your socks off," she said.

Kerry swallowed his first mouthful. "That might not be all. I think it's Sloe Gin," he replied.

Muriel gulped at her drink, knowing now that if she played her cards right she could have Kerry in bed within the hour. The thought of her own power over such a man was as intoxicating as the wine and would lend its own Dutch courage to her actions. She looked around. Props would be helpful. "No furniture?"

"Yeah, it's all in the other room." He motioned towards a doorway. "Piled high for some reason. Give me a hand and I'll bring the sofa in." He was obviously not unused to people doing as he said.

"OK," replied Muriel as she opened the door.

The room was a tip for all sorts of household junk, but just inside the doorway was an old, green and very tatty sofa.

Kerry came to Muriel's side and tugged on the sofa until it was clear of the doorway. Muriel began to walk to the other end of the sofa and whilst doing so with her back to Kerry, undid a couple of buttons on her blouse. Then she turned and bent low to pick up the far end of the sofa, her firm young breasts straining against the restraint of one button and a flimsy black lace bra.

They carried the sofa to the middle of the room, next to the bed. Muriel looked at Kerry's eyes before she straightened up. She watched them leave her chest and peer into her own eyes. She grinned wickedly before dropping her end of the sofa, climbing onto it and walking across the seats to Kerry, where she knelt on the arm of the sofa, bringing Kerry's head so close to her breasts that she could feel his breath upon them. She leant a little further forward, allowing his nose to disappear between them. Kerry kissed them both before sliding his hands beneath Muriel's blouse. Strong fingers massaged her back muscles then gently moved up and down the small of her back before wandering towards the fastening of her bra. She shivered at the touch of the rough hands. Muriel stepped off the sofa and Kerry pulled her further into his embrace. She could feel his state now as he began to kiss her neck whilst unfastening the final buttons on her blouse. He moved again, kissing a nipple as he lifted her breasts from the bra before lowering his aim. Muriel enjoyed the moment before she forced him onto the bed.

An hour passed before both needed to rest and, as darkness began to fall, the couple snuggled into each other to sleep a little and also to enjoy the warmth of each other's bare skin. Kindred spirits, Muriel hoped, that accepted life as it came to them.

Muriel curled into Kerry's back as he contemplated his weakness. He had expected this house to reap rewards, but was surprised by the speed at which the first had shown itself. When he had seen the house originally, a part of him had thought it a perfect hide away from the rest of the world, a hermitage that he could lock himself in, but he was wise enough not to deny his own nature.

Muriel was deeply intrigued by Kerry, already developing an infatuation, but Kerry was under no such delusional spell. In the past he had always entered relationships hoping that they would blossom into love and stay evergreen, but now he expected only what had gone before: a few weeks of summer before the autumn fall. Muriel after all was built for sex and not for him.

Muriel rolled over and stretched an arm out towards her discarded clothes, removing a small velvet sack from a pocket, before rolling back. "Let me read your fortune," she said.

Kerry turned to face her with a questioning look. Muriel opened the purse and showed its rune stone contents to him.

Kerry smiled as if he knew every trick in this dark girl's repertoire. "Go on," he said coaxing Muriel to continue.

"Pick a stone and place it on the bed facing up."

Kerry did this.

"That's the stone Raido; it's the journey stone. It could just mean that you're going on a journey soon or," Muriel tried to sound morbid, "it could refer to the journey of your soul from this world into the next." Muriel checked Kerry's expression. He seemed content with this game. "Put the stone back," she said.

Kerry did as he was told and Muriel shook the bag, before offering it to Kerry again. Kerry picked out another stone and placed it down. Muriel's eyes lit up as she saw the same stone again. "Definitely going on a journey," she said.

"Or dying."

Muriel smiled nervously. She wished he hadn't picked that stone. She had hoped for one about relationships. She knew she should have lied; the next stone she would lie about. With the stone replaced she shook the bag again, absentmindedly looking around the house. It seemed as if the veil was lifting again.

"What do you do for a living?" she asked whilst holding the bag out.

"Any work I can get. I travel around a bit, so I suppose I'll be looking to make some money on a more permanent basis here. What about you?"

"I'm still in the sixth for...m." Her reply had been punctuated by the surprise of seeing Kerry once again place the same stone down. She looked up at Kerry, his face was angry now.

"How old are you," he demanded.

"Eighteen," exaggerated Muriel.

"That makes you sixteen or seventeen."

"Eighteen," replied Muriel firmly.

"I thought you were older than that," he said as he moved his body away from hers.

Muriel felt a rush of alienation, first by Kerry and then, inexplicably, by the house. The flickering firelight made ephemeral objects dance in the corners of her eyes. "Why is age important?"

Kerry didn't really feel as if age was of terrible importance, but perhaps it was the route to getting his solitude back. "It's how I feel," he replied coldly.

Drudwyn, Kerry's dog, had been by Muriel's side of the bed but he now stood up and moved away from her. Whilst she looked into Kerry's face for compassion, a large family bible fell from the shelf above them and crashed to the floor with a thud that prompted a scream from Muriel. She looked around, only now noticing the wind that howled down the chimney. Like water flooding a sinking ship, it seemed to urge Muriel to abandon the room. The dog was staring at her, animating the hostility that the atmosphere now held. The panic of drowning set in and Muriel leapt out of the bed and began to bolt into her clothes.

Kerry watched calmly from the bed. Even in this strange mental state, Muriel looked good enough to eat, yet he was glad she seemed to be going.

"Get up!" Muriel begged. "Take me home."

The warm bed gripped Kerry's body and it was with reluctance that he stood up. Muriel had her boots on before Kerry had even taken hold of his jeans. A burning log noisily shot an ember onto the tiles. Muriel jumped again and ran for the door. By the time Kerry was in the doorway, Muriel was up the path and running, he watched her until she disappeared from sight and then returned to his bed. There would be plenty of time to contemplate the unusual turn of events in the morning.

Chapter 2

A few years prior to Kerry's arrival in Kirk Eaton (the name given to the small group of hamlets in the region), a resident would-be tabloid editor, started a local paper called "Something Strange". It carried articles from gig revues to studies of rural employment and whilst not being vastly profitable it had become a "must buy" each week for the local youth.

One particular drive of the paper had been to find somewhere for live music in the area. A lottery grant had provided the finances to convert a disused building to a club house, which was now capable of holding up to three hundred people without disguising its origins as a cow shed.

Kerry had not heard the band that was playing there this night but curiosity and a thirst for alcohol led him to the hall. He stood like a lighthouse as groups of friends, strangers to him, lapped at his sides at the packed bar. But the only lights not on the stage seemed to be the glow from the optics, which only filtered to Kerry's side of the bar through a haze of cigarette smoke. Only the lack of trendy dressers distinguished this club from one that might be encountered at the seedier end of a big city.

The compere walked onto stage. "Good evening strangers."

Some friendly heckling urged haste.

"Tonight we have some excellent home-grown talent, number thirty-nine in the charts today, rather a good band in fact, "The Dog's Bollocks"."

The curtain, which looked suspiciously like sellotaped bin liners, went back revealing the five piece "Dog's Bollocks", who went straight into a version of the Doors' number "When You're Strange".

When they finished, the petite dread-locked lead singer, Jane, awaited quiet from the appreciative audience. "Right, you may wonder what we're doing here. Well, my little brother is the latest editor of "Something Strange" and he told me if I didn't come down here and play he'd tell my mom the name of the band." She smiled playfully. "Anyway, this next song's written just for you lot and it's all about the tossers at Eaton Moor: "The Devil's Ring Piece". This one's for you, Ian." Jane's words seemed to have a bitter edge to them as she finished her sentence before going into a song that she tore to shreds with an aggressive power that her frame looked incapable of holding.

Kerry tried to concentrate on the words, but the first two lines were the only ones he could discern.

"The guide books call it Hafgan's Ring,
 but that's where they've seen devils sing."

The band played a few more numbers before taking a break. Jane and Animal, the drummer who did bear a resemblance to the muppet of the same name, started to push their way to the bar, but were accosted on route by a young man in a denim shirt with sunglasses lodged on the top of his head.

Kerry watched the threesome with interest. The young man turned his back on Animal and was obviously having an argument with Jane. From the body language of the two, it seemed as if Jane eventually conceded a point. The young man looked relieved, patted Jane on the back and moved off into the crowd, allowing his back to receive a masturbatory salute from Jane.

When Jane arrived at the bar, Kerry moved to one side making the only clear gap to the barman's attention. Jane passed no acknowledgement of the gesture and ordered two pints of Guinness.

Kerry looked at her from a corner of an eye. Close up she wasn't so enigmatic, a large nose detracting from that rock star look. He lent over towards her. " Hafgan's Ring is on my land," he said.

Jane turned to look at him. "Oh," she replied as if disinterested, and turned away to collect her pints.

"I just wondered why you wrote a song about it," Kerry continued.

This time Jane turned her head towards Animal, handing him his pint before walking away without giving Kerry an answer.

She was developing a real hatred for that song. It had really written itself during a studio jamming session, aimed at finding that last album track. But the record company manager had been in the recording room at the time and for some reason he had decided that it was about as commercial as the Dogs Bollocks were likely to get and persuaded the band that the track should in fact be their next single. Jane had protested, but once the decision was out of her hands, she'd thought it best to be as enthusiastic about it as possible. She hadn't anticipated such a disgruntled response from her hometown, where she'd been brought up on the urban legend of covens cavorting nakedly in the moonlight around the stone circle.

Chapter 3

The next morning, Kerry read from his book "Mabinogion and the Triads" as he pushed a few rashers of bacon around a frying pan he had been lucky enough to inherit with the farm.

It was the song that had prompted him to revise the subject. He new that Hafgan was a character in these traditional Welsh stories, a king of 'The Other World'. It was exciting to actually own land that had connections with the stories, however tenuous. He remembered the stories Etta had told him during the one week that he was allowed to stay with her at the farm as a child. They hadn't been like any bedtime fairy tales he'd heard elsewhere and his desire to recount the stories, perhaps with just a little childish flourishing, had landed him in trouble at school.

After breakfast, Kerry took Drudwyn for a walk aiming to find the stone circle. He hadn't noticed anything before but had spotted it on his map of the area. As he walked along he picked up a couple of twigs and held them out in front of him, dowsing for the ley lines that would surely emanate from a stone circle. After a minute, the lifeless sticks were discarded and Kerry returned his attention to the map. He should have been on top of it if he was reading the map correctly, but all he could see was a small patch of gorse and hawthorn.

Then he spotted a standing stone amongst the undergrowth. As he approached it, he noticed barbed wire tied to it and passing into the gorse. Further investigation showed that the hedge and barbed wire were most probably in position to protect sheep from the sheer drop on the other side, a miniature valley twenty feet below and only a few feet wide at the bottom where a stone slab, possibly an altar, lay upon four smaller stones.

Kerry scraped through the wire and undergrowth and gently slid down to the altar. He stayed there for a short while, examining the stone, but found nothing of interest. He had wondered if there might be something that was of relevance to what he had read that morning. The story said that a man called Pwyll had had to fight Hafgan, but would only be able to kill him if he stabbed him a single time. It wasn't very entertaining reading and he'd soon bored of it but it would have been nice to find what it was about the stone circle that had prompted someone to name it after such an odd character.

As Kerry climbed out of Hafgan's ring, followed by Drudwyn, he began to hear childish voices, carried to him by the wind. He cocked his head a little to one side to pinpoint the children's whereabouts and then headed towards a gorse-covered bank. The children would be at the top of it if he was right, obscured for now by the incline.

Sticking close to the gorse, as if to remain out of sight, he reached the top of the slope where the ground fell sharply away, leaving him completely visible to the young boys, playing with a rope swing in the sheltered copse below.

All the children were in the trees, their bicycles scattered below them. Like antelope having sensed a leopard stalking them, the children stopped their play and silently regarded Kerry's approach. They were not used to seeing anyone here, it was a place they went to get away from parents. Occasionally George Beck would go past on the road behind them, driving his Quad, but no one ever came that way on foot.

Kerry teetered on the brow, the children were now within earshot of a slightly raised voice, he called out in a friendly manner, "All right lads?"

A dumb silence answered him. Kerry didn't like talking to children. He saw little need for it in general, but there was a point to make. "I'm Kerry, I own the farm back there." He paused and nodded towards the farmhouse. "I don't mind you playing around here, but be careful."

From up in the largest ash, a high pitched voice replied, "Kerry's a girl's name!" It was a response designed to show bravado in the face of what may have been a veiled threat.

The tree was silent for a moment, then Kerry shook his head, turned and walked out of sight in the direction from which he had come. Drudwyn however lingered a while staring up at the children before he too trotted out of view.

Kerry was coming to the bottom of the gorse bank when Drudwyn hurtled past him and dived at a hare that was disappearing into the undergrowth. There was a little growl and a shake of Drudwyn's back end as it protruded from the gorse. Then the rest of his body emerged, the hare held loosely in his jaws. Drudwyn approached Kerry, wagging his tail and grinning.

* * * *

Kerry was in the kitchen skinning the hare when, without knocking, Muriel let herself in, intentionally dispelling the ghost of her childish fright the night before. Kerry looked up from the hare, repressing a smile. There was a wicked glint in his eyes today and they followed Muriel's gaze to the blood and fur on his hands. The skinning process had given the room a slight odour of urine.

Muriel said, "Hi," whilst tentatively flirting with a raised eyebrow.

The corners of Kerry's mouth rose a little, giving him the appearance of a man with evil intent. This kind of reaction was new to Muriel. Kerry wasn't the gagging for it teenager that she was used to. This was as alien as her first graceless steps into a sexual relationship. He certainly looked like he'd got over the age thing.

Kerry spoke, "I didn't expect to see you around here again." His tone of voice contradicted his words; he had known she would come back.

"Don't you want me …..here I mean?"

"I," stressed Kerry, "don't mind, and there's no one else, is there."

"What you been up to then?"

"Wondering how to get a lodger."

"I'll move in."

"I need someone who can pay their way, to cover my food bills, you see."

Muriel looked at the mess in Kerry's hands. "You do a bit of hunting then?"

"I have to be hungry."

"You won't mind the hunt going over your land then?"

"Bloody will!" replied Kerry. "Do they?"

"Yeah. It's only a small hunt though."

"Well I hope they don't try getting on my land without permission, because they'll get a little more than they bargained for. Are you into it?"

"No, it's strictly for the rich tossers, like Mom and Dad. I threw brake fluid on their cars last time they were out."

"Very constructive," Kerry replied sarcastically.

"Are you coming for a walk or what?" asked Muriel.

It wasn't the reply Kerry had expected to what he had thought had been an unnecessarily curt comment. "Where?"

"Well, I'm sure you've seen most of your land, so let me give you a tour of mine."

"Yours?" enquired Kerry.

"It will be when my fat fuck parents stiff it."

Two computing systems within Kerry's head analysed the data in front of him and gave him two views on what was happening. There was the obvious chance to have sex again, and it had been good the last time. The second computer looked for the less obvious. Muriel wanted to walk first; she wanted to be seen with him.

Now the two computers had to come up with one course of

action. Kerry had plans for his new life and although they did include sex, they didn't include a teenage girl.

"I think I'll have my dinner instead," he replied.

Muriel was silent for a moment as Kerry returned his attention to preparing the hare.

"I could make you something much nicer at mine," she eventually said.

"It'd be rude not to eat this now I've killed it."

Muriel moved towards him. Kerry kept his attention on slicing the meat from the bone of the hare. He didn't react at first as Muriel pushed her hand under his trousers. He let her fingers touch their goal before grabbing her wrist with his bloody hand and pulling her from his clothing.

Muriel stood back, shocked at Kerry's response. Ignoring her, he moved to place some meat in a frying pan.

This felt more like dealing with her father than a lover. She looked down at her cuff, now stained with blood.

"Twat!" she said and stormed out of the house.

"Yes, you're probably right," Kerry said to himself. It had been very tempting.

Muriel ran home again, this time only her sister Hazel was there to greet her.

"He's such a knob," she said vehemently. "He tried to scare me and I hate him. He's a creep; he's the worst friggin' neighbour anybody could have."

"You didn't get a shag then." It was Hazel's standard reply to her eccentric sister, who then ran to her bedroom screaming obscenities and slamming doors.

"Stupid cow," Hazel muttered.

Muriel's bedroom was small with little floor space. She walked over discarded clothes towards the desk lodged in the recess of a dormer window and opened a drawer. She removed cosmetics from the drawer to give her access to a large book hidden at the back.

With the book Muriel also took out a Tupperware box. She flicked through the book, her grimoire, before finding what she sought. The page was headed 'Banishings'. Muriel wasn't a real witch, and her spells never seemed to work, but this time, as she began to chant above the chicken giblets that she had removed from the box she could feel something happening, but it seemed to be to her.

No one interfered with Gwawl's plans and any body could prove useful at this stage.

Chapter 4

As Kerry settled down in front of the fire to eat his catch, he began to recall his one and only visit to the farmhouse as a child. Sitting in this very chair, Etta had bewitched him with fairytales.

* * * *

Etta knew that she would be the last resort for her desperate sister–in–law. Only when Grace could no longer bear another week with the incessant demands of her young son's overly inquisitive mind would she bring him to the farm, to the one person who could fill his mind from morning to night with stories that would satisfy his quest to discover the meaning of life.

Grace was aware of a few of her inadequacies as a single parent but still found memories to blame for her son's developing personality and the route that his character took away from her own. Her husband's parting gift prior to his death was to christen his son Kerry, which to her had always been a girl's name. Kerry was not as unusual a twelve-year-old as Grace believed. He merely had a desire for knowledge and a yearning to find the magic that made the world tick, whilst Grace had always lacked the imagination to see why anyone would like to believe that there really might be fairies at the bottom of her garden.

It was a new boyfriend and the chance of a cheap trip to Ibiza that finally broke Grace's resolve to keep him from Etta who she knew would only encourage his flights of fancy, playing up to the role of a witch in which Kerry had cast her.

Etta was in her mid-sixties and had never married or had children and so her nephew, Kerry was the closest person to an heir to her farm and knowledge. They had spent the first day of Kerry's stay working hard, "fixing sheep" as Kerry liked to call it. Kerry had assumed the day ended at teatime but instead they were back out on the Welsh hillside looking for lost sheep.

The day had been new and exciting for Kerry, even the weary feeling in his legs and the throbbing feet that he felt as he rested in an armchair after supper seemed like good things. The meagre log fire hissed rather than crackled but the little flames still danced and lit the room as Etta settled down to pass on the folk stories her father had told her. The stories weren't the kind that are found in children's books. Grace would surely disapprove but that didn't interest Etta who was as keen to keep Welsh customs alive as any daughter of the hills.

"You remember the large stone we saw peaking out of the hedge around the coppice today?" Etta asked

Kerry looked over at her in anticipation, his smile casting even more light than the fire dancing in his eyes, and off his shiny black hair. "Yes."

"Well, that's at the very heart of this story. Some people think they know the true story, but only I look after the land where it occurred. My father told me the stories, and his father's fathers have passed them down since the stones were first put in place. Yes, there is a whole circle and an altar hidden within that undergrowth." Etta checked Kerry's expression for interest and saw it in abundance.

"It all started many, many hundreds of years ago when this land was known as Glyn Cuch. In those days, men weren't surprised to find Other Worldly beings crossing into this world. And, one day, two men met, changing both worlds forever.

Pwyll was the Prince of Dyfed, a land not far from here. He had heard that a huge white stag from the other world had been seen in the woods that used to be around here. Glyn Cuch was famous as a place where the two worlds crossed and so Pwyll, wanting to prove himself to his father, headed out to hunt the stag. When

Pwyll eventually saw the stag, it was being chased by another pack of hounds. Charging at this pack with his horse and his own hounds, Pwyll drove them away from the stag. But these were no ordinary hounds and in front of Pwyll's very eyes, they disappeared, leaving only a grey-clad huntsman sitting astride a black stallion.

"Who are you that you dare to chase off my hounds?" asked the huntsman.

"Prince of Dyfed," replied Pwyll.

"This is not Dyfed, and that was not your stag to hunt," answered the huntsman. "I am Arawn, a King of Annwn, and that was my stag that strayed into this world."

Now, Pwyll hadn't met a man from the other world before, least of all a king and he realised that he had been caught trying to steal from this king. Pwyll was an honourable man and was saddened to think of himself as a thief, never mind what his father might say, so offered to make amends to Arawn. Arawn was a patient and forgiving man, but he did have need of someone brave enough for a task that he could not fulfil himself.

Arawn had an enemy, a rival for power in Annwn. He was called Hafgan by some, but," continued Etta, "do not expect him to always use that name."

Kerry looked puzzled but Etta enigmatically continued without further explanation.

"Now, Hafgan was an evil and cunning man who used all sorts of tricks and magic to try to take away Annwn from the good king Arawn.

Before Pwyll met King Arawn, Hafgan had fought with Arawn. Arawn had severed Hafgan's hand, but had shown mercy and left him to live. Hafgan, instead of taking defeat graciously, had gone to an old witch. who cast a spell. In exchange for promises and affection, the old crones incantations cast a spell so strong that Hafgan could no longer be hurt by blows from Arawn, and no one could kill Hafgan, except by his or her first blow.

Arawn explained this to Pwyll and took him to the other world to see the good things he had done as a king. Pwyll saw all the wonders of the other world, from the beautiful fairies to the deadly but thrilling vampires that Arawn protected his people from. And, most beautiful of all, the radiant woman who rode her white horse ahead of his and who was always just a little too fast to catch if ever he tried.

Pwyll became friends with Arawn and agreed to help him on condition that if he did survive the fight with Hafgan, he would at least be allowed the chance to speak to the horsewoman.

And so Arawn's magicians disguised Pwyll as Arawn and sent him out into the forest armed with just a sword. On his way through the forest, Pwyll felt that he was being followed, but each time he hid to see if anyone would ride by, he saw only a wolf or a hind. This happened many times until Pwyll realised that it was the creatures that were following him. So Pwyll decided to jump out in front of the wolf and confront it.

Pwyll waited patiently for the wolf and when it appeared in the path, he leapt from the undergrowth with his sword drawn and ready. The wolf turned into a young man called Manawyddan. Thinking that this must be Hafgan, Pwyll swung his sword at the unarmed man who tried to parry the steel with his bare arm. The sword cut deeply into Manawyddan but it was not a mortal blow.

"Wait!" shouted the injured man. "I am not Hafgan. I have come to tell you the truth."

Pwyll waited to hear the man's story.

"I am an admirer of the woman on the horse, as you are. Her name is Rhiannon and there is nothing that Arawn can do that will allow her to talk with you in the manner you would wish. She is betrothed to Hafgan, and although I do not believe that even she can see a happy union ahead, honour would not allow her to contemplate life with the killer of her husband to be."

"Are you a friend of Hafgan's?" asked Pwyll.

"I despise the man. He wants to enslave the people and banish all the creatures he cannot tame to your world. And I hope you do kill him, but I will not be the one who stands by and allows you to face him under false payment."

"Have you ever spoken to the woman?" asked Pwyll.

"No. She enchants me from a distance; I dare not say what spell she might cast upon me if I allowed her any closer. If I spoke to her I am sure I would lose all chance of happiness - unless you were to kill Hafgan, but I will take you back to your world if you wish."

Etta paused for a moment. "What do you think Pwyll did?"

"He fought Hafgan anyway," replied Kerry.

"That's right. He stopped and thought about the injury he had done to Manawyddan and how brave and kind Manawyddan had been to tell him the truth, and about what might happen in this world if Hafgan succeeded in the other world."

Pwyll left Manawyddan and walked deeper into this strange forest. Until, as he approached a branch across the path, he saw a giant of a man standing naked and covered in hair, holding one huge sword and an even bigger shield. Pwyll was not so quick to react this time having made the earlier mistake with Manawyddan. But this was Hafgan and Hafgan only saw Arawn.

Hafgan immediately flailed his sword at Pwyll, but Pwyll was small and lithe and ducked the blade, only to be caught with a hefty blow from the shield with all of the giant's weight behind it. Pwyll had failed. Semi-conscious he saw Hafgan raise the huge sword in both hands above him. But Manawyddan had been watching as a pine marten. Hafgan saw the marten run into Pwyll's sword hand and suddenly transform into Manawyddan who showed no hesitation in thrusting Pwyll's sword into Hafgan's hairy chest.

Hafgan grabbed his chest and pulled the embedded sword out, handing it back to Manawyddan, but Manawyddan remained still and waited until Hafgan fell to the floor.

He could have been the hero of his King and People, but

Manawyddan replaced the sword in Pwyll's limp hand and walked into the forest."

Even at twelve, Kerry had realised that life wasn't a fairy tale and sometimes there wasn't a really happy ending to every story, but he had grown to expect at least a moral where happiness was missing. At the start of Etta's story, he had placed himself in the role of Pwyll, but as soon as Manawyddan appeared, he had seen the true hero of the tale.

"So what happened to them all?" Kerry asked.

"That's a story for tomorrow. It's time for bed now," replied Etta.

The whole fortnight was filled with dark fairy tales, which Etta seemed capable of spinning around every hump and bump in the landscape. In-between work there was exploring to do, the whole moor being far safer than the city Kerry was more accustomed to.

Eventually the day came when Grace arrived to collect Kerry. He had missed her but knew he would miss Etta more. When they arrived home, Kerry found that Grace's new boyfriend had moved in and that soon his mother would deprive him of the status of "only child".

There were a few weeks before the summer holidays would be over and Kerry spent them recounting the goriest bits of his newly learnt stories, and questioning his mother over the intricate details and possibilities that the stories had posed. Instead of listening to the creaking of a bed, Kerry spent most mornings in the local library. He read anything that could fuel the fiery passion with which he had taken to folklore. Using his own vocabulary and imagination he wrote his own stories around the heroes that he read about.

The new term eventually arrived and Grace breathed a sigh of relief as she packed Kerry off to school. But by the Friday of that week, she was called in to see Kerry's English teacher.

Kerry's story telling had spilt over into his essay writing. Grace sat reading through the story in front of her. The class had been asked to write an essay, six hundred to seven hundred words long, with the beginning "Whatever happened to..." For a twelve-year-old, Kerry's essay sparkled like polished, wet jet.

"Whatever happened to Manawyddan?" was the title and his teacher had no idea what Manawyddan was.

...Whatever happened to Manawyddan after he slew Hafgan? Well let me tell you. The witch who had helped Hafgan had also been his mother's midwife and Hafgan had been born as a conjoined twin. The witch had cut off the weaker twin and kept it alive as a baby, and a secret from all but Hafgan. She was the first to find Hafgan's body and took it back to her hut where she cut it open and placed the baby inside of him, where it started to grow like a caterpillar in a chrysalis.

Pwyll was never sure what had happened in the forest and assumed that Hafgan had fallen onto his sword. He eventually met Rhiannon who, instead of being constrained by her honour, was pleased by Pwyll's advances and grateful to be free from her betrothal to Hafgan.

A year after their marriage, Rhiannon gave birth to a baby daughter, but one night the baby was taken by the creature that Hafgan and his twin had grown into and in front of Rhiannon's eyes was eaten.

Pwyll, eager for revenge asked Arawn to help him capture the creature. So, with the best hounds in the kingdom they chased this new Hafgan for many years, each period away from Arawn's kingdom growing longer. And the longer they spent away the less powerful the kingdom became and the more allies Hafgan made, resurrecting the rebellion in some of Annwn's poorer clans. Eventually, Pwyll died in an ambush by one of these clans and Arawn was forced to return home, to save himself and his kingdom.

Rhiannon was distraught. Pwyll had left her pregnant, and in fear that Hafgan would be back when this child was drawing its own breath. One day she persuaded Arawn to hold an open court where Arawn's subjects could come and offer suggestions as to how to deal with the threat to their kingdom.

Manawyddan appeared before them, his hunting hound by his side.

It was the first time he had attended court since the meeting with Pwyll and the first time he had ever heard the wise and strong words that flowed from Rhiannon's mouth.

Arawn's face lit up to see his greatest warrior alive and well.

"I can find Hafgan and with your powers we can banish him from this world until he repays the debt he owes Rhiannon," said Manawyddan to Arawn, too bashful to address Rhiannon directly.

"Why would you not kill him?" Arawn asked.

Manawyddan recounted his tale and in front of everyone assembled, the reasons for his actions and explained what had brought him to court that day "I knew nothing of what was happening here, having exiled myself to a foreign land until horse after horse ignored my will and led me back here to their goddess."

Rhiannon's heart was warmed by Manawyddan's tale and she agreed to his suggestions. The next day Manawyddan rode out with Rhiannon and Arawn's best magicians to track down Hafgan.

Manawyddan's hound took just three days to pick up the scent and another to track him down to a small village where a baby had just been taken. They found Hafgan asleep, gorged on the flesh of babies, in bed with the witch who had resurrected him. Manawyddan and Rhiannon called upon the woods and earth around them to raise Hafgan from the ground onto an altar. Around this altar grew a cage of standing stones and briar. The giant awoke and tried to escape but the briars tore at him and ripped the outer skin away, leaving in place the weak, small child that the witch had placed within Hafgan's Belly.

Arawn pierced the witch's heart with his sword but before she died she swore that if the child were not given a chance to amend its ways she would return with Hafgan and an army from the grave. Manawyddan wanted, the Hafgan child, dead and didn't like the trickery that the witch was trying in her death throws. Arawn, however, was more fearful for himself and his subjects but believed himself wiser than the old crone. After consulting with his magicians Arawn came upon a punishment that would safeguard his kingdom and a chance for redemption that the child would never be able to grasp. He cast the child from his world into this one. "Until you can give her back a child!" he shouted as the infant disappeared, pursued by Manawyddan's hound.

"Whatever happened to Hafgan? Well that's another story."...

* * * *

Kerry could remember the incessant questions that were asked about what films and TV he was allowed to watch, and how things were at home in general. His mother never took him to see Etta again and she had become no more than a vivid childhood memory - until a solicitor had tracked him down with the news of her death.

Chapter 5

Christopher Hannay related the story of a strange man who had approached him and his friends in the copse to his parents and, like any nine-year-old, he made a good story of it.

Christopher's older brother, Billy, a stocky shaven-headed nineteen-year-old was also listening to the conversation. "Nut him in the bollocks next time." he said apparently oblivious of any possibility that this wasn't a good course of action for a child.

Billy's mother chastised Billy as best she could before giving Christopher the 'don't talk to strangers' speech.

It took little over a day for the news to travel around the residents of Kirk Eaton that Kerry had had sex with a teenage girl and had invited young boys to play on his land. So it wasn't without a little suspicion that P.C. Walters, investigating the disappearance of Muriel, knocked on Kerry's door nine days later.

P.C. Walters was in his penultimate year of service and, like a tree, his girth had grown in size each year. Walters explained his business to Kerry politely. Muriel had failed to return home three days ago, having last been seen by friends who dropped her off in a car at the top of the Beck's farm track.

Kerry could see an eye of suspicion upon himself, although this was actually a misjudgement of P.C. Walters's habit of always having half a mind on what would happen if the person he was talking to 'cut rough'. Kerry's arms were on show, and although their length elongated his muscles, P.C. Walters could still see that Kerry was what he called a 'truncheon job'.

"I haven't seen her for over a week," said Kerry, unconcerned.

"Oh well, she's probably off gallivanting; she's gone missing before." Walters handed Kerry a card with a number on to ring if he did see her.

Three hours after P.C. Walters's visit to Kerry's house, the constable was aimlessly driving around his patrol area when the radio call that many officers long for, but dread when it arrives, came through.

"Foxtrot Alpha, three two, are you receiving from NA?"

P.C. Walters replied, "Go ahead NA."

"Foxtrot Alpha, three two, proceed directly to Kerry Taliesin's farm at Kirk Eaton. A body has been found, believed to be that of Muriel Beck. Mr. Taliesin will meet you at his house and take you to the scene. Protect the scene; assistance is on its way. Keep us informed – over."

"10/4 received." P.C. Walters had been a police officer in rural areas for most of his twenty-year service and had never been the first officer at the scene of a murder and now every organ in his body was in confusion. His brain rallied enough to inform the rest of him that nobody had said it was a murder; probably just a false alarm.

P.C. Walters was at Kerry's house in minutes. Kerry and Drudwyn were waiting as he got out of the car.

"What have you found, Mr. Taliesin?"

"Muriel" he replied bluntly. "I'll show you where she is."

P.C. Walters followed Kerry, his brain working overtime. If Kerry had found a dead girl he was calmer than P.C. Walters would have expected. He decided that questioning could wait until he saw whatever Kerry had seen. The two men had walked for only a couple of minutes across Kerry's land when Kerry headed for a solitary oak tree. Some crows were startled from the ground as the pair got closer.

The P.C. prepared himself for a body on the other side of the tree, but he was not ready for what he did see as they rounded the oak. For there, sitting neatly against the tree was the barely recognisable body of Muriel. She resembled a fox after the hounds had had it. Her head was intact but only attached to the rest of her body by a spinal column. Her torso was just bone and remnants of organs, her black blouse just ribbons, too laden with blood to flap in the wind. It was the legs and hips that became the focus of Walters' attention. They were perfectly intact, still inside a pair of black jeans. He could look at those legs and imagine the rest of the girl lying there, perhaps asleep. But Walters had to face facts, and vomited.

Kerry's land soon became off limits, even to the owner. Police officers and scenes of crime experts scoured the ground, whilst two detectives interviewed Kerry in his house.

The junior detective, Detective Inspector Renshaw, a man in his late thirties with a battered but friendly face, was asking most of the questions, whilst D.C.I. Smegvick seemed quite happy to sit in the rocking chair and listen.

D.C.I. Smegvick was almost completely bald and a much larger man than Renshaw, but to Kerry they both seemed far too similar, and relaxed in each other's company to the point that Kerry thought he was being treated to some psychological mind game.

As the interview went on, Kerry began to relax into the question and answer session. It was almost enjoyable, and Renshaw's no nonsense manner was quite endearing.

After about half an hour of questions, in which Kerry was unable to shed light on the cause of Muriel's death, the detectives began to ask questions that, to Kerry, seemed to be going over old ground, whether to waste time or catch him out he wasn't sure.

Renshaw and Smegvick were, as Kerry could see, a double act. Although Smegvick was the silent partner at the moment, both detectives knew what the other was thinking: Kerry Taliesin didn't seem to give a damn that there was a dead girl on his farm.

A scruffy man in cords and a tweed jacket walked into the room. D.C.I. Smegvick looked up at him.

The man in tweeds spoke. "No need for an exam. There's no

sign of a sexual assault. In fact, her knickers are about the only things intact. Of course we'll know more after a post-mortem."

An R.S.P.C.A. inspector, squeezed past the scruffy man to get into the room, "Hi, I'm told you want us to take a dog in."

The two detectives looked at each other.

"Who called you?" asked the D.C.I.

"Inspector Wilks," replied the R.S.P.C.A. officer.

Smegvick's and Renshaw's faces screwed up, both clearly annoyed by this interference with their work. Smegvick rocked himself onto his feet, walked into the hallway and shouted for Inspector Wilks.

Inspector Wilks was the local uniformed inspector, the 'boss' at the nearest police station, under normal circumstances. Wilks followed D.C.I. Smegvick into the living room. "Ah! The cavalry," he exclaimed as he set eyes on the man from the R.S.P.C.A. "The problem is," he continued, addressing the man, "we need this dog holding for evidence, and a vet to see if he could be responsible for the death of a girl."

Smegvick had taken up a standing position in front of the fire. He outranked Wilks and was the officer in charge, but sometimes the temptation to allow his underlings to hang themselves was too great.

Smegvick watched as Kerry showed his first hint of emotion.

"You can't think my dog did it! He wouldn't, and what did he do with all the meat?"

Renshaw looked a little queasy at the question.

Wilks responded to Kerry. "Sir, I believe you, but we have to check it scientifically."

Kerry didn't like Wilks. He was a plump pear shape with grey hair and schoolmaster spectacles, but it was the way he had said "sir" that had raised Kerry's neck hairs. The word had come out of that thin mouth as if it was sour food being politely spat into a serviette.

"Don't talk like this is all routine. I bet you've never done this before. I bet you don't even know if they can check that it was my dog. This is a bloody moor! You get all sorts of stories about wild animals up here, don't you? I've even heard people talk about panthers."

Wilks ignored Kerry's outburst as if it hadn't happened and, turning to the R.S.P.C.A. inspector, instructed him to carry on.

The man stooped a little and, facing Drudwyn, slapped the side of his leg, giving a whistle and a "come on boy."

Drudwyn stayed put and snarled. The man had spent long enough with dogs to know which ones to treat with respect, but it was rare to come across a big dog so indifferent to the presence of strangers one moment and powerfully aggressive towards them the next.

"I'll just get the stick and rope out of the van," he said, and soon returned with a six-foot pole with a rope noose attached to one end.

Kerry shook his head in disbelief.

The R.S.P.C.A. man hooked the noose around Drudwyn neck; Drudwyn contemptuously shook it off. After a few attempts, the rope became too tight to shake off. Drudwyn didn't seem too bothered by this until the man tried pulling on the pole. Drudwyn resisted a bit and just as the man thought he'd got Drudwyn, the dog ran forward, straight into him, causing him to land on the floor, no longer holding the pole. Drudwyn skidded to a halt and calmly walked back to Kerry with the pole still attached.

The police officers wisely offered no assistance.

Kerry felt it was his turn to speak again as he removed the noose from Drudwyn's neck.

"Look, I'm sure this is a situation without rules, so let's use some common sense. I'm the only person that Drudwyn obeys."

Kerry was cut short by Inspector Wilks.

"Drudwyn?"

"Yes, Drudwyn," continued Kerry. "So why not just place us

both under some kind of house arrest until you can find a vet who can tell you that Drudwyn didn't do it."

Inspector Wilks replied, "We can't really do that because we've no reason to suspect you at this point."

"Actually inspector," said Smegvick, "we've no real reason to suspect this dog and as I'm the officer in charge here, I think we should accept Mr. Taliesin's offer of a kind of house arrest."

"Erma," grumbled the scruffy man from forensics.

"Yes?" asked the D.C.I.

"Well, couldn't our friend from the R.S.P.C.A. just tranquillise the dog so that I can take a scraping to check for blood on his teeth and take a sort of dentistry record."

"Don't you want to check his stomach?" asked Renshaw still contemplating where the meat could have gone.

"Well yes, that would be conclusive I suppose, but I've got some good bite marks on the body and I could rule the dog out quickly on dentistry alone."

The detectives looked at Kerry, unsure as to whether they needed his permission to tranquillise his dog.

Kerry nodded.

Half an hour later came the preliminary confirmation that Kerry's dog didn't have the teeth formation that caused the puncture marks on Muriel's body.

Inspector Wilks and the two detectives convened to another room of Kerry's house, having left four uniformed officers with Kerry and the bewildered and sleepy Drudwyn.

Inspector Wilks spoke first. "We can't say it wasn't him just because it wasn't his dog. He's only been here for a few days and we've got the strangest murder case we've ever seen."

"Who says it's murder?" asked Renshaw.

"What else?" asked the D.C.I.

"An escaped zoo animal perhaps. Alice's husband studies things like that," replied Renshaw.

"Oh, is Alice married to Jim Farrier?" the D.C.I. replied surprised.

"Yeah, I didn't put the two together for a while."

"Who's this Alice and Jim?" asked Inspector Wilks, convinced that the discussion had taken a sidetrack.

"Alice is a D.C. with us, and Jim is an inspector over at the city, but he's written a book on mystery predators in Britain, big cats and that sort of thing. He might just like an attachment on this case."

"How did Jim get a cracker like Alice?" asked D.C.I. Smegvick. Renshaw shook his head.

"A crying shame."

"Can we get back to the current problem please," asked Inspector Wilks. "Do I arrest him or not?"

"There's no good reason to. Just ask your local lads to keep an eye on him," replied the D.C.I. "And," turning to Renshaw, "organize some proper statements from those that last saw her and her parents, and let's have some media coverage."

"Is that wise, with talk of wolves and such like?" asked Wilks.

"No one's talking about wolves." Replied the DCI irritably. "The official line is we found a body. I mean, there really isn't anything to connect the animal that ate her with the reason she's dead, but it's definitely suspicious. There'll be no arrests until we have all the info possible. So let's get investigating. I want everybody she knew and everybody in the village talking to. I'll make a decision about Jim Farrier after the P.M. results.

Chapter 6

Five days later D.C.I. Smegvick was at his desk. The calm air that he had shown on the day that the body had been found had left him. He had all the information at hand now. The post-mortem report put the cause of death as a bone-breaking bite to the neck, with no forensic sign of human interference, but there was the matter of the location of Muriel's body and the time. She had been missing longer than she had been dead.

The D.C.I. had placed himself under the microscope by appealing for information on a local news programme. He hadn't gone into detail as regards the death, but people were starting to ask questions that he wasn't going to answer without talking to Inspector Jim Farrier, 'the cat man', as he was known in the force.

Smegvick took his hands from his eyes and rubbed them over his balding head. What exactly could Jim Farrier say that could help him?

When Jim walked into Smegvick's office, moving with military precision as if on parade, he was already fully briefed on the intricacies of the case.

Smegvick nodded a hello and looked up at Jim through bleary, bloodshot eyes, his eyebrows slightly raised, inviting Jim to divulge some thoughts.

Jim remained standing, his well-groomed, baby face complimenting his full tunic uniform. "I'm afraid I can't cast much light on the case," he said and not awaiting or looking for a response continued, "Like any moor in Britain, the area has its sightings of large, unidentified animals, probably pumas, which are no real threat to humans, certainly not adults anyway." His speech had the lilt and occasional inflection of a man who had spent his formative years in the local farming villages.

"You'd be looking for something like a leopard for this job. One did escape from a zoo in a German bombing raid and was shot later somewhere in Snowdonia. The simplest explanation would just be two or three dogs, acting like a pack. I'm sure that's what half the sightings are anyway."

Smegvick could detect a slight I told you so hint in Jim's demeanour as he listened to explanations of the various methods that could be used to track and trap the range of suspect animals. Coppers had laughed at Jim for years for his hobby of keeping track of all the big cat sightings across Wales, so it was with a certain feeling of redemption that he left Smegvick's office, assigned to the case.

That night Kerry gazed out of a window. He could see the oak tree that marked the gruesome spot where a strange young girl had met the grim reaper. He could even hear the branches creaking in the wind, like church bells mourning Muriel's passing.

Kerry lifted his gaze to the clear sky, to the full moon. The wind picked up a little. The door behind him opened with a bang, inviting him into the night. Kerry turned to face it. He did nothing for a minute and then left the house, with Drudwyn on guard and the wind the freedom of his rooms. Like an animal tracking it's prey, he cocked his head listening to a faint murmuring carried on the breeze. He started to home in; there were humans on his land in the middle of the night. He could hear where the rhythmic noise was and followed it to Hafgan's ring.

He peered into the hole and then secreted himself in the hedge above the altar, the wind hiding the rustling noises he made. The pit was no longer empty. Tonight there were thirteen cloaked figures, thirteen faces hidden by monk-like hoods. The wind concealed their words as it concealed Kerry. He could only hear a chanting but could not discern the meaning. The chanting stopped and one of the figures stepped on to the altar and spoke passionately above the noise of the wind.

"I have heard the rings on her fingers and the bells on her toes. She is coming to fulfil her cycle, but this time there will be no eating of her son, we can break the chains of Clas Merdin, the whelp, their sword will be our eyes."

The wind drowned out any more words and the low chant that seemed to vibrate the land began again. The figure on the altar turned to step down. He wobbled on the brink of the altar and instead of stepping off, turned and called out above the chanting.

"Manawyddan, can you hear me?" He was calling to the banks of the pit, perhaps to Kerry or perhaps to the world, "We will hunt her down."

He then stepped down and led the others out of the pit. Kerry held his breath as the thirteen took different paths away from and around him. He could see two of them clearly as there backs faded into the night. They hadn't been wearing habits, but characterless hooded sweatshirts. Kerry pondered the significance of this for long enough to let the trespassers leave his land and then made his way back to his shelter.

The next morning D.I. Renshaw and Inspector Jim Farrier were sipping coffee in the mobile police station, which was now acting as an incident room in Kirk Eaton. A uniformed constable tapped on the fragile partition of the inspector's office. D.I. Renshaw waved the young officer in.

"What is it lad?" asked Jim, somewhat condescendingly.

"Err, well, it's the local newspaper, sir." The constable handed Jim that day's edition of 'Something Strange'; the headline was 'Murder?'. Jim started to read it. It was standard coverage of the found body, which had been in other newspapers.

"So what?" asked Jim.

"Well sir, it goes on to mention a wolf."

The two inspectors were interested now; they sat up on their seats, concentration on Jim's face as he read on, anxiety in Renshaw's features as he waited for Jim to finish reading.

"It's got everything in, right down to the last detail," Jim said, "and it reads badly like they're blaming a werewolf."

The constable coughed to attract their attention. The inspectors looked up at him.

"That's just that paper's style sir, it's kind of a studenty cult thing."

"A studenty cult thing," ridiculed Jim.

"Thank you, Constable," said Renshaw. The constable acknowledged the D.I. and left the room.

"Well," said Renshaw, "I'm sure there must be a better way than using a load of hounds, but you'd better get your hunt organised P.D.Q, before the media circus arrives. I'll find out how the hell this reporter got his story." Renshaw had been very successful as a detective, having always kept his hands clean and with the help of Smegvick had dealt with any controversy well, but he had the feeling that this case was the one just waiting to blow up in his face.

"Well, it's Wilks really that gave me the idea of using the hunt, I didn't even know there was a local one or that he was in it."

"Pleb," replied Renshaw, as a comment on Inspector Wilks.

Jim shrugged his shoulders in agreement. "Any way I'm off to see The Master of the Hounds now, so I'll let you know how thrilling that was later."

Renshaw left to see Ian Fast, the editor of 'Something Strange' at their expansive office above a hairdresser's in Becksworth.

Ian, a twenty-one year old student of journalism rocked on a chair, sunglasses on his head, feet on the desk and a cigarette dangling from his mouth. Renshaw found it hard to suppress a smirk when he set eyes on Ian's attempt at looking like a journalist and it became even harder when Ian tried to talk like a tabloid editor.

"Well, what is it Inspector? I'm a busy man."

"Tell me where you got your information for the piece on the murder," demanded Renshaw.

"Yes, I wrote that piece. Good, wasn't it?" replied Ian.

"Where did you get the information?"

"A source."

"Who?"

"Just a source."

Renshaw stood up, leaned over the desk and put his face to Ian's.

"This," he spat, "is not a game. Even the real editors on Fleet Street don't piss you about when you're talking murder. Now, where did you get the information?"

Ian didn't even take a second to decide that he would divulge some information. "OK, look, we, well, I get phone calls now and again. A chap gives a password and a story. He says he's in the police and he's never given us duff info before."

"Who is it?"

"I don't know."

"Accent?"

"He's local."

"When did he ring?"

"Yesterday, middayish."

"Right, I'll organise a B.T. trace for you and when he rings again we'll have him."

Ian didn't look too thrilled at the idea, but he didn't argue. D.I. Renshaw had a look about him that suggested he never played good cop in the good cop, bad cop game, although in fact it was just a look.

Meanwhile Jim Farrier, accompanied by a WPC, was gliding up the gravelled driveway towards Lord Smith-Kurr's mansion, past the wide lawns, peacocks and gardener. The sun lit up the windows giving the whole building a warm and inviting look that rarely accompanied such grand houses.

The car parked at the foot of the short flight of steps leading to the main entrance.

Upon reaching the front door, the constable lifted the doorknocker, a large ring held in a lion's mouth. Inspector Farrier coughed and pointed out the doorbell. The constable, still in her probation period and easily embarrassed by small mistakes in front of senior officers, blushed a little and rang the bell.

The couple did not have to wait long before a traditionally dressed young butler opened the huge doors.

"Good morning," said the butler chirpily. "Can I help you?"

"Yes, good morning, Inspector Farrier and P.C. Horricks to see Lord Smith-Kurr."

The butler lead the pair into an entrance hall, a marble floored affair with a sweeping staircase to the right. From there the officers were taken into a large carpeted room with deep red leather armchairs, rows of book cases, a bar and a relaxing view over the sun-lit gardens.

"Please take a seat," said the butler. "I shall inform Lord Smith-Kurr of your presence." With which the butler left the room.

"This is smart i'n't it," commented the constable as she surveyed the room.

Jim had not had a chance to reply when their host entered the room with a broad welcoming smile. Jim blinked as he stood to shake Smith-Kurr's hand, the sunlight catching hold of the huge lord's blonde hair giving his head an ephemeral, ethereal halo. He was a very large but elegant man in his early thirties, immaculately dressed and groomed.

The constable was certainly pleased with his appearance and thoughts of Lord Smith-Kurr in her handcuffs flashed across her mind's eye.

"Good morning officers." The voice was deep, smooth and classy, but void of the closeted lilt that affected some of the county's titled landowners. "Would you like a drink?" He started to head towards the bar. "I'm afraid it's the barman's day off."

"Err, no thank you. We're on duty and all that," replied Jim.

"Quite wise. I'll get the butler to arrange tea and coffee." At which Smith-Kurr rang a bell behind the bar.

"Now, what is it that I can do for you?"

The constable considered the reaction she would get if she told him what he was already doing for her.

"Well," started Jim, "it's an unusual request really. You see, we think that the girl who was killed at Kirk Eaton was attacked by a wild animal and we wondered if we could persuade you to use the hunt's hounds to try and flush it out." Jim didn't like the idea much, even if it had been his suggestion. He felt as if there had been pressure on him to provide solutions to the problem of locating the animal, so he had provided a solution and now awaited the ridicule that would follow and the possible, no, probable failure.

Smith-Kurr furrowed his brow a little and rubbed his chin.

Jim awaited his first disparaging comment.

"Would tomorrow be soon enough?" replied Smith-Kurr eventually.

"Yes!" Jim was almost embarrassed at the eagerness of his own reply.

"Do you ride, Inspector?" enquired the Lord.

"Err, yes I do. My wife taught me, but I don't often get the chance to practise these days."

"Will you be joining us tomorrow then?"

"No, I'm afraid not but obviously Inspector Wilks will be with you." Jim wasn't in fact sorry at all not to be joining the hunt; he had no time for them and had actually expected to take an instant dislike to the master of any hunt. However Smith-Kurr in some ways reminded him of a burglar he had dealt with on a number of occasions, in that he hated all thieves of whatever description but had never felt any animosity towards this particular burglar. Indeed, he had to admit to himself that he quite liked the man.

"What about your wife? We could provide a horse if she doesn't have access to one."

That was a comment more typical of the type-casting Jim had given to Lord Smith-Kurr prior to meeting him. The thought that he would bring his wife out to enjoy a hunt that's aim was purely professional seemed ridiculous.

"No, I'm afraid she won't be joining us, she's on duty tomorrow as well. She does have her own stallion though, a grey, so perhaps some other time."

"I look forward to it already," replied Smith-Kurr.

"Thank you, very kind of you to invite us." More excuses to come up with. "Getting back to the hunt, Inspector Wilks will be with you and have radio contact with a large number of strategically placed officers. We've also arranged for the R.S.P.C.A. to attend with tranquilliser dart guns although the main aim is to stop the animal at any cost. And we will have a helicopter on the ground ready to take off when we have somewhere to direct it."

Jim and Lord Smith-Kurr spent a few minutes longer discussing various details of the hunt before Jim and the WPC left.

Gwawl was not given to modesty although he had been around long enough to meet and talk to men and women with truly humbling intellects. Now, even with half a mind on his past failures in entrapping Rhiannon, it was hard to contain his excitement. To begin with he had done no more than track down that vengeful hell hound, that part, of what had become his life was an obvious direction to take, brave but unavoidable. From that point on he had felt that his plan had always seemed clumsy, with too many variables, and yet it appeared to be working.

Chapter 7

In the evening of that same day it began to rain. Kerry had been shopping at the mini-mart in Becksworth. With the prospect of a drenching and having already seen one teenager lose their footing trying to run on the shining cobbles of the market place, the lure of the nearby Green Man pub was stronger than the need to walk the five miles back to Kirk Eaton.

It was a long and narrow pub, with a crowded bar area. Tobacco smoke assaulted his lungs as Kerry attempted to get served. The clientele covered a range of drinkers but many looked to Kerry as though they had stepped straight off the tractor, making him feel happy about bringing his carrier bag full of shopping into a pub on a Saturday night.

Kerry bought himself a pint of bitter and then made his way through the crowd, looking for space and enjoying the warmth. The pub was a corridor of four small rooms; the fourth had the only spare seat in the pub, in a corner with a small round table. Kerry sat damply down, before taking the first gulp of a long desired drink.

Beside his table was a much larger one, with benches on either side. This was occupied by a small group of young men, holding half-drunk pints and talking in hushed voices. A couple looked up at Kerry as he entered the room, but with a mournful look of disinterest they had quickly returned to their conversation.

A man with a dangerously large nose was speaking whilst Kerry eavesdropped. "I suppose, like, that.... Well, you know, she's always..." The man was clearly drunk, but eventually managed to convey the feeling that Muriel had been an accident waiting to happen.

A stocky man, still carrying the acne of adolescence, answered him, only a little more coherently, expressing an opinion that the man with the nose shouldn't have been talking about the dead like that. "And if you do it again I'll kick your fuckin' head in." The respectful volume of the voices started to rise.

The shaven headed Billy Hannay joined the conversation at this point. He was the most sober yet to speak. "If you're going to give anyone a kicking it should be that pervert that killed her."

A small tattooed teenager now chirped up. "I thought they said it weren't 'im."

"Couldn't prove it more like," replied Billy. "Anyway, he's a perv. He tried to chat my little brother up." Billy's speech started to rise into an aggressive shouting. "I say we go and do 'im. Fire his house, kill that dog and string 'im up by the bollocks!"

"Yeah!" replied the small lad.

Billy ordered him to fetch his car to the front of the pub. Titch obediently rose from his seat.

Kerry held his pint glass on the table, appearing as though he might be able to ascertain the meaning of life just by watching the bubbles rise. He contemplated what course of action to take, Titch helped him by cutting his thinking time down.

"The car's outside," he said obviously having just remembered where he had parked it.

Kerry couldn't let them near Drudwyn or the house. "Excuse me lads," he said smiling and worrying. "But I know the man you're talking about didn't chat anyone up or kill that girl."

Billy asked the obvious, "How?"

"I'm Kerry Taliesin."

Kerry anticipated a "Who?" But the reaction was quicker and more furious than that. The youth closest to Kerry whipped the back of his fist onto Kerry's windpipe. As he gasped for breath, Billy, in one smooth motion, broke a pint glass and shoved it into Kerry's face.

These boys fought every Saturday night. They weren't just the loudmouths that Kerry had hoped. He tried to stand and lash out but a torrent of punches knocked him to the ground. Kerry covered his head with his hands and, as kicks arrived at his midriff, he could hear people shouting, a girl screaming and his own rasping, gasping breath. One kick caused a sickening cracking noise. That was the last blow before the landlord and a bar man were allowed to drag the gang away from Kerry's body.

The yobs left before the ambulance arrived, convinced in their pea-like brains that they had been the heroes of the people. Kerry was taken to the city hospital, where his broken arm was put in plaster, his face stitched and his swelling treated. He was asked if he wanted the police called but at 10 o'clock the following morning he merely enquired the way back to Kirk Eaton and started walking without having contacted them.

Kerry's motion highlighted his pain and once he hit the open road he decided to start hitching. He'd walked about two of the fifteen-mile journey when a driver finally took pity on the hunched up form ahead of her.

The hatchback stopped about fifty yards further on than Kerry so he did his best to run to the car, but had to stop after a couple of attempted strides. The car waited and Kerry finally opened the passenger door. There was one lone female driver whom Kerry instantly recognised as Jane, the singer from the Dog's Bollocks. Jane did not recognise Kerry. She had only met him briefly and now he did not resemble his former self so well.

"Hi," Kerry said and tried to smile but only succeeded in hurting his face. "Are you going towards Kirk Eaton?"

"Yeah, jump in," replied Jane, in a much friendlier mood than she had been on their first meeting.

"I'll get in, but I'm not sure about jumping." Kerry cautiously lowered himself into the car and Jane set off. After that neither the passenger nor the driver spoke for a mile, Kerry's gaze was on the road ahead. Jane glanced at Kerry occasionally without him noticing. She quite liked the rough look and it was hard to imagine anybody looking rougher than Kerry did right then.

"I heard you singing at the club the other day," Kerry said breaking the short embarrassed silence.

Jane smiled. "Oh, did you like us?"

"Yeah. I tried…" Kerry paused, and then continued, "I tried to talk to you about your song, Hafgan's Ring."

It was like a knife in the stomach to Jane as her mind made the connection in a split second. She remembered the man at the bar, realising later that it was the man suspected of murdering Muriel. What the hell was she doing picking up men in an area where someone had just been eaten to death, let alone the man who was suspected of doing it. It occurred to Jane that she was very, very stupid.

"I just wondered what you knew about Hafgan's Ring," asked Kerry.

"Nothing," squeaked Jane.

Kerry sensed Jane's fear, but he wanted information not blood.

"I'm just curious. Why write lines like 'that's where I've seen devil's sing?'"

"It's just a line, just something to sing about, it doesn't mean anything, like, err, there's a ghost in my house."

"Yeah, there's one in mine too," said Kerry.

"No, like the song 'There's a Ghost in my House' by the Four Tops; it doesn't mean anything." Jane was panicking. She turned the radio on; a record was playing.

"But you must know something."

"No."

"Look," Kerry was showing just the slightest sign of anger, "you must know something."

"No."

Kerry forced himself to relax a little.

"Look, I've seen something strange going on in the ring, I'm just interested. I won't interfere."

Jane could see Kerry wasn't going to give up.

"It's nothing, just rumours you grow up with, urban myths with no urban bit"

The song on the radio finished and went into the news.

"Residents of Kirk Eaton are being warned by the police to keep children indoors and not to travel alone, after the report of another missing person. This follows the discovery of the body of Muriel Beck, last week in Kirk Eaton. Police are now looking for a nine-year-old, blond haired boy, who hasn't been seen since seven o'clock yesterday evening. The police have stated that they are looking for a man in relation to the disappearance."

The rest of the news was background noise to Jane and Kerry's thoughts. Neither of them was in any doubt as to who the police were looking for. Jane had the gift of calmness that came from having little imagination and a simple plan.

Kerry contemplated talking about the newscast, but there was always a chance that Jane hadn't connected him to the disappearance. As they drove through Becksworth, that illusion was shattered. Jane suddenly slammed on her brakes, before leaping out of the car, Kerry hadn't even seen her undo her safety belt. He stayed in the car not attempting to follow her with anything but his eyes.

Jane had parked outside the police station and ran straight in. Kerry could see no point in trying to go anywhere and was staring out of the window at the station doors when Wilks accompanied by two burly constables and Jane came scurrying though them.

Wilks interviewed Kerry thoroughly, asking questions not only about Kerry's movements the previous day but also about his lifestyle in general, using a seemingly endless flow of constables to check up on Kerry's alibis and recently made acquaintances. The cashier in the mini-mart remembered his being in at around eight, Tom the landlord had him in the pub a short time later, and the hospital had the rest of the night covered. There was a gap though.

Wilks looked down at the piece of paper on which he had been jotting notes throughout the interview. "So you walked five miles to do some shopping. It took you about an hour, the hour in which our lad's gone missing."

"If that's when he went missing, yes."

Wilks stared at Kerry, in a strangely intense manner, as if trying to solve a long equation written in Kerry's eyes.

"Well, did any cars pass you on the road?"

It struck Kerry that Wilks wanted someone to have seen him on that road.

"Probably, but I don't remember any specifically."

Wilks returned his attention to the equation.

Kerry felt the pressure exerted by the silent puzzling and found himself volunteering the details about the people he had seen in Hafgan's Ring. It seemed to help Wilks reach a decision; he looked at his watch and spoke.

"I think we can rule out witchcraft, but if you do see them again then give us a ring straight away and we can at least see what they're up to. Now I think I've detained you as long as necessary. Obviously we've no grounds to hold you on, but to keep suspicion off yourself and to help us with our enquiries I don't expect you to leave the area without telling us."

He hadn't planned on going anywhere so Kerry nodded an agreement.

"Good, now if you can hang on half an hour I'll get a constable to drive you home."

Kerry thought it odd, that the flood of constables had dried up, but he'd tried walking earlier and although he suspected some delaying tactics there was very little for him to fear from the police. That was the beauty of being such a single man. Wilks took Kerry through to the reception room and asked him to wait there.

Wilks now had to consult with Jim Farrier and Renshaw. They had organised the hunt to go across Kerry's land that morning but that had been before the boy went missing. A professional search for not just the boy but forensic clues would take at least a day to organise and another day could mean another death. Officers had already searched Kerry's house and found nothing, so it was reluctantly that D.I. Renshaw made the final decision and despatched Wilks to join the hunt.

The hunt in all the traditional regalia was milling about outside Kerry's farm. Inspector Wilks was sharing a joke with Ian Fast and Tom, the hulking landlord from the Green Man. The Becks were trying to help keep the hounds in order. Apart from the huntsmen, there were a large number of hunt followers on foot or in cars, and a small contingent from the R.S.P.C.A. who were not at all happy about some of the people they were shoulder to shoulder with. The crowd on Kerry's land was further added to by a number of apparently disorganised police officers eyeing some of the rougher looking terrier men with great suspicion.

A signal from Lord Smith-Kurr and the horses and hounds set off across the Taliesin farm.

Kerry was driven home a short time later and viewed the horseboxes and Range Rovers with dismay. There were small clusters of people awaiting news from the hunt, but no one apparently in charge. Kerry found a sedated Drudwyn in the house with an R.S.P.C.A. officer, and stormed back outside, determined to find the man in charge. He spotted the pips on Jim Farrier's shoulders and approached him.

"I want a word with you," Kerry's voice was quiet but full of commanding rage.

Jim had met more fearsome adversaries. He could see the light of intelligence in Kerry's face and the weakness of his wounded body. "Mr Taliesin I presume."

"I own this land and I want the hunt off it now," replied Kerry.

"You wish to obstruct the search for a missing nine-year-old boy and a murdering animal?"

Kerry' eyes raged more, but he had to concede that he didn't.

"I do understand how you feel," said Jim

Kerry thought otherwise.

"But in this instance," continued Jim, "it's different. The hunt has an indisputable use."

Kerry's shoulders sagged a little further as the fire left his eyes. "Well, I'm going in for a coffee," he eventually said before starting to turn away from Jim, and with a casual look at Jim said, "Are you coming?"

It was not the most inviting offer Jim had ever received, but the quick change from aggression to acceptance was intriguing enough for Jim's feet to follow Kerry into the house.

"Are you in charge of it all?" asked Kerry handing Jim a mug.

Jim explained his role and why he had landed the job. It pulled a memory from a filing cabinet in Kerry's head.

"I've read your book; I've got it in the box somewhere."

And that was all it took. For the next two hours, Jim and Kerry chatted about the various theories on big cats in Britain. Half an hour into the conversation Jim realised he had enthused about his pet subject so much that he hadn't been sharp enough, and was failing to make the most of this meeting. Jim wondered if Kerry had played the schoolboy trick of getting a teacher onto their pet subject and off the syllabus, but if that was what Kerry thought he was doing, Jim let him and sank right back into his passion.

Kerry and Jim were very different men. Jim appeared stiff and regimental with jagged little edges, whereas Kerry was more like a pebble in a stream, but both increasingly believed that they were only seeing the tip of the iceberg and in some battle of wits and in an understated ego way, it was fun.

The two of them were still talking when Jim's radio interrupted them.

"Foxtrot India Five receiving Foxtrot India Four."

Jim answered, "India Five go ahead India Four."

"We've found the boy's body."

Jim looked at Kerry's reaction. It was faint and hard to interpret, but Jim couldn't help but feel that Kerry had had to think about what facial expression would be fitting.

Again, the whole investigation team was soon on the scene. This time the body was in the middle of the moor, but as before, there was little more than a skeleton left.

The hunt was despatched from the scene by D.I. Renshaw and trekked past Kerry's farmhouse. Jim and Kerry walked outside.

Smith-Kurr was at the front of the group. He looked down at Kerry. Kerry stared back with his one good eye and addressed Smith-Kurr between clenched teeth "Come on my land again and it will be the last thing you ever do." The words were immature but the hatred in them was frightening.

Smith-Kurr carried on his way not deigning to respond. Ian fast followed a few horses behind and took the opportunity to snap a picture of an aggressive looking Kerry.

The remainder of Kerry's day consisted of answering question after question from Renshaw and Jim Farrier.

After leaving Kerry's farm with no useful leads to follow, Renshaw and Jim drove to Becksworth police station, where they rendezvoused with the D.C.I.

"So Inspectors," said the D.C.I., "what do you know?"

There was a short silence as Jim and Renshaw hoped the other would answer first.

The D.C.I. eased the situation. "Jim, is it an animal?"

"There's definitely an animal involved sir and judging from the two kills, if it's wild, its range is restricted and perhaps it won't venture further than the two farms, the Beck's and Mr. Taliesin's. But of course it may not be wild, it could be someone's pet and if it's food source dries up, who knows?"

Renshaw took over from this point. "We know it's not Mr. Taliesin's dog from the teeth marks. We're currently having Mr. Beck's sheep dogs checked, but obviously we don't expect a result there. Questioning of the Becks has turned nothing up at all. Inspector Wilks told me that he knew the Becks well and that they were as down to earth and as sane as any couple he'd met, and as far as Mr. Taliesin goes, how can you suspect a man when there's no evidence of any human activity. But we questioned him. He's not seen or heard any animal and says that his sheep all seem to be alive and well."

"Are you ruling Taliesin out then?" asked the D.C.I.

"No sir, there are connections between both victims and Mr. Taliesin. In the second case, Chris Hannay was spoken to by Taliesin when the lad trespassed on his land and we've discovered the lad's older brother was involved in a serious assault on Taliesin."

"Is Taliesin pressing charges?" the D.C.I. queried.

"No sir. He says he understands their anger."

"A guilty conscience or a hippie?"

"Hard to tell, sir. Gypsies sometimes look for their own revenge rather than having to bother with us," replied Renshaw. "He is our only connection, but in a village of this size, everyone's connected to everyone else somehow."

"So, what are we going to do?" questioned the D.C.I.

"Well sir," replied Jim, "D.I. Renshaw and I thought a little surveillance wouldn't be amiss, on Mr. Taliesin and his land, killing two birds with one stone."

The D.C.I. nodded his head a few times before giving his verdict on the suggestion. "Yes, I think that's a good idea. I'll sort out three shifts of two officers and have them liase with you two. But don't just leave it at that. I want reports and an ongoing enquiry."

"Yes sir," replied the inspectors.

The surveillance team was despatched to Becksworth, a simple affair of two plain-clothed constables parking a car where they could see Kerry's farm and focussing binoculars upon it for eight hours at a time.

But unfortunately, no one had really thought the surveillance approach through. With a farmhouse in the middle of nowhere, Kerry could quite easily disappear in the dark and, in fact, did so on the second night of surveillance. It was only noticed that he had slipped away undetected when he returned, as one officer reported it 'smirking and taking the piss.' Kerry had in fact made a point of being seen on his return.

Nevertheless, a log was kept of Kerry's actions for four days. In that time he sold his handful of sheep to George Beck, tended his vegetable garden, went for short walks around his land and Eaton moor with Drudwyn, posted a couple of letters in Becksworth and placed an advert in the Becksworth News asking for a lodger.

Again the Inspectors discussed a course of action.

Renshaw addressed the D.C.I. "The problem, sir, is that Taliesin knows we're following him. He walks everywhere; it's impossible to follow him on anything but foot and because he walks so slowly our men just can't appear natural when they're following him. We're not getting anywhere, but whilst we've got an eye on him, things aren't getting any worse. I recommend we give him a lodger."

"Don't you think," said the D.C.I, "that he would have thought of that?"

"Well yes, but it's a risk he's taking. He obviously needs the income and if we can convince him that we are one hundred percent sure that it's an animal and that we've called off surveillance, then we might be able to fool him. I mean, there're already a number of animal traps on his land and I don't think we can risk letting him get a lodger that doesn't know what they're letting themselves in for," replied Renshaw.

"Mmn." The D.C.I. thought, rubbing his hands over his face. "Well, I've got to admit I'd be happy to call off the twenty-four hour surveillance. It's a lot of money to waste on someone we're not even sure is involved and it's not proving anything."

Jim decided to speak. "I agree. I don't think Kerry is involved and we're wasting valuable manpower when just one lodger will do and as cynical as it sounds, we have to keep a mind on what will be said when we do catch the killer if Taliesin is involved. We can't be seen to be letting civilians be put at risk."

A vindictive smile crossed the D.C.I.'s face. "I'm glad you think like that, Jim, because we need a detective in there who isn't going to get rumbled easily, and that doesn't mean a middle-aged man with a pony tail or a cocky youngster in a drug dealer's jacket, so you won't mind if we use Alice."

Jim shifted uneasily in his chair. He didn't think Kerry was a murderer, but that was all. He didn't know for sure and the thought of his wife alone with Kerry and himself alone without his wife was horrendous, but it was not his choice. It was D.C.I. Smegvick's and he had obviously decided prior to this conversation.

"You see Jim," continued the D.C.I. rather sadistically, "she's genned up on the big cat theory and I'm sure you've discussed the case with her. And he's bound to assume we'd send a man for safety. We've already found a good cover that would suit her better than most. She can be a lecturer in psychology at Leeds University who's taking a sabbatical. She has after all got a degree in psychology." The D.C.I. was a professional; he always knew the resources available to him. "You see, Jim she's ideal. Not only can she keep an eye on Taliesin, but her opinion of his state of mind would also be helpful. Meanwhile we can continue looking for another suspect and if we can get a…"

There was a knock on the door.

"Come," boomed the D.C.I.

PC Walters stepped around the door.

"There's another body sir, on Eaton Moor."

"Shit," was the general response.

The body was that of Jane Fast the 'Dog's Bollocks' singer, and this time it was rape and murder.

The following days consisted of the police painstakingly searching the moor, waiting for the post-mortem results and other forensic evidence and sending Alice Farrier to answer Kerry's advertisement.

Chapter 8

DC Alice Farrier was not alone as she drove down the track to Kerry's farmhouse for she had the company of a crowded room listening on the other end of well-tried and tested surveillance technology. One microphone was hidden in her car's interior light, one doubled as a belt buckle and a third was disguised as a pendant. Alice knew all this, she knew that both bugs and officers on the other end were reliable, but she was still scared, fearful of what lay ahead and fighting hard to suppress panic. She'd been to the toilet almost as many times as she'd checked her story that morning. She tried calming herself with music and with kaolin and morph. Neither had worked.

She was pleased though that she had been asked to undertake the operation. It was a chance for her to show her so-called superiors exactly how a professional went about her work. Her self-confidence had been bolstered, not because she was under delusions of why she had been picked, but because at least now she had some justification for her career choice. Her father had expressed surprise when, instead of following him out to Australia to help on his new stud farm, Alice had decided to study psychology. After finishing her degree came the cultural and less than obvious leap into the police service.

She pulled up outside Kerry's house and stepped out of the small van. The scene wasn't as Alice had pictured it. She had seen herself walking up to a door and knocking. She'd then imagined her words as Kerry answered the door, but in reality the door was wide open and a huge dog was lying in there. Alice knew about Drudwyn; she knew his teeth didn't configure to that of the killer, but right now she also knew fear. Alice braced herself; if she was a hard-bitten cop, then she should be able to face a dog.

Alice walked towards the door. Drudwyn stood up. Alice paused. Drudwyn opened his mouth, a tongue rolled out of one side and his tail swung gently from side to side. Alice relaxed and walked forward; Drudwyn took a couple of bounds and was at Alice's side.

A ripple of fear flowed through Alice's body, but it quickly subsided as Drudwyn muzzled into her, jumping a little in a clear display of welcome. Drudwyn then bounded back into the house, barking as he disappeared around a corner.

Alice stopped in the doorway and knocked on the rotting wood. Kerry appeared from a side room. Jim had described him as a 'gypo' and knowing what her husband usually meant by this, she had expected something more scummy and less alive than Kerry.

"Hi," said Alice, stretching out a steady hand towards Kerry. "I'm answering your ad for a lodger."

As Kerry shook the hand in front of him he smiled and Alice caught her first sight of the wicked glint in his eyes, but it disappeared as he realised Alice wasn't another horny good looking neighbour but a financial prospect, food on the table. The only resemblance to Muriel was Alice's jet-black hair, but even that was void of the hint of blue that came with whatever dye Muriel had used.

A large, baggy jumper covered any curves to Alice's body that Muriel might have put on show.

"I am looking for a lodger," replied Kerry, "but I'm not sure you'll like it. I mean, the house is a bit ramshackle and I presume you've heard about the trouble that's been going on around here. I had hoped to get a male lodger."

Alice's green eyes fired an angry glance.

Kerry continued, "I don't mean to be patronising; it might not make a difference, your sex that is. It's just that there's been two girls murdered not a stone's throw away from here and well, I might…" Kerry broke off his speech momentarily, shrugged his shoulders and continued. " Sorry, I guess you know all this."

Kerry's sudden change of tack threw Alice a little and left her wondering if that last comment had been a direct threat to her cover. His eyes were looking straight into her prying at the wrapping paper around her thoughts. "Look, I've spent the last three years in Leeds. Three murders is hardly significant."

She did know about the murders then, thought Kerry. She'd added one. "Okay then, come in and I'll show you what's on offer." He turned and Alice followed him through the hall and into the kitchen, where he put the kettle on before continuing the tour.

It certainly wasn't the kind of basic accommodation Alice was used to, although it did have an attractive simplicity. Her mind had already sanded and polished the bare floorboards that were in every room. Perhaps in the middle of nowhere curtains weren't the norm but the wind that rattled the windows suggested otherwise.

The musty smell had gone now and as Alice entered the sitting room she found the smell pleasant, provoking a memory of boyfriends' bedrooms, a singularly male odour.

"So what brings you to these parts?" asked Kerry.

"I'm a lecturer at Leeds University and I felt a little stressed, so I'm wondering whether to take a year's break, a sort of sabbatical, get out into the fresh air, away from academia. I've heard one too many people complain that all lecturers know is school-university-degree-lecture."

"Well, it's definitely another world here." Kerry started to climb the stairs. He stopped and turned, "I'm Kerry by the way." He put his hand out. Alice took it again. He had met beautiful women before. Muriel for instance had been no dog's dinner, not metaphorically anyway, but Alice's touch, warm and soft on his callused, swollen hand felt magical, almost as if, if he left his hand in hers long enough, his cuts and breaks would vanish.

"Alice," she replied having felt the handshake last just a second too long for comfort. The hand that had engulfed hers was strong, rough and attached to a murder suspect.

"What do you teach?"

"Psychology."

"You don't speak any foreign languages do you?"

"French."

"Pity," he said. "I inherited some of my aunt's notes with this place but they're in Welsh so I can't read them."

Kerry opened a door and allowed Alice past him into the room. "This would be your room."

The room was large. A double bed was by a curtainless window, which overlooked a stable area and the rugged moor. There was a sturdy oak wardrobe and dressing table and nothing else but the dust caught in the sun's glare.

"Well, what do you think?"

Alice looked around for a few seconds, feigning an interest that would be expected of a lodger. "It's not exactly what I was hoping for but I think it will do me good." Alice produced a perfectly acted, relaxed smile. "It'll certainly take my mind off the City. It'll do just fine."

Kerry wanted her in, but wasn't going to make a mistake with someone who he might well end up spending a lot of time with. "What do you intend to do for money during your sabbatical?"

"I've hardly spent anything for the first couple of years of working so I've got well over three months worth of savings, but the idea is to get a job as soon as possible, just something that gets me enough money to pay my way and sort of practise what I preach in a real work environment. There seems to be a lot of grooms' positions available round here if you don't mind the pay and have a little experience."

"You like the hunt crowd?" Kerry had tried to ask the question in a manner which would suggest that he would like her more if she was of that persuasion, but he realised that it came out a little hurried and flat.

"No, but the horses don't choose what they do and I'm not out just to find people who think as I do to work with. That would defeat the whole purpose."

Kerry dissected Alice's answer in his head; the pause was a little too much for Alice. "I do have references," she said

"No need," he replied. "When do you want to move in?"

Alice smiled. "Now, if that's okay."

Kerry had considered doing a bit more of an interview, but Alice's smile on the doorstep had shown as much as he would have discovered in a twenty minute question and answer session. It was a smile that fitted Alice's features so well that Kerry doubted if, under normal circumstances, it ever left her face. Perhaps it was not a permanent fixture now, only because she was scared. He did suspect her pale colour was not her usual look.

"Yeah, no problem, I'll put a curtain or something up."

"I'll just bring my cases in then."

" I'll give you a hand."

Alice followed Kerry and watched his denim-covered bottom descend the stairs. Her first impressions were that Kerry seemed a little gruff, slightly suspicious and very confident. She wished for some of that. A few minutes later, Alice's cases were in her room, the door was open but Kerry knocked all the same.

"Can I come in?"

"Of course," Alice replied, appreciating Kerry's courtesy. Kerry entered the room with Alice's coffee and a large tablecloth, he handed Alice the mug and draped the tablecloth over the curtain rail.

"It's not much," he said, "but it's the best I can do." Kerry moved to the door.

"Aren't you having a drink?" she enquired.

"Yes, but it's downstairs. I didn't like to impose, it's your room now."

"I'll come downstairs with you and you can tell me what there is to do around here." Alice was already interested in Kerry's mannerisms. They jarred against each other like sand paper and wood.

"After you then," said Kerry.

Alice braced herself and walked out of the room and down the stairs in front of him. She felt very strange. Behind her was a possible triple murderer and although no police officer had mentioned anything about werewolves, the 'Something Strange' newspaper article had been brought to her attention. But she was aware of more than just fear; there was also a sensation of ease with this stranger, in a way that she had previously only experienced with nice, soft Jim. She likened it to interviewing one particularly forceful football hooligan in whom she had seen a likeness of her cousin, a soft, easy-to-talk-to man, and she had consequently found the hooligan easy to talk to and subsequently help to send to jail for four years.

Alice and Kerry sat down at the table in the kitchen.

"I'm not really the best person to ask about what to do around here. I've only been out socially twice. Once this happened," Kerry indicated his plastered arm, "and the other time I met a girl who's dead now. I've not been around here very long. I tend to read or just go for walks, with Drud…wyn." Kerry had said Drudwyn in quite a confused manner.

Alice was a little unnerved; inside she was shaking like a leaf. "What's up?"

"Nothing really," Kerry still sounded puzzled, "but I've just noticed that he's lying underneath you."

"Yeh." Panic was setting in again but the surface was still.

"Well, I've never seen him this friendly towards anybody; I find him hard enough to handle myself, but, oh well." Kerry resigned himself to accepting the new situation and shrugged.

"Why do you call him Drudwyn?"

"Well, when I was travelling I kind of acquired him from a bloke called Dog who called his dog, dog. Daft as it might sound, I dreamt about the dog on the day I took him and in the dream I called him Drudwyn, and because I didn't want a permanent reminder of Dog I went with Drudwyn. I know it sounds a bit hippy, dreaming about a name and all that, but I did."

"Where did you travel?"

"Oh, just around, more of an itinerant worker than anything."

"Yeah? What kind of work did you do?"

"Anything, labouring mostly."

"You surprise me. I thought with all those books around you'd have had a more, er, a job where you'd use your brain more."

"I like to think about certain things but I wouldn't want to have to think about set things for a living."

"So you're a man at peace with himself."

"No. Is anyone?"

"Sorry," replied Alice. "Must stop being a psychiatrist."

"Very Bridget Jones," Kerry laughed.

"What fat and frumpy?"

"No, talking as if you were writing in a diary."

Alice's smile widened, an appreciation of the Jones's diaries in a man, even just the film version, was a good point.

A quiet moment, expected between two strangers followed as each looked momentarily for something in the other's eyes. The eye contact was broken almost immediately by Alice who, inexplicably, began to fear that Kerry's probing eyes might be able to see her secrets. At first it was just her true identity, but then there were other things, feelings and stupid thoughts that only came to her mind if she wondered what the worst thought someone could read from her mind could be.

"Will you be getting many visitors?" Kerry asked, wondering if he dared enquire about a boyfriend. He had not seen any rings on her fingers but her skin seemed too pale to betray any marks left where one might have been.

"Hardly anyone knows I'm here. How about you?"

"Just the police," replied Kerry with apathy, then picked up a bit. "But I've got a couple of old friends coming to visit tomorrow."

"Travellers?"

Kerry smiled mischievously. "No. I'm about to make some stew, do you fancy some?"

Alice let Kerry's evasion of her question go and went to unpack whilst Kerry prepared the stew. It was quiet in her room. Every noise she made sounded foreign. It seemed bizarre to be hanging clothes up in this man's wardrobe. Ten years she had lived with Jim in the same house with familiar views from the windows. It seemed to her memory that she had never watched the sunset from any window in her house, but now she sat on the edge of this bed, apprehension growing inside her as the daylight faded, making the oak tree a far more sinister sight. She thought about the dead body that had been found beneath that tree and remembered how, as a child, she had picked out human forms in the shapes of winter trees. The memory triggered Alice's imagination and the oak seemed to be a giant, horned man facing over the moors away from the house. But as suddenly as she had seen that image she saw another. The tree was now facing the house, facing Alice's window, staring at her staring out. The change was so sudden that Alice almost believed the tree had turned around. Swiftly Alice drew the tablecloth across the curtain rail to block out the devil in the tree.

Alice turned away from the window and noticed a massai mara mask hanging on the wall, she hadn't noticed it before, the hard shape of its wood cast harsh shadows, the elongated face with its eye and mouth holes chilled Alice but she couldn't take here eyes off it. She felt as though she had to watch the mask for if she took here eyes off it, it would somehow make its move. She remembered taking her eyes off the tree. A loud knock on the door made her squeal and jump. Her heart was pounding but she recovered her composure.

"Yes?" she called.

"Stew's ready. Do you want it in there or downstairs?"

"I'll come down in a second."

Chat was polite and pleasant as they consumed the stew although Alice was grateful that there was no meat in it. They washed the pots together afterwards then adjourned to the spacious living room that now had a couple of large uncoordinated armchairs; Kerry's makeshift bed had vanished. He lit the log fire and poured Alice some of the wine that he had inherited with the house.

Kerry didn't put any lights on, but Alice didn't mind. She began to feel safe. The open fire was comforting and the wine soothing. She patted Drudwyn and drifted into a world of her own as she watched the flames dance. This was a life that she could have become accustomed to. She felt too mellow to continue her secret interrogation of Kerry and both Kerry and Alice felt comfortable with the silence.

Then, a BANG! Followed by a whooshing noise and "Bastard!" Someone had thrown a petrol bomb at Kerry's house. It had missed a window and was ablaze relatively harmlessly on the ground below. It was followed by a shout of "pervert" and a stone smashed through the same window. Kerry jumped up a little too fast for his injured body and looked out of another window.

"It's a couple of the wankers from the other night. Stay here with the dog." Kerry finished his sentence as he stepped out of the door, baseball bat in his good hand.

Alice went to the window. It was hard to see what was occurring. There was little light to see by. She thought she saw two figures running away, but she couldn't make out Kerry. She waited by the window; Drudwyn by her side. Five minutes of eternity passed. Alice considered if she should be out there, watching Kerry, but she felt that to go out into the night now would be foolish. Besides, it was cold out there. She went upstairs to her room to fetch her torch. When she came down the stairs, she saw the door wide open and Drudwyn gone. Again, the vulnerability of her situation became blatantly apparent.

No sooner had Alice closed the door than it opened again and Kerry and Drudwyn walked in.

"I lost them," said Kerry. "I'd have kept on looking but Drudwyn came out, and I didn't like to leave you alone. I'd be prime suspect again and I think I'd care this time. Are you alright?"

"Yes fine. How about you?" Did he mean, care about her or care about being prime suspect? Wondered Alice. Probably just the rent she concluded.

"No problem, glad I didn't catch them really. I suppose they can't have heard about what a good job they did last time otherwise they wouldn't have run off and I'd have got a bloody good kicking. Still, an Englishman's home is his castle. Anyway, I think I need a bit more wine before I settle down for the night just to calm me down."

Kerry and Alice returned to the log fire, finished off the remainder of the bottle and started on a second. Alice had started drinking to ease her fear but one drink had led to another, each one increasing her courage. Kerry stumbled a little on his way upstairs to his bed and raised a small giggle from Alice who followed him at a respectable distance.

The first night alone in the house wasn't going to be the frightful experience she had imagined, for now the devil himself could walk into her room and she would ask him to join her for a drink. She was pleased though, when, at the top of the stairs, Kerry headed straight for his room without a backward glance.

The next morning, Alice awoke when the light of the sun ridiculed the tablecloth curtain.

The first coherent thought in Alice's mind when she awoke was what Kerry's body would look like, the second thing was a mild hangover and the third was that she was still alive. She drew the curtain back to view the moor and its solitary oak, so strangely out of place amongst the heather and gorse. But, for all its singularity, the tree no longer held a fear, not in the daylight. Alice smiled to herself, as she realised she was at work and she didn't even have to get out of bed to earn her crust, but the smile vanished when she looked around for the object that had chilled her blood the previous day. The mask had gone. Alice assessed the situation. Kerry must have entered her room in the night and removed the mask. Alice was scared again. What kind of a man was Kerry? Why would he remove the mask and what else did he do last night?

Gwawl clapped his hands and laughed aloud. He had almost certainly found the object of his two old desires. One check would help to confirm that his vigil over the hound of Manawyddan had finally born fruit.

Chapter 9

It had been a sleepless night for Jim on duty in the listening station. There had been a couple of anxious moments through the night and two thoughts repeated their complaints over and over again. Alice was not an actor and yet she seemed to have thrown herself into the role of Kerry's lodger wholeheartedly. There was also the anger that raged within him, caused by the arsonists who he was powerless to arrest.

Jim was preparing to go off duty at 9 a.m. when he was summoned to the D.C.I.'s office. Jane Fast's post mortem results had arrived. When Jim entered the office where the D.C.I. and D.I. Renshaw were already in discussion, the mood was serious and pleasantries weren't bothered with.

"It's not human semen," said the D.C.I staring at Jim, awaiting a response.

Jim stared back unable to produce a coherent reply from the host of thoughts within his head, all of them upon the unmentionable possibility.

The D.C.I. did not wait long for Jim to comment, seeing the unease in Jim's face.

"What we seem to have must be a complete sicko with some bloody big animal that, somehow, he's caused to shag the corpse. They're running tests on the semen to identify it better. I think that it'd be worthwhile now to get a sample of semen from the dog at Taliesin's place, so if you fancy a chance to see your wife you can go and get it."

"Thank you sir. I'll contact the vet."

Perhaps it was paranoia about his wife's predicament but Jim wasn't happy about the way everybody investigating the case, including himself, had been so dismissive about the suggestion of a supernatural force at work. He still didn't believe there was anything vaguely like a werewolf involved but the villagers had mentioned it and Kerry had talked about the occult, so surely it was worth looking into. Jim knew well enough how many nutters there were out there. It wasn't beyond belief to think that one of them could be committing these crimes with the intention of raising the dead. Of what? Jim questioned himself as to where that last little bit of rambling thought had appeared from. He knew what he meant and he knew where to start looking into the matter.

Jim, whilst researching for his book, had talked to a local university lecturer in anthropology on the possibility of ancient Britons having anything to do with big cats. It had been a long shot the first time Jim contacted this Dr. McNatley but he had been very useful; perhaps he could be of help this time. He remembered McNatley for being the first to suggest that any large cat roaming Britain in prehistoric times would have probably been given religious significance by the humans of the day who seemed capable of worshipping anything and then eating it. Jim also recalled that McNatley had gained an interest in the occult through his study of anthropology. So, before leaving for Kerry's farm with the vet, Jim rang the university and arranged a meeting with the professor.

Jim wasn't the first to arrive at Kerry's farm that day. Alice heard a knock at the front door from her bedroom. She had already dressed and headed for the stairs to see who was brave enough to call on Kerry at 8 a.m. There was no chance of padding quietly down the creaky stairs, even in the worn out old trainers on her feet, so after two attempted steps she opted for a casual saunter.

Alice was near the bottom of the stairs that led almost directly to the door when Kerry opened it. Alice could see that Kerry wasn't pensive about opening the door; he must know who was calling. The door opened across the path of Alice's vision. She could not see the callers but she could hear Kerry's reaction; it was new.

Kerry spoke one word, loudly and with exuberance. "Hey."

Alice heard movement that caused her to envisage Kerry hugging the caller and then a feminine response, muffled, but clearly the voice of someone glad to see him. Then there was the voice of a young girl, a sweet and sour voice.

"So, I hear you've been up to your old tricks," said the girl.

"Come in," replied Kerry, whilst moving out of the way.

Alice watched as anyone would as the two callers entered. The first through the door was the girl, fourteen maybe fifteen, her multi coloured hair tamed to look untamed. Denim shorts over stripy stockings wedged into Doc Marten boots and a man's black woollen jumper drowning her torso. But the clothes were unimportant. To Alice it was all about the face and her actions. The girl was clearly at home; no hint of unease crossed her brow or slowed her legs as they carried her into the hallway with her carpet bag, and away from the safety of her companion who was struggling in with two more bags.

Kerry took one bag out of her slightly callused hand. The older woman was in her late fifties and of a much more reserved appearance. A subtle floral dress covered her slightly plump body, while a black cardigan gave her somewhere to stick tissues.

The older woman was the first to acknowledge Alice as she looked up to where she was standing. "Hello." The woman's expression was one of greeting, and her face oozed warmth and flickered with a soft candle-like light. She didn't express surprise at Alice's presence. The young girl in silence stared at Alice as if making sure that she would remember the face next time she saw it before disappearing into the kitchen.

"Hello," Alice responded as she finished her descent of the stairs and put out a hand for the woman to shake. "I'm Alice."

The woman was about to respond when Kerry spoke up. "Alice, this is Emily and that," he said whilst indicating towards the kitchen, "was Lucy, a little more shy around strangers than she admits."

"Pleased to meet you, Emily," said Alice. "Is she your daughter?"

Emily smiled even more. The smile indicated a dismissing of the question, but without a hint of ridicule, as if it had been asked many times.

"More of an apprentice," she replied with a soft rural, Cornish accent.

"I'll put the kettle on," said Kerry moving away.

Alice was a little suspicious of the platter, upon which Kerry was handing her the opportunity to question Emily, but a gift horse was needed right now. He might think he was an evil mastermind, but Alice felt she would be more than a match for him.

There was a brief awkward silence, as two strangers thrust together with nothing to sell, could be expected to exhibit. Alice's brief silence was fake and timed to perfection.

"So, have you come for a break?"

Lucy appeared from out of the kitchen and answered before Emily had the chance.

"Would you come for a break in the murder capital of Britain?"

Alice wondered how to respond to the sarcasm but Emily was more forthcoming.

"We're old friends of Kerry and he thought we might be interested in what was happening up here."

Alice frowned. "I didn't think he was interested in what was happening up here too much... You do mean the murders?"

Lucy disappeared again.

Emily sensed Alice's uncertainty about the situation. "Well, I can't really speak for him dear, but yes I do mean the murders and the stone circle people and other odd things." Emily could have waited for the next question but she knew what it would be. "We're interested in this kind of thing because there's a suggestion that there might be a witchcraft connection and, as one practising and one trainee witch, it got our interests up." Emily lowered her voice and leaned into Alice a little. "To be honest, it's Lucy who wanted to come most, she doesn't really seem to get the need for fear."

Alice was surprised by Emily's revelation, not because of how far-fetched she found witches but because she found Emily so thoroughly credible. "I'm sorry if I seem a little ignorant, but what exactly does being a witch entail?"

Lucy re-entered the hallway clutching a bottle of wine, closely followed by Kerry carrying two mugs of coffee.

Lucy again interrupted the conversation. "You know, turning people into frogs, eating babies, flying on broomsticks and stuff."

Kerry handed the mugs to Alice and Emily and deftly removed the wine bottle from Lucy's lips, leaving a dribble of red down her chin. "You've still not grown any," he said as he lead the way into the lounge.

Emily walked through with Alice. "We can't really do all that," she said. "It's more a way of life than anything else. A healthy respect for nature and other people but there are your traditional methods to improve the harvest or undoing curses, although the undoing curses side of the job doesn't really get called for much these days, which is nice. The spells don't always work and Lucy isn't anywhere near getting me to teach her the major things like that. Adolescent witches have a hard enough time of it as it is and until she pulls that blanket down she's not getting anymore training other than in social skills."

Emily noticed Alice's questioning expression and backtracked a little. "A blanket's something you kind of put up to stop other people being able to read your heart. It's something all adolescents do to a certain degree, deliberately in Lucy's case. They just get paranoid at that age, not surprisingly when you think about some of the thoughts they do have. Of course a pinch of salt, some garlic, a lock of hair and a flame and you can burn the blanket right down, but that's considered to be inappropriate behaviour in certain circles, so I just leave her to it."

"Let me get this right," said Alice, but she was interrupted by Lucy lunging for the bottle of wine that Kerry had placed by the side of his chair.

"Alcohol!" she proclaimed in mimicry of a Mexican accent.

Alice looked at Lucy disapprovingly. It hadn't been that long since she'd been in uniform clamping down on underage drinking.

"Don't worry Alice," said Emily. "She doesn't get it regularly enough to get addicted."

Alice was going to get things straight but there was a knock at the door. Emily was closest and opened it to reveal the uniformed Inspector Jim Farrier accompanied by a vet.

"Quick boys," shouted Lucy up the stairs. "It's Dickless of Greendocks. Flush the video down the toilet. You'll never take me alive copper."

She then dived into the kitchen and slammed the door behind her. Alice was to say the least, surprised, but wasn't going to say any more until asked to. Jim looked a little puzzled by Lucy's performance.

"Inspector Farrier. How can I help you?" asked Kerry, accepting Lucy's behaviour as stupid but not unusual.

"The, err," Jim looked at the respectable looking Emily and then back at Kerry. "Could we talk in private?"

"There's nothing to hide from Emily, Inspector, she was a nurse."

Jim wondered what that had to do with anything before saying, "Very well, this is Mr. Hen, the local vet."

Emily, Alice and Kerry all repressed a grin.

"The problem is, that last body," explained Jim. "Jane Fast, was… well, to put it bluntly, we found traces of semen that weren't human, so we want to take a sample from your dog."

"No chance," was Kerry's irate response.

"Come on, it'll rule your dog out," pleaded Jim.

"I was under the impression he had been ruled out."

"Well yes, Kerry but that was…"

"But nothing, my dog has been poked and prodded and drugged so much in the last couple of weeks that I don't want to put him through anymore."

"I could get a warrant."

"Could you?" asked Kerry, still aggressive.

Jim wasn't sure if he really could get a warrant. Taking a sample from a dog wasn't something he'd been taught during his inspector's course.

"Come on Mr. Hen, we're wasting our time here."

Jim and Mr. Hen left. As they walked to their car, Lucy hung out of an upstairs window and sang some lines from the song 'I fought the law', but in her version she won.

Alice just wanted to go to her room and wait until the world made sense, but she knew she couldn't. She had to be around Kerry as much as possible and now was a time to study how he related to people he knew. Kerry was clearly tense. It was Emily though who caught Alice's interest with a drop of anxiety in her formerly easy face as she waited, ever so briefly for the sign of an explosion from Kerry. It didn't come.

Alice blew away the expression when she asked "Would you like me to make us some drinks?"

"I'd love a cup of tea," replied Emily.

"I'll do it," said Kerry. "I've already boiled the kettle."

And so Emily, Alice and Kerry sat down to a cup of tea in the kitchen whilst Lucy continued to explore the house.

"She seems a bit of a handful," said Alice to Emily.

"You wouldn't believe it. She was a real quiet, nice girl until a few months ago. Then she started reading a comic about someone called Tank Girl and she's gone berserk; probably her age."

"So what are your plans whilst you're over here?" asked Alice.

Emily stared at Alice in a way that Alice could not interpret. In fact it felt as though Emily was studying Alice's expression, mapping every contour like a remote probe on Mars. Kerry's eyes then joined in the silent gazing. Kerry looked from Alice to Emily and back again. Neither seemed to know how to break the stare and Kerry, for once, looked worried.

"Emily," Kerry broke the silence, "has come to see if she can interpret the notes I was telling you about."

"The Welsh stuff?" asked Alice.

"Yes."

"I'd like to see that as well. Where is it?" asked Alice.

"On top of the box of clothes in the living room." Kerry hoped she'd go for it. He wanted to know what was wrong with Emily.

"I'll get it." Alice stood up and left the room, closing the door behind her, but remaining on the other side of the door listening.

"What's up?" asked Kerry.

"She's not what she seems," replied Emily.

"What is she then?"

"I don't know."

Alice went for the manuscript, found it and returned to the kitchen. Although she had been able to hear through the kitchen door, the police listeners had not managed to pick it up.

"Here it is," announced Alice holding the red plastic wallet and placing it in front of Emily. Emily opened it up removing the dozen or so pages and began to read. Kerry and Alice watched as Emily's lips moved in time with her finger on the paper, waiting eagerly to hear the verdict. Emily turned to the next page and read a little more. Again Emily looked up.

"It's your aunt's writing, I think. She seems to have been continuing the Cyfarwydd tradition."

"The what?"

"A Cyfarwydd," Emily explained, "is the name given to the storytellers in ancient Welsh history, they were more than just bards, they were also seen as having the gift of sight, of being able to see into the other world."

"That's one of my few memories of her. She usually just told stories from the top of her head but I do remember her pulling out bits of paper and reading me stories from them. I never realised she was translating them from Welsh. So is it stuff from the Mabinogion or stuff she's made up?" asked Kerry.

"The Mabinogion, yes it is, or at least of the ilk. I'll have to read the rest of it though. The stories are always different depending on the teller, like folk songs, because they're handed down verbally, or at least they used to be. Different singers have different versions. I mean these stories are based a good two thousand years ago and the first English translation wasn't done until the nineteenth century by Lady somebody or other."

Chapter 10

A little later that day Jim sat in the office of Dr. McNatley. McNatley was a short, slim, middle-aged man, dressed in the uniform tweed jacket and brown cord trousers. He was pouring a coffee and spoke to Jim with a delicate hint of a public school accent.

"The second time in the same week. I'd almost suspect I was under surveillance if I was a paranoid man."

Jim could only offer a puzzled look in response to McNatley's statement.

"I saw you at the hunt," explained McNatley. "A pastime that I keep quiet from my students."

"Oh, I'm sorry, I obviously didn't recognise you in your riding gear."

McNatley shrugged his shoulders without offence.

"I assume this is to do with the beast. You are hoping for one of your big cats perhaps?"

"Well, it's getting very serious now," replied Jim a little tersely in response to McNatley's less than concerned tone. "Obviously what I have to say mustn't go further than this office."

McNatley nodded his consent.

"We've had three murders now and non-human semen at at least one scene and I wondered if you could think of any occult connection. It's been suggested. I don't mean that I believe in all that rubbish, but some loony might be carrying out some fantasy."

McNatley didn't reply at first, in fact he didn't give the faintest sign of replying. Jim remembered this as one of McNatley's personality traits from the last time they met. It was annoying and as much as Jim felt that it was some psychological test of his patience, he couldn't wait. "Well, do you think it's possible?"

"It's possible, probable in fact. It's no great secret that some tribes across Europe used drugs to induce horses to copulate with women, sometimes as a form of punishment. The whole cult of Epona the horse goddess had references to the fact that she, the goddess that is, was forced to have sex with a horse and that's linked to a similar group of stories from Wales about a woman called Rhiannon. I've always thought that the chalk horses were something to do with sex. Now," McNatley smiled enthusiastically, "do you know anyone in the area with a penchant for horses?"

There was sarcasm in Jim's response. "Just about half the population."

"Sorry, I mean anyone new, anyone with a white stallion, they seemed to be the horse of choice."

"No," lied Jim, there was a newcomer with a white stallion but she was not involved and technically it was a grey.

"Well, I don't know what else I can tell you. I'm sure you know as well as I do the kind of sick videos that are out there, animal farm and the like. Maybe it's more to do with snuff videos than the occult. You could always buy a white stallion and see if it attracts any interest."

Jim could see that McNatley had put some thought into the whole business. Although the plan obviously needed some work. Perhaps, thought Jim, this would be a way of involving Alice more.

"Are there any books you could recommend on the subject?" he asked.

"Oh no, there's bits and bobs of research in thousands of pieces of work but no book on the subject that I know of."

"What about the fact that an animal seems responsible for the killing?"

"Probably a large dog drugged up on some other potion."

"Do you know of any cults in the area?"

"No, they won't be from this area anyway. Occultists will travel miles away from home to avoid detection. But I do recommend you try the thing with the horse out. You're best off with the horse's real owner as well, I mean they'll be able to bluff it better if approached."

McNatley made a show of reading the time from his pocket watch. "I'm afraid that I have a class waiting for me. You'll have to excuse me."

Jim could not suppress a look of irritation. "For the sake of my investigation," Jim paused not happy with reverting to an aggressive line of speech that he normally reserved for the most stubborn criminals, "your class can wait."

McNatley blinked at Jim with an expression that Jim interpreted as feigned surprise and deduced that he had control of McNatley's time now.

"I only have a few more questions to ask," Jim maintained a firm, domineering tone to his voice, just in case McNatley thought he might push his luck.

"Have you ever come across people doing anything like this in recent times?"

"No, I can't say that I have, but if it was going to happen anywhere it would be in an interbred, backwoods community like Kirk Eaton."

"So you're not too sure about your theory that these occultists would not be from around here?"

McNatley stared at Jim for the briefest of moments. A little anger at not being infallible showed on his face, "No, I'm merely throwing suggestions at you inspector. Now I really must go."

Jim ignored this final point, "What drug would they use?"

"I don't know," snapped back McNatley. "I'm not a bloody pharmacist."

"Well, find out and you might save a few lives." Jim looked at his own watch. "Now I have to be going too, so here's my card if you find anything out." Jim handed McNatley a grubby card and left the office. He hadn't had to leave but he wasn't going to let that fool of a lecturer go of his own accord. There were still questions unanswered, but he hadn't as yet formulated them. After all, he had just received some of the strangest information of his career and his mind had started to stick a little on the anatomical feasibility of the more gruesome point.

* * * *

Emily's study of the Welsh notes took a few hours as she constantly cross-referenced what it said with a couple of books out of Kerry's collection. She couldn't even be prised away when Kerry, Alice and Lucy sat down for dinner around her, and she didn't look up until Alice left the room.

"This is all very interesting Kerry, but it's not why you asked us here," she said.

"It might be," replied Kerry. "I want to know what this group who use my land are up to. Now I know that's part of the Mabinogion, it might mean something because the man shouted something about Manawyddan and I know he's a figure from the Mabinogion."

"They might be white witches of course," said Emily. "They might know something the police should know, because if they are accusing Manawyddan of something they may believe magic is at work. Manawyddan is seen as a shape-shifter in the Mabinogion. If this coven has got the idea of a werewolf, they may believe it to be Manawyddan, but that seems unlikely because nowhere in the Mabinogion is Manawyddan presented as anything but a hero, even in this version," Emily indicated the notes before her, "which is slightly different from the common story."

Chapter 11

The following day when Alice awoke, she was surprised to find the house so quiet. It had taken on a peaceful air. No doubt, she thought, all this would change when one of the others got up. She washed, dressed and ate and still not a soul stirred in the house. Alice went into the living room, waking Drudwyn as she started the fire. She looked through a box of books wondering if they might contain a clue, but she found nothing of interest. Alice was bored. There was nothing to do, no one to talk to and she couldn't go out.

She sat herself down in the living room and began to gather her first impressions. Unfortunately, she was denied the ability to write her thoughts down. Any recorded material that could be found by Kerry would throw the whole operation into disarray. Alice wasn't prepared to allow her ideas to free-flow into the microphones. She was a professional and had to have a clear line of thought before committing anything to the listening room.

Alice started with her first impression upon meeting Kerry but unable to focus her thoughts on paper her mind soon started to take tangents.

Alice tried to disentangle the knowledge she had of Kerry before meeting him and how she would feel about him if their had been no suggestion of a murderous streak. She had turned up, a lone single woman, asking to live with a single man in the middle of nowhere. Her mind looked for points of reference, comparable moments in her life. She retrieved memories of her time living in student digs.

She had thought, naively that the two male and three female students would just get along as friends. She had spent a lot of time with James; his sense of humour and easygoing nature made him a good friend when home seemed so far away. They had both got drunk one night and although it went no further than a snog, James had a girl friend and Alice woke up the next morning a little less naive.

The point here, she felt, was that James had not really wanted her, but if she had let him, he would have had her anyway. She was living with a man again now, even though she was a lodger and she couldn't shift the thought of a few drinks leading to a kiss. She wondered how she would handle that this time. But instead of wondering how she would react, her mind contemplated how it would feel, the taste of fresh lips, rough hands, passion.

Alice wondered if it was her turn to be James. She shook her head, dislodging thoughts and refocused on Kerry's position in the enquiry. She began to fit standard profiles to him but soon realised that she knew far to little about him to even begin. For instance, was he faking the mysterious side of his personality in some vague hope that Alice would find that attractive? Or was he hiding something? Alice felt neither option really fitted.

Where was he right now, what was he thinking? Alice couldn't help but think that Kerry's mind was on her. She tried to concentrate again but found that keeping her train of thought on the right rails was stimulating a headache.

Perhaps, she thought, something of Kerry could be learnt from his books, Bram Stoker's 'Dracula' rested open on the opposite chair. An hour into the book she began to become disturbed at the failure of the rest of the household to appear. The previous day Kerry had been up and about by eight o'clock, but it was eleven o'clock already. Worrying thoughts entered Alice's head. If she checked their rooms, would she find them all murdered in their beds, or a strange menage a trois? Perhaps they had all been out the night before, satisfying their blood lust. Alice could picture them all as vampires flying through the night.

Twelve o'clock came and went. Alice made herself some dinner. She finished her meal and still the house was silent. She considered her options in her mind and decided to knock on Kerry's door. But what would happen then? A few scenarios ran through her head.

Alice brushed her teeth in the bathroom. She did so whilst trying to convince herself that the reason for this midday hygiene was to waste time, hoping that Kerry would awaken soon, but she knew elsewhere in her body that she was brushing her teeth for an entirely different reason.

Alice waited outside Kerry's door. She walked away without knocking and then back to the door, away and back a second time. She forced herself and knocked quietly on the door, her heart pounding more than her knuckles. There was no answer from the other side. She knocked harder, a grunt emanated from inside, followed by Kerry's voice, croaky with a hint of annoyance. "Come in."

Alice slowly opened the door; she hadn't seen Kerry's room before. It was as large and bare as her own. There was a freestanding candelabrum like those found in churches, a few boxes and a huge four-poster bed. The curtains of the bed were closed around it, but they were of a translucent, white material and the sun shone through the window lighting up the bed.

Kerry appeared as a silhouette within the bright glow from the bed, sitting upright.

Alice paused before speaking, staring at the outline of Kerry's torso.

"Sorry," she said, "but I was worried when no one got up. It's the afternoon and what with all these murders."

"Thanks Alice," said the silhouette, "but I'm just a bit of a late riser." There was still early morning gravel in his voice. "I'd best get up now."

Alice watched as Kerry's silhouette cast off the bedclothes, he was naked she was sure, her eyes picking out no modesty. A pair of feet appeared at the edge of the bed. Alice stared, not entirely surprised at her own excitement but maintaining a calm exterior. If Kerry was going to act as though this were normal behaviour, so would she. A hand appeared on the curtains and Alice's morals got the better of her as she closed her eyes. In that moment she realised that closing her eyes took more confidence than keeping them open. She could not see Kerry but she heard him approach, desperately she wanted to look, she could feel his breath on her neck now, how close was he?

Kerry had been unaware of the translucent nature of the curtains and had pulled on a pair of jeans from under the bed, whilst Alice had her eyes shut. He saw her now, standing motionless in his room, her eyes shut, her lips slightly apart, he could almost hear her heart pounding. Nothing she could have done would have made her more alluring.

He couldn't help himself, crossing the room and standing so close to her, wondering why those eyes were hidden away. Her lips demanded it and just as they began to frame a word, he succumbed, kissing them as gently as Alice's vulnerability required. Time seemed to stand still. She wanted her lips to move in response but instead she pulled away with a sharp intake of breath as her eyes flashed open and she bolted from the room, taking in just enough of Kerry's attire to feel that she had made a fool of herself.

Alice slammed the door behind her, symbolically stopping Kerry from following her. She reached her room feeling stupid, almost childish. How must she have seemed, how could she feel this way and how could she face Kerry again?

Kerry was at a loss to account to himself what had happened and why. Kissing those lips evoked no memories in Kerry, for nothing that had ever gone before could compare to something so simple yet so arousing. It was so right that although he desperately hoped that his lack of self-discipline wouldn't lose him a lodger, he knew that given the chance, he would repeat the event over and over again, in the hope that her lips would move with his just once.

Kerry dressed and decided to confront the situation.

Alice was in her room when there was a knock on the door. She knew it was going to be him and briefly considered not answering. When she did, she kept her eyes fixed on the floor.

"I'm sorry," he said. " I wasn't sure what was going on and found it hard to resist, but I don't want to have to look for another lodger. It won't happen again." He wanted to add, unless you want it to, but managed to keep the thoughts inside himself. After all, he could be making a fool of himself in front of a police spy.

Alice's answer was abrupt. "It's okay, I'm staying." And she closed the door in Kerry's face. Behind the door, Alice felt herself glowing with embarrassment. Kerry had flustered her plans. She knew she had to stick around him but right now she couldn't face him. Instead she waited for over an hour until she was sure that she had heard Emily and Lucy up and about.

Alice had decided that each day was to have a specific goal and today it was going to be spending time with Lucy. She was the one most likely to be found alone and could be the easiest to obtain information from. She needed to know Kerry inside out and one of the most intriguing aspects of his life was his relationship with this precocious young girl.

Alice found Kerry and Emily sipping coffee around the manuscript.

"Any joy?" she asked.

Emily answered her. "The story's a well known one, but it's not quite the same as the popular version. What I'd really like to do is find where Etta copied it down from or if it was done from memory."

Alice couldn't help but like Emily. She was the kind of person that only existed in childhood dreams of a perfect world. She always seemed happy and interested in the people around her. A bit batty perhaps, but that was her charm.

"Try the loft, that's where I'd have kept it."

"I never thought of that," said Kerry. "But that's probably because I've never seen a hatch into it."

"It's in my room," said Alice.

"Do you mind if we have a look?" asked Kerry, finding it hard not to grin each time Alice spoke.

"It's your house."

"But it's your room."

"Feel free." What was that rule about not inviting a vampire in?

Kerry and Emily headed for Alice's room, much to her delight. Now she could have an uninterrupted conversation with Lucy. Alice tried all the rooms before concluding that she must be in the bathroom. But there was a lock on the bathroom door. Kerry must have fitted it and it showed vacant. Alice knocked all the same and from within Lucy called her in.

Alice was shocked to find Lucy using the toilet, one of Kerry's books on the Mabinogion in her hand.

"Oh, I'm sorry," Alice said, "I thought…"

"It's alright, I'm not proud," Lucy responded. "Did you want the toilet?"

"Err, no. I was looking for you."

"Why?"

"I'm just confused by everything. Kerry's a bit weird and these murders and talks about ghosts. I just want somebody who'll tell me anything that will make me feel safer."

Lucy wiped, stood and pulled a baggy pair of hipster jeans up.

"Do you fancy him?" asked Lucy.

Alice blushed, remembered the police and replied, "No, I just wonder."

"Well, Alice, to tell you the truth, Emily thinks he's a harmless, nice guy, but Emily is a few cans short of a six pack." Lucy turned the shower on.

"And what do you think?" Alice asked.

Lucy started to undress. "I think he's a hot bit of totty and I can't wait to give his broomstick a test drive, but I wouldn't trust him not to have something to do with these murders." Lucy stepped into the shower knowing that she wasn't being entirely honest. She had never expected the things that had been done to her would have had such an effect upon her sexuality so long after the event. She wondered if the perpetrators had known exactly what they were doing. Her life since then had become an act but it was one she had learnt enjoy.

"Why?" asked Alice.

Lucy winced a little as the first cold water assaulted her skin. "He's deep. He's not the type of man you can read easily. I mean, if you could see into his soul it might be whiter than white, or as black as the devil's own and, having heard a little about his past, it's hard to think of him as pure. I mean, you can tell just by looking at him that he's a bad'n."

Alice decided to check out her assumptions that Emily thought Lucy was a witch.

"How did you know it was me at the door?"

"I didn't," replied Lucy.

"So why shout come in and why not lock the door?"

"Because, beautiful Alice, you're not the only one who wants to jump his bones. I figure that I'm not such a hot looker with my clothes on, but if I can trick him into finding me in a compromising position, he might just take me roughly from behind."

Alice was astonished. "But how old are you?"

"Old enough to want it." The water had turned to hot now and steam rose from around Lucy's small feet.

"Can't you just cast a spell on him?" That was a clever trap thought Alice.

"Please! Alice," Lucy replied feigning offence, "I do have some morals."

"Could you do it though?"

"If I can know that you own a horse, I certainly know how to make a fool fall in love."

Alice stared at the grinning girl in front of her, unable to formulate a response to what she had just heard. If Lucy's aim had been to shock then it had worked.

"How did you know I had a horse?"

"I used to ride horses, mangy, knackered ponies on the sites and I just felt an empathy with you, as if whatever I found beautiful and exciting so would you."

"As simple as that?"

"Well, us witches are known for our extra intuition," Lucy replied. "Bring your horse here. Kerry wouldn't mind. You could keep it in the stables. They're a bit messy but I'd help you tidy them out for free rides."

Alice smiled, acting out a compassionate role. "Okay, I'll ask him, but I've not really been here long enough to ask favours."

"Don't worry about that, I've never known him say no to anyone."

"What sites are you on about, anyway?"

"Travellers."

"Who looked after you?"

"I don't need anyone to look after me." Lucy paused, aware that her response was a slight exaggeration, experience had taught her that much. "I was on my own mostly, except for Dog, the friend I left the home with."

Alice responded, not needing to search for a question, "You must have been very young."

"I was; Dog was about twenty."

Alice was intrigued but felt that the path she was going down didn't lead in the direction she wanted to go and time might be important. "Did you meet Kerry travelling?"

"Yeah. Dog had been travelling the previous summer, just playing at it really and had made mates with Kerry. We met him after a couple of months on the road. We were a bit hard up because of

Dog's H addiction and he thought Kerry would lend him the money to get by. But he ended up having to swap his dog for Kerry buying a fortnight's worth of food shopping for him. Not really what the twat wanted but that's how Kerry got Drudwyn and I just preferred the dog to Dog, so when Kerry moved on I asked him to take me with him. A couple of weeks later I realised that we had been working our way down to Emily's where we stayed for a bit and where he left me."

At last Lucy had given up the battle to hold her secrets. Alice guessed she had intended telling her the tale anyway.

"So was Dog your boy friend then?" Alice asked, backtracking a little now that she could.

"I think that's what he thought," replied Lucy in a matter of fact way. "Dog was sort of raping me as soon as he'd got me away from the home."

"And Kerry?" Alice knew the reply she wanted to hear.

"You can't fancy someone you think's capable of that can you?" replied Lucy.

Alice was unsure as to who fancied whom in Lucy's answer.

Lucy stepped out of the shower and towelled herself off. With a hint of Vanilla, the scent of damp hair and clean skin cut through the steam.

"Did you go to the police when Kerry took you away?"

"No proof by then and Kerry dished out a little summary justice when he found out."

Alice changed tack a little. The police ears had something to investigate and she could go back to the rape later. For now, incriminating Kerry in vigilante activities wouldn't help stop the murders. "So how does Kerry know Emily?"

"Don't really know." Lucy pulled on her knickers. "So is there a Mr. Alice back in Leeds?"

"No." Alice hoped her acting was up to the job. She was sure it would fool your average human, but not so sure about someone with pretensions of having supernatural powers.

"A boyfriend then." Lucy watched Alice's thumb touch the base of her bare ring finger in a habitual movement.

"No."

"So what drew you to this one little spot in the middle of nowhere?"

"Fate, I guess."

Lucy smiled. "Yes, you're probably right. Anyway, I'm off into town."

Chapter 12

The conversation was immediately brought to the attention of Jim and D.I. Renshaw who held a meeting an hour later with the D.C.I. A typed transcript and a new piece of evidence. Jim read the transcript out trying to keep his voice passionless even when reading Lucy's accusations regarding Alice's feelings for Kerry.

"Right," said the D.C.I., "get hold of whatever police station covers Tiley. Ask them for records about travellers in their area from three years ago to one year ago. Get them to find out what home that girl's gone missing from. I want her full record. Find out if there's any intelligence on a traveller called Dog. I daresay there'll be a dozen with the same name but check for one that's from that area. I want surveillance photographs of these two visitors sent around the country and Jim, get your wife sorted out with her horse tomorrow."

"Yes sir."

Arrangements had been made for Alice to leave the house, drive into Becksworth and meet Jim and DI Renshaw in a hotel room every Tuesday and Saturday.

The next day arrived and Alice left the house at ten a.m. She was sure that no one noticed her leave; apparently Kerry, Lucy and Emily were sleeping in again. She arrived at the hotel and waited in the room for Jim and Renshaw.

Alice was sitting in a harsh, red fabric armchair in the family sized bedroom, a little on edge for the moment, neither in her role as a police officer nor acting as a lecturer on holiday. She didn't like much about the room. It was cold and sparse and something else that it took her a little while to put her finger on: it was spotless and regimental. There was no smell of dog, no fiddle on the floor or blankets covering the windows.

As the door opened, Alice felt her heart in her throat, for the split second it took Jim and then Renshaw to appear from behind it. It was at the moment of seeing the familiar and safe faces that the armchair suddenly became more homely. She relaxed into it for the time that it took Jim to cross the room, to her beaming face.

Jim and Alice made a habit, for the sake of professionalism, not to show much affection whilst on duty in front of colleagues, but this time was different. Alice moved to stand and hug Jim, but he moved slightly to one side, stamping his requirement to keep the professionalism even now. And it was Renshaw who placed a large soft hand on to her shoulder in the warmer of the two greetings. Alice's heart sank a fraction but at least neither Jim nor Renshaw were likely to turn on her and eat her. It was the first time she had felt entirely safe for three days and it was an enormous relief.

Jim relayed the details of what he had learnt from Dr. McNatley.

"I've heard some strange ideas in my time," said Alice, "but that takes the biscuit."

"The D.C.I is keen on the idea, especially since those two weirdoes turned up."

"Oh well, I suppose I'll have to ask Kerry if I can keep a horse there. I can't see him saying no though."

"Why's that?" asked Jim.

"Well, he's being helpful and coming across as quite a nice guy really."

"That," said Jim suspiciously, "is probably what Muriel Beck thought when she met him."

Alice shot Jim a dirty look.

"What's your opinion on your three friends' mental state?" asked Renshaw.

Alice was glad to talk to Renshaw who at least didn't have any vested interests.

"Lucy, the young girl, is badly damaged. She could be lying about the rape, but I feel she's telling the truth and I think it's affected her a lot. I'd say she's in need of a lot of counselling. I really have never met any girl quite like her. Mature one minute, five years old the next."

Jim noticed Alice's concentration switch to the window to watch a magpie perched on the window ledge shake a little drizzle from its feathers before flying off. Alice's attention returned to Renshaw as she continued her report.

"I can't really say much about Emily. She seems to genuinely believe she's a witch, but doesn't define what one is, but she seems quite normal otherwise. And as for Kerry, well, like Lucy said, he's deep. I'm sure the other two aren't up to anything, but Kerry I'm not sure about. He doesn't let much out, but there again three days isn't long enough to decide if a pleasant eccentric is a murdering psychopath at heart."

"There's some new evidence," said Jim.

"Oh."

"Yes, the elder sister of Muriel Beck has told us that Muriel was dabbling in witchcraft a little as well. Apparently she, the elder sister that is, found Muriel doing something strange with hens' blood. The sister, Hazel I think she's called, said she didn't think it was important at first, so we may possibly be closer to ascertaining the motive for her murder. If she was involved in witchcraft, she could have been killed either by other witches or some sort of vigilante witch hunter, or by whoever. Anyway, it's given us another avenue of thought."

"Don't tell me sceptic Jim's starting to believe in witches," said Alice.

"I believe," answered Jim, "that there may well be people who think they are witches."

Jim and Renshaw continued to brief Alice on the investigation so far. A phone call on Renshaw's mobile was handed over to Alice.

Smegvick expressed his appreciation of her efforts but left her in no doubt that they as yet weren't enough. She had better come up with a lot more information about Taliesin or she would be out of the farm.

Alice wanted to impress Smegvick, a man who was talked about in the highest terms by everyone who worked with him, but right now Alice wasn't too impressed with his man management skills. She had to find something of relevance to the case at the farm, preferably incriminating evidence. For this she needed Kerry to be involved in the murders and although she was reasonably sure that Smegvick was playing it straight, she had the nagging feeling that he would be happy with a result – the right result some of her older colleagues called it.

Alice returned to Kerry's house with groceries that Jim had given her at the meeting. The household was just stirring. Emily entered the kitchen in her dressing gown as Alice was putting away the food.

"Been shopping, Alice?"

"Yes." She looked at Emily's attire. "Another late night?"

"Just a late riser; I read a lot at night."

Tonight, thought Alice, I will see what you do after I go to bed.

"Morning." Kerry walked into the room.

"Kerry?" said Alice, lengthening his name into a sort of plea.

"Alice," replied Kerry.

How do you bring horses up in conversation subtly, considered Alice. "Well," she continued, "I was wondering, you know the outbuildings?"

"Yes."

"Well," continued Alice, "one of them could be cleared out to be a stable and I've got a horse and wondered if I could keep him here. It'd be better you see to have him here with me than in some strange stables."

"Yeah, no problem. I'll give you a hand moving some of the

junk about."

"Thanks."

"Do you want to do it now?"

"Sure, if you're not busy."

"I could never be too busy to go into a dark stable," Kerry was about to say "with you" but instead he stopped himself, changed his tone and said, "and shift a load of old junk with giant spiders hiding underneath it."

Kerry pulled on his boots and led Alice to the outbuilding. One in fact looked like it was a stable. Inside were rusting farm implements, boxes and even some horse tack. Kerry and Alice peered over the half stable door.

"Right," said Kerry. "We'll shift all the junk into the next one along."

"I'll pay you know, for the use of the stable," said Alice.

"No, it's not necessary. It's not like I was using the stable."

Alice was intrigued by Kerry's humble lifestyle. She wanted to insist that he accept some payment but as it would come out of the force's coffers and they were listening, she decided against it.

Kerry seemed in an unusually conversational mood.

"You were the only enquiry I got about the room."

"I hadn't heard about the murders." Alice could not believe the stupidity of her reply; even on a desert island it would have been difficult to miss the publicity surrounding the deaths. She had answered too quickly and now, although it might have been paranoia, she wondered if some inflection in Kerry's voice hadn't urged her to speak before thinking.

Kerry said nothing as he pushed a rusty old lawn mower in to the light of the day. There was no ripple of connivance on his battered face or signal that he found her reply damning. She was watching for it now and on guard against any further verbal trickery.

They went back into the stable again. The dust visible in the shafts of light produced its threatened sneeze from Alice.

"Gazuntike."

Alice smiled at Kerry as he watched her bring a tissue to her nose. He smiled back almost lecherously. It brought to Alice's mind memories of old movies, the stable or the barn, sometimes a garage, that was where the passions climaxed in those films. This little room with its mixture of straw and old tools was the essence of all those scenes. The romantic side of her personality wanted to re-enact one of those movies now whilst her sensible side wanted Jim to be her leading man. She wondered what thoughts crossed Kerry's mind and consciously looked in to his spider web eyes, resting there just long enough to let the spiderman think that she was trapped, before alighting to a corner of the room and pulling at some tack.

"Don't I warrant a 'bless you'," she said into a corner. "I would have thought that was the least you could do with a marauding beast about."

"Bless you," replied Kerry.

"What do you think about the deaths?" Alice asked, whilst making a show of continuing with the job in hand.

Kerry started to tug on a handle of a large chest with his good arm, testing it for ease of movement. "Just some escaped zoo animal or something," he replied absent-mindedly.

Too absent-mindedly Alice felt. "No you don't, you don't think that at all, I can tell."

Kerry straightened up and gazed at Alice with a face that carried only the slightest hint of surprise. He took his time to think before even responding to Alice's claim.

"Are you another witch?" he asked despondently.

"No," replied Alice. "Just not another idiot."

He seemed troubled now, but still replied in a blasé fashion.

"Maybe it is an animal, maybe it's not. I don't know and I'm not really bothered until it starts affecting people I care about, and there's not a lot of them about."

"Bullshit," said Alice.

Kerry could detect no anger in Alice's words, just a determination not to be fobbed off. She was thrusting herself to new heights in his esteem.

Alice's questions were not framed as demands but friendly inquisitiveness.

"You care about Emily and Lucy, but you invited them up here, putting them in danger. Why?"

"I acted on impulse," he could see from her eyes it was not enough. "Don't you ever feel fate urging you to do something?"

If she did her body language was only saying continue. He could stop of course but his own fatal argument was pushing him to continue, answering questions he had never even asked himself.

"It's like you, when you first came here, I said no, but fate invited you in."

Alice folded her arms, light-heartedly starting to play a game, the prize being Kerry's thoughts.

"I've never asked Emily to read my fortune or give me a mojo, or reveal her secrets to me, but I've known her for years. I felt as soon as Muriel died that the reason I knew her was for this, for something big. Now if it's just a cat, common sense can protect them, but I can sense the evil in my every bone, like nothing I've ever felt. It grew on me slowly at first and I thought I might be imagining it. I'm still not sure, but you see if I am just imagining it, then we're all safe. If not and you start believing down another road, you have to go the whole hog and call in people who believe they are here to help. It's just like getting a metal detector to a field where you think there's treasure."

Alice frowned not fully appreciating the analogy.

"I mean if there is evil here they might find it, if they can do half of what Emily claims they can."

"Why do you think you can feel it and what do you mean by evil?" Alice was starting to feel a little like Pandora with a box in front of her. "Do you mean Satan worshipping kind of stuff?"

"Satan's just the name of a god that got associated with evil, but I don't know what I mean. Evil…" Kerry shrugged his shoulders, struggling for the right words, "Evil's, evil, whether it's a child molester or a supernatural thing. It's a force and it's here."

Answering these questions didn't seem such fun anymore. Alice could see that he was becoming a little uncomfortable with the situation.

Alice was satisfied. She had a little to go on now. She needed more of course but she had been pushy enough and she wanted time to assemble her thoughts on Kerry and his state of mind.

She started to move junk again. Kerry seemed relieved by this and returned his attention to the chest.

"Sorry Alice, but I think you'd better get Lucy to help us move this," Kerry had dragged the chest no more than an inch, his bad arm lowering the muscle power he could put into the job.

"Open it," Alice said.

"It'll only be junk. Probably full of spiders," replied Kerry.

Alice stepped over the chest, unlocking it with the key, which had been left in its hole. The rusted hinges screeched in defence as Alice pulled the lid upwards. She greeted the contents with a look of bewilderment. The entire chest was full of what looked like salt and desiccated garlic, and on top of this bed lay a few rolls of parchment.

Alice lifted them out, giving each a little shake before handing them over to Kerry. Cautiously he unrolled a little of one of them. It was the same as the writing that he had found in his aunt's notes.

Kerry told Alice that he would send Lucy out to help her finish clearing the stable whilst he showed the rolls to Emily.

Emily soon identified the story on the parchment as that from the wallet.

"What's the story then?" Kerry asked.

" Gwawl, a king of the other world, fancies Rhiannon. Rhiannon marries Pwyll and has a baby, which Gwawl eats. Gwawl gets banished to this world, by his enemy Arawn, who's also Pwyll's friend, which was a punishment because he could be killed if struck by a single blow from a mortal. He could only return to his kingdom if he found Rhiannon in this world and gave her the baby he'd eaten. Pwyll dies and she goes on to marry Manawyddan."

Kerry quietly laughed. "And they say your religion's far fetched."

Lucy and Alice came through the door, Lucy rubbing the dirt from her hands onto her jeans, Kerry's jeans Alice suspected judging by the rolls at the bottom and the size of the waistline.

"All cleared out," said Lucy. "Now what about these parchments?"

Emily patiently repeated herself.

"So nothing to do with the murders then?" asked Lucy.

Emily shrugged her shoulders, about to say that she couldn't think of a connection, when one occurred to her. But Lucy was there first.

"Gwawl is like an archetypal character, like the grim reaper. He appears in different stories with different names, but at the end of the day it's Gwawl, and he does get called," Lucy paused for pantomime-like effect, "Hafgan. They are both kings who have what's rightfully theirs stolen"

Alice was only a little interested in the conversation. It certainly wasn't about to catch a killer, but she believed that under normal circumstances she would have asked a question around about now. "Why would this bloke have two names?" she asked.

"The devil," replied Emily. "Satan, Lucifer, Old Nick, Mephysto, all the same bloke," Emily hesitated raising her eyebrows a little, "according to some."

The conversation seemed to take a sidetrack at this point, Lucy and Emily contesting which of them could think up the most people with more than one name.

Alice whispered to Kerry, "I'm going to get my horse."

He nodded and she left the room as Lucy gave a shout of delight as she remembered, "Rhiannon and Epona."

The three left in the house heard Alice's car leave the farm. They looked at each other, able to speak more freely now, but unsure where to start. Lucy showing the impetuous nature of youth began, "Shagged it yet then?"

Kerry laughed, "No," he replied.

"So why keep her around? You know she's up to something."

"She's nice," Kerry replied lamely.

"You'll be eating those words when she turns into a hairy monster," Lucy said. "Or when you do and she's standing there with a police issue silver bullet."

"Time to take the hairy monster for a walk," said Kerry before calling Drudwyn.

Chapter 13

Kerry had been roaming his land all afternoon with Drudwyn and he now stood at the top of a gentle incline, surveying the panorama of his purple, heather covered moorland, gaining vigour from the wind that tugged at his unkempt hair. Slowly he let his mind absorb the fact that this beautiful wilderness, almost void of human thought, was his to do with as he pleased.

He was contemplating how different it might have been if no human had ever set foot upon those hills, when softly but perceptibly the earth began to vibrate beneath his feet. The vibrations continued as a thudding, clattering noise joined it. Kerry searched the horizon in front of him. He could see nothing but sensed that something large was heading in his direction with some speed. He turned around to look back at the house to see Alice cantering towards him upon her stallion. Relieved Kerry waited for her to come to him.

Alice halted the horse by Kerry's side; he looked up at her and smiled. It amazed Kerry how different Alice appeared on the horse, so perfectly relaxed and full of joy in her saddle that it was hard to think of horse and rider as two separate entities. Alice was not wearing the required hat and instead her hair, like Kerry's, blew in the wind. Kerry compared her to Bodicea in his mind, for although there was no warrior aspect to Alice's appearance, she certainly held a noble bearing upon the horse and yet she did not have the manner of one who would look down upon the serfs.

"I didn't expect it to be quite so big," said Kerry as he put out a hand to pat the horse. The horse neighed and side stepped a little before a gentle word from Alice brought it to rest.

Alice felt an alien emotion, she said nothing for the split second that she considered it, it was jealousy, she wanted Kerry's attention on her not the horse. Alice shook her head trying to dislodge the thoughts, wondering what effect this case was having on her.

"Have you ever ridden?" The emotions were clinging on to the sides of her consciousness and she knew that the horse always brought out the wilder side in her, perhaps because up there she could entertain more basic thoughts than might seem proper, since until she dismounted, they would only be thoughts and perhaps some words.

"No, but it's not a bad idea, now I've got this land I suppose I could get one. We could ride together," he said playfully.

"I'd like that," Alice realised she had replied a little too enthusiastically. She wasn't here to flirt and her words had probably never been listened to by so many people at the same time. But it seemed so hard to avoid playfully amorous thoughts when looking down into those eyes. They danced about with so much life that it seemed unnatural not to entertain them.

"I don't think I will get one though. It's probably more of a responsibility than I've got time for at the moment."

"I'd give you a lesson, but B.A.'s not the horse for learners."

They began to walk back to the house. The thought of flirting with Kerry had given Alice an idea about digging for the extra information that Smegvick had demanded. After all, the two dead women had probably both flirted with him and it seemed obvious that at least Muriel wouldn't have been very subtle about it.

"I was speaking to a friend at uni about you on the phone," she said.

Kerry didn't look up this time. He felt a little massage of his ego, but wasn't about to fall into an embarrassing misunderstanding again.

"She wanted to know if she could come and visit."

Still Kerry kept his head pointing in the direction of home, allowing Alice to raise her voice enough to carry to his ears from her position in the face of the breeze.

Alice continued in a light-hearted tone, "I told her, she could wait her turn."

Kerry gave in and grinned, possibly with a hint of a blush on his swarthy face.

It wasn't going to plan yet but she was going to persevere. "When you kissed me…"

Kerry looked up, he wanted to hear every word of this, however embarrassing it was going to be.

"I was flattered."

Flattered, thought Kerry, was not the word he had hoped for.

"Do you like me Kerry?" she asked.

"Of course," he replied his brow furrowing.

Alice was going to use a psychology that she would never have been allowed to use on a patient. She halted her horse and bent down towards Kerry's ear. "I know we have a long time together and that it's only been days so far, but I've spent a lot of time with you in those few days and things go through my mind. I wonder what goes through yours when you catch my eye and hold it for that second too long?"

Kerry was at first shocked by a forwardness that he had not expected from her and then searched for some hint as to the thought process going on inside her brain, but there was no clue. Alice drew herself up again and faced forward, not looking in his direction, her face ignoring the question that her mouth had set.

"If you thought I was a werewolf or the killer, would you sleep with me?" Kerry responded.

That wasn't an answer Alice had expected; it threw her a bit, but encouraged her in the direction she was taking. "If I thought you loved me and I loved you, but I'd need convincing to fall for a murderer," she replied. There was a pause, "Do you love me?" she asked in a matter of fact kind of way.

"No." Kerry was unnerved. In his experience women who talked about love within four days of meeting him could generally be classified as bunny boilers. He hoped Alice wasn't about to fall into this category.

Alice used a silence to push Kerry along.

"I think it's an overused word anyway. I don't know what you think it means, but to me it means someone you would want to spend the rest of your life with."

Alice was enjoying this line of questioning too much for her professional liking. Although Kerry wasn't saying anything specific, she was now seeing the slightest glimpse of a soft underbelly.

"If you loved," she said, smiling mischievously, but with a hint of coldness that came from forcing a conversation that she would rather have had in private, "you would tell your love everything. That's what it is, not being scared to reveal your worst secrets because only then can you feel comfortable with someone, when the fear of being found out has gone and that person is still with you."

Kerry began to feel from Alice's tone that he had misread the situation and that in fact Alice was having a general conversation with him about the meaning of love, not about his feelings for her in particular. "Why?"

"To love would be to trust implicitly, or at least not to care if let down. To love would be to have no secrets."

"That answers your question then. I obviously don't love. Now why don't you just ask what you want to?"

Alice turned her head to look at Kerry. "Are you the murderer?"

"Why are you out here with me if you think I am?"

"I don't think you are, but I don't know you're not. The psychologist in me reckons that you might tell me the truth, even if that meant admitting to murders and letting me live to know the story."

"Are you sure it's not the copper in you?" Kerry's stare was icy cold.

The police ears waited with anticipation. Cars were put on standby, ready to respond to any incident that occurred on that tiny patch of moorland where Kerry and Alice stood in a deadlock of their own making.

"What?" asked Alice, still feigning cheekiness.

"Are you a copper?"

"No." Alice dropped the playful approach. His distrust of her had actually offended her. She would have to think about that one later.

"Then I'm no killer."

The questions had brought an acted but chilly mistrust between Alice and Kerry and dampened down the conversation. As they travelled back to the house, Alice ceased her questioning. Professionally she had received a setback rather than any pertinent information and emotionally she felt downhearted by the sudden twist that the conversation had taken by going from flirting to accusations.

As they came to the house, a Landrover drove down the drive and stopped outside. Lord Smith-Kurr stepped out of the vehicle wearing a long, waxed cotton coat. Kerry did not immediately recognise him as the man he had threatened at the hunt meet. Alice had not met Smith-Kurr before and presumed him a friend of Kerry's. Smith-Kurr looked at Alice briefly. Alice smiled at him, a friendly smile was returned before he turned his attention to Kerry.

"Mr. Taliesin," Smith-Kurr moved to shake Kerry's hand. Kerry accepted the hand. "My name is Geoffrey Smith-Kurr. Actually its Lord Smith-Kurr but that sounds a little pompous, don't you think?" Alice dismounted keeping an interested eye on Smith-Kurr. "I came over specifically to apologise to you and your beautiful wife," he nodded towards Alice who stood holding her stallion a little back from the two men.

"Alice is my lodger," corrected Kerry.

"My apologies, madam."

Alice smiled pleasantly back at Smith-Kurr, realising as he stood by Kerry that Smith-Kurr was in fact an extremely large man. Kerry was not small but Smith-Kurr had more than a few inches on him in height and width.

"As I was saying, Mr Taliesin, I wish to apologise for our intrusion the other day. I had no idea you did not know that we were on your land."

"You were with the hunt," Kerry's hackles started to rise.

"Yes, but as I say I do apologise and, unlike some Master of Hounds, I do fully understand the anti-hunt argument. I don't agree with it but I respect those that stand up for what they believe in and so I give you my guarantee we won't intrude again unless by mutual agreement with the police."

"If you understand the arguments it makes your crimes all the worse. Now get off my land before I set my hound, on you."

"I'm sorry you feel that way. It took a lot for me to come here, what with all the rumours about you."

Smith-Kurr climbed back into his Landrover and drove away whilst Kerry watched scowling.

Alice thought about Kerry's reaction to Smith-Kurr. On the one hand, surely someone who protected foxes was unlikely to kill young women, on the other hand her experience had taught her that love for animals did not guarantee a love of the human race. Perhaps Kerry hated the hunt because he was the quarry.

Alice led the horse to the stable. No sign of extraordinary interest had been shown in the horse by anyone. Still, there was tonight.

Time moved slowly for Alice for the rest of the day. Kerry seemed to avoid her as she sat about reading, occasionally visiting her horse even though she could see the stable door from her room. It was an awful feeling, just waiting for something to happen. She felt that tonight something would have to break the almost stagnant waters of the murder enquiry and she decided to follow Kerry to watch his actions that night. As the day wore on she began to fear what she might see and concern also grew for her stallion.

That evening Emily made a large casserole for the four of them, which they ate around the kitchen table. With the food, Kerry's frosty air disappeared. The meal and light conversation also eased Alice's worries a little as she allowed a homely feeling to lap at her shores, but there was still that edge, a tsunami in the distance.

"Emily," said Kerry, "that was excellent. I think you ought to stay longer."

"Thank you," Emily started to collect the plates.

"No, leave them, I'll do that." Kerry took the plates from her and prepared to wash up.

"Do you fancy a game of chess, Alice?" asked Emily.

At last, something to take her mind off the situation, thought Alice. "Yeah, why not?"

Emily and Alice retired to the living room where Emily set up a fine chess set with intricately carved pieces on the top of one of Kerry's boxes of books. Lucy was already in the room, keen to avoid any domestic duties. She sat on the edge of a chair, fiddling with Kerry's baseball bat and a violin bow.

Alice was aware she couldn't see Kerry but hoped he wouldn't turn into a wolf whilst washing the pots.

"You can be black if you like, dear," said Emily.

Alice looked down at the board and moved a pawn, then looked over at Lucy. She was now listening to a personal stereo, still clutching the bat in one hand and a book in the other.

"Expecting trouble?" asked Alice.

Lucy did not reply. Emily looked over at Lucy, picked up a paper back book and threw it into Lucy's lap.

Lucy sprang to her feet, propelling the book onto Drudwyn's head and looked around startled. When she was happy that all was as it should be, she removed the headphones from her ears.

"What?" she demanded angrily.

"I just asked," said Alice, "if you were expecting trouble?"

"Trouble?" Lucy repeated.

"The baseball bat."

"You never can tell," said Lucy.

"You seem nervous enough," continued Alice.

"Yeah well, I was thinking about the murders."

Emily shot Lucy a reproachful glance, but Lucy continued, "What if those people in the stone circle are involved and that there's two sort of forces fighting it out. I mean, if they're using Hafgan's ring, they've probably been using it for a while."

Emily interrupted. "I don't think Alice wants to hear all this."

"Bollocks," replied Lucy. "I've got nothing to hide whether she's a pig or not."

"Lucy!" Emily was getting flustered.

"I'm not," said Alice.

"Whatever you reckon," Lucy continued regardless. "Anyway, if it's them, you should have had murders before. But if they're using Hafgan's ring and worshipping Hafgan or Gwawl then they would hate Manawyddan, so maybe a Manawyddan cult has moved onto their territory and they're fighting it out."

"A bit like Frankenstein meets the Wolfman you mean," said Emily sarcastically.

"It's just a thought," said Lucy apologetically.

"Well it's a stupid one," chastised Emily.

"No dafter than you thinking it could be a werewolf."

"Well I can disprove any power in the Mabinogion," said Emily. Lucy looked worried.

"It says here that anyone who wishes the sword of Rhydderch the generous to come to them can get it by calling for it by its name, Dyrnwyn; only problem is it should burst into flames."

Lucy expression turned to smugness. It was quite obvious that Emily was planning to put the theory to the test.

"So," said Emily, standing up and moving to a clutter free part of the room, "Rhydderch, send me Dyrnwyn."

Nothing happened.

Lucy shrugged her shoulders. "Perhaps you have to be from the other world," she said. "You know, the reincarnation of Gwawl or Rhiannon. Or, perhaps the sword would have to have been in this world, or…"

Emily appeared content to listen to Lucy's rambling suggestions. She loved Lucy and on the occasions when Lucy acted childishly, it brought out maternal emotions in her thoughts.

"Or, perhaps the Mabinogion is just a bunch of stories, with no magic connections, which is my bet," concluded Lucy.

Jim, in the listening room, scribbled down a note for D.I. Renshaw who was coming on duty in the morning. He wanted Renshaw to contact Dr. McNatley at the university and find out if Lucy's words meant anything to him.

"And," continued Lucy, "who's new to the area and showing an awful lot of interest in the Mabinogion?"

"He's always been interested in it," Emily said, fighting her own doubts that Kerry was deceiving her perceptions.

"Shape-shifters have to start somewhere," said Lucy. "Why not here? We never see anything when he drags us out to Hafgan's Ring every night. Perhaps that's because he's with us."

Alice at least knew the cause of the late rising now, but she found it hard to believe that Lucy could seriously doubt Kerry if she was prepared to watch Hafgan's Ring for hours waiting for a coven of witches to turn up. It brought back some childhood memories when she would argue for the sake of arguing, usually about which was the best of her father's horses.

Kerry entered the room. As he did so, Lucy realised how openly she had been talking; for some reason it had never crossed her mind to lower her voice in Kerry's house.

"I suppose you'll be wanting to come with us tonight then, Alice," Kerry said.

"No!" said Alice. "It's bloody cold out there for a start, and I'm not really sure I know what you're all talking about."

Of course she knew. Kerry had told Wilks about Hafgan's Ring and she understood there was a connection with the writings, but why would a lecturer on a sabbatical leave the house in the middle of the night? Of course the curious detective would, but today she was a university lecturer and besides, it was cold out there.

Kerry told her about the people he'd seen in the ring and the words he'd heard, words connected to the Mabinogion story. "And now that I've told you our secrets, perhaps, you would have the decency to tell us yours."

It was another tense moment at the farm, and in the listening room. Kerry's face was stony and determined, yet to Alice there seemed a hint of weakness about the expression that she had not seen in him before. Perhaps his ego was expecting a dent. She was not so hard herself as to take pleasure in thinking she had some part in this cracking of his exterior. Alice felt no hint of danger as his eyes stared at her, bereft of their previously permanent sparkle. She knew things could blow up now, but felt her head shake at the thought that Kerry could possibly be involved in the murders, or even have ever posed a risk to her. How could he be a suspect? He had alibis and, for God's sake, he was human.

"You think I'm a copper?" she asked.

Lucy answered, "What makes you think we're stupid? We can sense deception you know."

Kerry didn't seem to need any more evidence of Alice's guilt.

"Why Alice?" he asked.

Alice searched for a hint that Kerry might be waiting for confirmation of her guilt but she saw none; he simply knew. The case was as good as over for her. Going back to her home and spending a night in safety beckoned, but not strongly enough. She had to leave this place with some level of professionalism. She felt the word professionalism in her head. It was different now, having taken on new meaning during her time with Jim. It had grown to mean the controlling of her urges, urges to slob, to kiss, to shout, even just to run. She could do all those things here, but hadn't and regretted it now.

Kerry repeated himself, aware that Alice seemed to be daydreaming at a time when he would have expected a little more concentration. Whatever she said next he would know she had planned out in her head. "Look," he continued, "I invited you in and all you do is spy on us, try to trick us and keep doing so in the face of our efforts to make you feel at home. Why?"

Alice remembered a colleague from her training school days who had once expressed surprise at why criminals got so irate at the police when they got caught. It hardened Alice's emotions but broke her resolve.

"Why do you think?" she said, angry at such a stupid question. "You are a suspect, dead bodies, serious stuff, my job."

Jim held his breath, fraught with worry. Never had an undercover operation he had worked on been blown out of the water like this. People were going to think his wife was incompetent. There was her safety as well of course. He despatched cars to stand-by at the farm gates.

Kerry turned to the witches. "Can you give us some time alone please?"

It was a lot to ask Lucy. She didn't owe Alice anything and despite her words, she was probably the greatest believer in Kerry's innocence that ever lived. Emily however needed no time to think and, taking Lucy by one hand, led her from the room.

Kerry, still standing, stared down at Alice, far enough away to give the impression that he was standing off, his face a dormant volcano with the tragedy and rage out of sight, but not out of mind.

Alice could see that Kerry now had feelings that he didn't know whether to or how to express. She thought he had always suspected and she never imagined that confirmation of her role would have quite such an effect on a man who, to the outside world, seemed about as fazed by adversity as the Himalayas.

Kerry's lips formed a syllable but it was Alice who broke the silence, mindful of the listening room staff.

"I suppose you want me to go now?" she said and for a moment thought she saw the slightest glaze in Kerry's eyes.

"No. You can at least be my alibi for the next murder. It'll save you having to put those morons back outside my front gate, watching me though their binoculars."

"You really want me to stay?" Alice asked, inwardly relieved that at least she had a lifeline to Kerry now.

Coldly he replied. "You'd have to tell me your real name of course. That's one of your rules, isn't it?"

"D.C. Alice Farrier," she said.

Kerry regarded her with incredulity. "You're Jim Farrier's wife?"

Alice nodded, a little afraid that if she spoke the lump in her throat would be picked up by the police ears. Without any other reaction, Kerry turned and left the room closing the door behind him.

Alice sank deep into her chair, silent tears forced their way through her steel eyes, but she had no time for this. She had to think of what she should do. She was a police officer and there was still a murder investigation centred on the house. Alice dried her eyes and spoke quietly into the pendant around her neck.

"I'm going to stay here. At least that way we have an officer near the crime scene at all times."

For the rest of the day Alice saw nothing of Kerry, but to her relief Emily and Lucy did not change their attitude towards her, perhaps, thought Alice, because they had always known. Lucy, who Alice had expected to alienate with her disclosure, seemed more interested in slagging off Jim for allowing her to be put in such a position, rather than any reprisals against her.

Emily confided in Alice that tonight was to be the last time she would bother going out to Hafgan's Ring. They couldn't go every night and any coven worth its salt would be out on a full moon. If they weren't there tonight they would never be there again until the whole murder business was sorted out.

That night Alice watched the threesome leave the farmhouse for the moors. It was the first time Alice had known that she was alone in the house. At first she had no problem with that. She knew once she was in bed with the covers wrapped tightly around her, that any fear would leave her.

Alice entered the hall heading for the stairs when she heard a noise emanating from the kitchen. She glanced at the kitchen door before running up the stairs. She knew it could only have been Drudwyn, but every noise was suspect.

In her bedroom, she only had to make it from the light switch to the bed. She removed her shoes, flicked the switch and made a dive for it. The room was dark for only a few seconds until Alice's eyes grew accustomed to the moonlight. She could see the sky from her bed and having forgotten to close the curtains, the moon shone down at her; a full moon. Folklore bore heavily upon Alice. She would just jump up, close the tablecloth curtain and so protect herself from the evil moon. But as she reached the window it was something more earthly that brought a scream and backward leap from Alice. A flurry of feathers in the form of an owl landed on the window ledge. It flapped twice, steadying itself and then peered in through the window at Alice. She stared back, calmed at first to see a bird, but growing steadily more anxious as she personified its stare.

Alice took the one last step forward and pulled the curtain across the window; the owl remained motionless. She climbed back into bed, fighting her fear with childhood prayers. The covers weren't working their magic this time. A scraping noise started at the door, a whimpering joined it and identified the cause as Drudwyn. But the realisation did not calm Alice's fears. She ridiculed the thoughts that came into her head, but once there they would not budge.

Why did he want to come into the room? Was he scared of something out there with him? Or something in here with her? If it was possible for a person to turn into a wolf, which of course it wasn't, couldn't a dog do the same?

She called out to Drudwyn in a reproachful manner; the scratching stopped. Silence never came, as the wind outside seemed to take over from the noise at the door, rattling the window. Alice could imagine it giving way and spraying her in shards of glass. Then, above the gale, she heard her horse whinny. She leapt out of bed and wrenched the curtain back, the owl was gone but something darted into the shadows of the stable block, too quickly for Alice to make out. The threat to something other than herself, to her precious horse, gave her a new vigour. She ran out of her room. Drudwyn was not there and as she ran to the door adrenaline pumped around her body. She began to shout out to the police ears, explaining what was happening. As she ran into the yard in her stocking feet the wind momentarily subsided, leaving her in a spine chilling silence. The stable door was a little ajar and she slowed down on her approach to it. Her horse stuck its head out giving it a good shake when he saw Alice. She patted the horse and peered in to see Drudwyn making a nest in the straw.

The sound of a cough took Alice's eyes towards the moor to see the threesome emerging from the darkness. Alice waited for them, a wave of relief washing over her. Never had she been so relieved to see a murder suspect. As Kerry and Lucy walked past her, not staying in the cold any longer than necessary, Lucy explained that again they had seen nothing at the ring. Emily hung back a little, taking Alice's hand and looking into her petrified face before speaking.

"You really do like him don't you?"

Alice didn't speak, unsure of what to say.

"When all this is over and you've caught yourself a perfectly ordinary mass murderer you'll kick yourself for doubting Kerry, but you are doing your job and I think you're doing the sensible thing under the circumstances. Very brave too."

Alice smiled, relaxed by Emily's presence. She was such a sweet lady that her confidence boosted Alice's own.

Chapter 14

When Renshaw came on duty the next morning, he read the list of salient points made in the transcript of the tape recording from Alice's evening. He wasn't impressed at the note left to him by Jim requesting he contact Dr. McNatley and with a dislike of conducting enquiries on the phone Renshaw found himself dropping his own plans to follow Jim's whim and driving over to the university.

When Renshaw arrived at the university offices, he found the receptionist unclear as to the whereabouts of McNatley.

"I'll just ring his department." She listened to the music until one of the professors answered on the other end. "Hello," chirped the receptionist. "I've got a police officer at reception who'd like to talk to Dr. McNatley……… No, I didn't think so…hold on I'll just ask." the receptionist addressed Renshaw. "Can anybody else help?"

"Does anybody know where I can find Dr. McNatley?"

"Yes, he's taken a chair at Aberdeen University."

"Well, does anybody else here study the occult?"

The receptionist gave Renshaw a puzzled look but passed the question on.

"Professor Webb says he's coming down if you'd just like to take a seat."

"Thank you."

Renshaw sat down but didn't have to wait long before the diminutive Professor Webb was addressing him, shaking very slightly like a small lap dog in a draught.

"Are you the police officer?"

"Inspector Renshaw." Renshaw held out his hand.

"Professor Webb. Now Inspector, I'm not sure if I can help but

I'll certainly try."

"Well," replied Renshaw, "I really wanted to speak to Dr. McNatley as he's already spoken to one of my colleagues about a certain situation."

"Yes, well myself or my colleagues may be able to help without Dr. McNatley."

Renshaw thought he sensed some animosity in Webb's voice. "Could we go somewhere less public?"

"Certainly," Webb replied. "I seem to have inherited McNatley's office," Webb escorted Renshaw to McNatley's old office. "Now then Inspector, fire away."

Renshaw explained the situation as Jim had done to McNatley. He then reiterated what advice McNatley had given Jim and finally handed Webb a short extract of Lucy's outburst about Hafgan's Ring, Manawyddan and Gwawl.

Webb looked perplexed. "I'm a professor of anthropology and some of what you say McNatley told you is true, to the best of my knowledge. But this question about white stallions and female owners sounds like pure fantasy. Do you mind if I try and get hold of Mr. Neil from the history department? I think he may be able to help us."

"Sure," replied Renshaw.

Webb left the room and returned a few minutes later with Mr. Neil. Mr. Neil said nothing at first but studied the transcript that Webb handed to him, his old and fragile fingers following the lines.

"Inspector," said Mr. Neil, "I understand you believe there is some form of occult practice that needs investigating. The thing is I'm a historian pure and simple. I have never studied the occult past any effect it may have had on society as a whole. However, I can help you with the factual side of your problem. For a start the names Manawyddan, Hafgan and Gwawl all come from the Welsh folk stories named the Mabinogion. They are similar to the tales about King Arthur and Merlin. The stories date back to a time in

Europe when certain strange traditions apparently did exist and it seems quite likely that there was a ceremony in which horses were forced to commit acts of bestiality. That ceremony relates, if memory serves me well, to the cult of Epona the Horse Goddess, who is linked to Rhiannon the Horse Queen in the Mabinogion."

"What do you mean "linked to"?" asked Renshaw.

"Well, because stories were spread by word of mouth, names changed, although the stories often remained the same. So, in one part of the country a character may be called Epona, and further north, or in Wales, Rhiannon."

Renshaw let out a deep-depressed breath. "So what about this idea that two cults are fighting it out?"

Mr. Neil shrugged his shoulders. Renshaw looked at Webb who also shrugged.

"I tell you what though," broke in Webb, "I know who could help with your investigation."

"Who?" asked Renshaw.

"Emily Marthson. She's a writer of some highly intellectual studies of the occult. She also wrote a biography I read and she apparently helped West Mercia police with a problem once. You could probably contact her through her publishers. I met her once at a lecture; she's quite a character."

Renshaw opened his briefcase and delved around inside it for a while before producing a surveillance photograph of Emily and showing it to Webb.

"Is that her?"

Webb looked at the photograph and took a second to make his decision. "Yes, that's her. Are you going to tell us what this is all about then?"

"Sorry gents, I can't,"

Webb and Neil weren't bothered. Helping a police investigation would probably be the highlight of their year. Renshaw left the meeting and made his report to the D.C.I.

"That certainly presents us with a quandary," commented the D.C.I. referring to the presence of Emily at Kerry's farm.

"Can it hurt to talk to her?" questioned Renshaw.

"We might as well. She could be very important to us. Or on the other hand we could get Alice to talk to her."

The D.C.I. mulled the point over in his mind.

"No, I think we're better off being up front and getting her in on a professional basis. Go and get her; tape record an interview with her if she'll let you. If not, try to get a statement and if she appears to be on our side, try and avoid any reference to her being a witch, because that wouldn't go down too well in court."

"Yes Sir."

Renshaw left the office and drove over to Kerry's farm. As he drove down the farm track, Drudwyn ran alongside the car, barking until it came to a halt outside the house. Renshaw contained a look of surprise as he spied Lucy and Kerry both playing the fiddle. The dog was standing close to the D.I's eye level as he sat in the comfortable safety of his car. He stared back at Drudwyn looking in and found himself wondering what those canine eyes had seen. The dog seemed to come to an acceptance of Renshaw and trotted out of sight around the house.

"The devil went down to Georgia?" asked Renshaw, recognising the tune as he got out of his car.

"If he did," replied Lucy ceasing to play for a moment, "he stopped off here for lunch."

Kerry stopped playing and waited for Renshaw to explain why he had called.

"I understand Emily Marthson is staying here."

"Yes," replied Kerry suspiciously.

"I'd like to speak to her."

"It would be wiser to speak with her inspector."

"Whatever. Is she about?" asked Renshaw.

Emily had been listening from the kitchen and came out of the front door. "I'm Emily Marthson. How can I help you?"

"Good morning, Mrs. Marthson, I'm Detective...."

"Miss," corrected Emily.

"Sorry, Miss Marthson. I'm Detective Inspector Renshaw. I wondered if I could pick your brain on a professional basis, regarding the murders around here. I'm told you are an expert on the occult."

"Well, I know a little of interest and yes you can have my help on a professional basis," Emily turned to Lucy. "Professional means I get paid, doesn't it?"

"You'd better," replied Lucy.

"We can discuss finance back at the station."

"Oh, you want me to come with you."

"If it's convenient," replied Renshaw.

"If you're paying it's convenient."

Emily walked over to the passenger door of Renshaw's car and waited for him to open it for her, which he did. As they were driving away, Renshaw brought up the subject of payment. "Actually we were hoping that you would help us out of a feeling of public duty. We're a little strapped for cash in the force and this enquiry is a big drain on resources."

"If we keep it quiet I don't mind not being paid, and to be honest I only made a fuss about it for Lucy's sake. She'd give me hell if she thought I was fraternising with the enemy without taking their money."

"Do you see us as the enemy?"

"No, not at all. I'm definitely on your side in this. I hate to see so much sorrow in one place. It leaves a physical scar on the land, you know."

"We were put on to you by a professor at the local university, Mr. Webb. Do you know him?" Renshaw had always had an open mind and wasn't about to close it the minute it was put to the test.

"No, can't say that I do."

"If it's all the same with you, Emily, I'll ask you questions on tape. It's easier to write down the important bits later that way."

"No problem."

When Renshaw and Emily arrived at the station, he led Emily through to an interview room and fetched her a cup of tea. He made sure Emily was at her ease and began the interview, or 'exchange of ideas' as he had been instructed to call it by the D.C.I.

Renshaw opened the questioning. "Tell me everything you know."

Emily resisted telling him everything she knew but instead told him what she knew about the murders. She explained about the Mabinogion, as the lecturers had and about the newly found notes which she had translated.

"The notes state that Arawn, one of the kings of the other world, befriended Pwyll, a mortal. This allowed Pwyll to marry a woman of the other world and he chose Rhiannon, the horse Goddess. This angered a former suitor of Rhiannon, Gwawl. When Rhiannon had a son by Pwyll, Gwawl killed the baby and ate it. Arawn and Pwyll banished Gwawl from the other world and punished him with a spell, which would force him to live in this world until killed by a mortal or until he could find a reincarnation of Rhiannon and impregnate her. So, Rhiannon would conceive the very son that Gwawl had murdered and eaten. But Pwyll had another trick up his sleeve to stop Gwawl getting Rhiannon pregnant. It doesn't say what that was though."

This, thought Renshaw to himself, was a case to write a book about and retire.

"So does all that have any connection with the murders?"

"At best, no, or at least just one nutter who thinks they do, or, at worst," Emily paused for effect. "At worst the story is true. Gwawl is still alive and he wants to find Rhiannon. Perhaps he thought that last girl was her."

"I think," said Renshaw almost convincingly, "that we can rule out a two thousand year old king of the other world wandering about."

"You'd think you could, wouldn't you?" replied Emily.

"And what about the werewolf suggestions?"

"Well, the original idea was that shamans and other magical people could turn themselves into other things. The wolf was a favourite, as was the eagle and salmon. It could have been derived from an astral projection, a sort of controlled, out of body experience, where a person chooses to resemble a wolf instead of a person. Theoretically, some powerful magicians could make their projections more than just something to see through. They could make them solid and as real as the real thing."

"Do you believe that?" asked Renshaw.

"I've never seen it," replied Emily.

"So what about these people Kerry claims to have seen in Hafgan's Ring?"

"A coven of witches more than likely. There are a few of them in this country even now. Some work white magic, others black and some, like those in Hafgan's Ring, I suspect work a strangely twisted kind of grey magic. They may think they are doing good, but if it's to their benefit only, is it really good?"

"And what about Kerry?"

"You mean, do I think he could be the killer?"

"Yes."

"No, I mean it's not Drudwyn, so he'd need another animal and there isn't one, unless he was a shape shifter. But I think I'd sense it if he was."

"Do you think Alice is in danger?"

"It's hard to tell without knowing the nature of the beast. She's probably less at risk than the surrounding households."

"Why?"

"Because Kerry likes her. In all the time I've known him he's never been violent except when it was absolutely necessary to protect Lucy, and then he was like a wild…."

"Animal?" finished Renshaw.

"Just a terminology, Inspector."

"Is there anything else you'd like to add?"

"Yes. I've told you what I know, now you tell me."

Renshaw told Emily everything he knew, which didn't amount to a whole lot. Emily listened intently and when Renshaw had finished, she looked quite concerned.

"I just don't get the bit about them leaving the horse alone. It definitely doesn't fit with anything, but there again, the occult's a large subject area. I suppose I can't be expected to know everything."

"Do you see any pattern in the murders?"

"Well, I suppose you have to look at it from different perspectives. If it's Gwawl, for instance, he's being very stupid in attracting all this publicity to himself, seeing as mortals can kill him. If it's a sicko then that's your department, so no."

Suddenly Emily shuddered. She got up and moved swiftly to the door, which she opened and went into the corridor. A door at the end of the corridor was swinging, as though it had just been used; no one else was in the corridor.

"Miss Marthson," said Renshaw, a little surprised at her action.

Emily turned back to face Renshaw. "Even in the police force," she said to Renshaw.

"I'm sorry I don't follow you," he replied.

"Oh nothing, it's not important."

In fact it was, but Emily was of the impression that D.I. Renshaw would rather not hear about the fact that one witch can recognise another and that she was sure a witch had just walked through the corridor.

"So can you think of anything we should be doing?" Renshaw asked.

"Well, speaking from common sense and not as an expert on the occult, I'd say continue to keep an eye on Kerry, not because he's a suspect but because he may well have been the catalyst. Things only started to happen when he moved here. Somebody's either using him as a scapegoat or he's the real reason for the murders starting. And if I find anything else out I'll pop in."

There was little more to say so Renshaw wrapped up the interview and had a P.C. drive Emily back to the farm. An hour later, Renshaw was briefing the D.C.I., Inspector Wilks and Jim on the little he had learnt from talking to Emily.

"She sounds like a fruitcake to me," Inspector Wilks said when Renshaw had finished.

"Maybe," replied Renshaw, "but she doesn't come across as one, she seems very sincere."

"Well, all I can say then is let's hand the job over to a priest."

"Thank you, Inspector Wilks," said the D.C.I. "I think we can do without the wit."

There was a knock on the door. It was Alice. The officers, including Jim, were surprised to see her. The D.C.I. waved her in.

"Morning Sir."

"Alice," responded the D.C.I. questioningly.

"Well, they know I'm in the force now so I thought there wouldn't be any harm in coming in for more regular updates, and there's no great need for a secret rendezvous either."

"I suppose not," said the D.C.I. "So, have you anything to report?"

"No, not if my bugs are still working well."

"Right then, I've got a press conference. I'll let Jim bring you up to scratch with developments." the D.C.I. turned his attention. "Renshaw, Wilks, back to work."

The D.C.I., Inspector Wilks and D.I. Renshaw vacated the room. Alice kissed Jim on the lips.

"You look like shit," said Jim.

"Thanks."

"And what was all that stuff, asking Kerry if he loved you? It sounded a bit over the mark."

"Well, I wasn't getting anywhere, so I thought I'd try a different track," she said brightly.

"He certainly sounds very taken with you from what he said. And there's one or two silences that sound a bit suspect on tape."

"That's probably when I'm on the bog." Alice was quickly losing her cool in the absence of support from her husband.

"No, you came across loud and clear when you were on the bog."

"Look, you volunteered me for this job. I'm sitting there scared stiff, thinking any moment someone is going to be biting chunks of flesh out of me. I'm trying to pump a murder suspect for information, it's freezing, every man and his dog is listening to my ablutions and the first thing you can do when you see me is have a go."

Jim wanted to say sorry and explain the stress he was under, but he imagined Alice turning it around, showing how much more stress she was under. Alice looked Jim up and down. As ever he was immaculately turned out, a stark contrast to Kerry.

"If you spent less time polishing your uniform you'd have more time to relax and maybe you wouldn't bite my head off every time you see me."

"That's it though, I don't bloody see you. You're happy spending time with Kerry Taliesin even though there's no need now that your cover's been blown. What's your plan now? Get into bed with him to see if he's the murderer, or would that be something you've already tried?"

"You're a twat Jim, and if you want to lose me you're going the right way about it."

"Oh yes, I can see it now." Jim was shouting. "You leave me and say it's my fault that you're shafting the biggest criminal this country's ever had. It won't be me that breaks up this marriage, it'll be your libido."

Alice gritted her teeth. "You stupid bastard," she said quietly and left the room.

The problem was Jim knew he was being stupid and horrible and although he loved Alice most of the time, he had bouts when he thought more of other people's opinion of him than he did of his marriage. Jim was paranoid that his wife was having unfaithful thoughts, although he had no real grounds for his paranoia. But his attitude also meant that he was afraid that others would think he'd married a slut, even though his new colleagues had a high opinion of Alice. But that just made things harder. He wished he'd paid more attention to the song that recommended "Marry an ugly woman".

The tiredness was burning at the back of Jim's eyes and he wasn't sure when water entered them whether it was because he had just hurt Alice or because of the lack of sleep. He rubbed them and left the office but Alice had already gone. One thing Jim couldn't stand was lack of professionalism and the fact that Alice left without being updated on the situation brought out an anger in him that dried his eyes and temporarily overshadowed his remorse.

The rest of Jim's miserable day passed without incident and he returned to his home in the early hours of the next day. Jim and Alice's house was a large modern building, part of a newly finished housing estate for the middle classes. Jim unlocked the door and went inside locking it behind him. He thought about the old farmhouse his wife would be spending the night in. He looked at the safety of his double glazed door and contemplated what it would be like to stay in a house with the door falling off its hinges. Still, he thought, what good is a door when you're living with the very thing you would wish to lock out. The more Jim thought about Kerry, the more he convinced himself that Kerry was the killer and had evil designs on his wife.

Jim took a swig of water then walked up the shag pile carpeted stairs. He realised in his own mind that Kerry was the killer and yet no one could prove it. He was actually committing the murders and laughing at the police's inability to put him in the frame, laughing at Jim and his wife. Jim walked into his bedroom and switched the light on. The room was tastefully decorated and the furniture all built in teak. There was a TV, a midi system and a huge, inviting bed. This place was the safe haven from the outside world that Jim was always glad to come back to, even on his own as he so often was, because Alice's shifts and his rarely coincided.

Tonight, like so many in the past, he would sleep alone, not that he minded. It at least meant a better night's sleep; he could toss and turn to his heart's content. He undressed, put the bedside lamp on and the main light off, got into bed and pressed the remote control on the TV.

He watched the last half hour of the late film, which, frustratingly for Jim, didn't have huge numbers of double D sized girls running about. But it did take his mind off Kerry and Alice and made him tired enough to go to sleep. He turned the TV and light off, put his head down and was soon snoring away with plenty of rapid eye movement.

"**Pwyll**," a soft masculine voice was calling out, "**Pwyll.**" Jim looked around to see where the voice was coming from. He realised he was in a huge room with a tiled floor cold upon his feet and although it was indoors there were fires burning. A fire-eater blew a flame in front of Jim's face and when his view returned he saw a large metal-caged ball in front of him with a naked woman inside. He'd seen the balls before in sleazy clubs and TV films. Underneath the ball and back a few feet he could see steps leading up to something central but he couldn't see what for the ball.

"**Hello Pwyll**," the voice came from behind the ball from the top of the steps. Jim tried to move forward to see who was speaking but he couldn't move. He started to become aware of the situation.

"**That's right, it's just a dream for now,**" came the voice.

Movement, far to his side caught Jim's eye. Two leather-masked men were turning something on a spit over heated coals. It looked sickeningly like a roast human.

"Ignore that, Pwyll and watch the girl in the ball."

Jim returned his sights to the ball. It had started to swing like a pendulum. The tattooed girl inside sat cross-legged and motionless.

"Watch it, Pwyll and relax."

Music started playing, low, rhythmic, evil.

"Drift into a state of complete ease, feel yourself sinking deeper and deeper, falling into happiness. Close your eyes and imagine yourself falling backwards through time. Enjoy the experience. Feel the rush of years blowing past you as you fall out of this life and into your previous one, falling faster and faster. The faster you go the better you feel. You're flying at speed backwards through past lives, you can feel the power of time and you're desperately waiting to reach your most exhilarating speed. Now you're looking for a better life, a time when you were Pwyll, the wise one, Prince of Dyfed, Chieftain of Annwn. Rush towards that time of power. Now Pwyll, open your miserable eyes."

Jim's eyes opened.

"Gwawl," he said with a Welsh accent.

"King Gwawl," the voice lost its soft melody and now the words he uttered were deep, gritty and spiteful.

"What is this?" Jim spoke in Welsh and was answered in the same tongue.

"Do you know who you are, weak, arrogant mortal?"

"I am Pwyll, Prince of Dyffed, Chieftain of Annwn." These were proudly spoken words.

"So why aren't you there now?"

"I, I do not know," Jim's voice faltered.

"I shall tell you why, oh Prince of Fools. It is because you died, like all mortals do, but I shall not be cheated by death for the revenge I seek on you. Think hard Chieftain of Annwn. Recall that day when your vast brain dreamt up the punishment for my crimes, you and Arawn, King of Annwn. Do you remember?"

"You were sent to live with mortals," Jim replied, and then hung his head grasping the situation.

"That's right Pwyll, and you thought merely transforming me into a weakling would render me defenceless and incapable of becoming a sire. Well it didn't and I've had a great time gorging myself on the pleasures of the flesh. It was no punishment; it was an opportunity to find your wife Rhiannon and fuck her senseless! And now, after only a few hundred years, I've found you and Rhiannon. So, I'm going to kill you soon and you can watch all the non-fatal abhorrent mutilations that I'm going to perform on your wife's creamy body from wherever mortal spirits spend eternity. I must also add how grateful I am that you actually married her in this lifetime. I may not have found her without your help, so not only do I get to eat your child, kill you and take your wife, wolf-fashion, I also get to laugh at Arawn when I return to the other world. And whilst you have no powers in this world, I have many. I am indestructible. Do you recall the vampires that claimed so many lives in my kingdom? How we thought they were undefeatable? Well, I play with them now, like you would with a hare. Take a look behind you."

Pwyll looked over his shoulder. Fear gripped him but when he turned there was no vampire, not immediately anyway. And then a small circle of candles to his left drew his attention. Sitting within this circle of miniature flames was a pathetic looking man. Pwyll stared at him; the man stared back with deep, sunken, dry, very sad, colourless eyes. The man's paper white skin was tightly stretched over his skeleton. The expression skin and bone had never had a better home than in this man. How could this sorry thing be a vampire thought Pwyll? But he knew it was for there, protruding from its mouth, were the unmistakable fangs.

"You see, Pwyll, I can capture them and sentence them to an eternity of starvation and ridicule. I keep this one to demonstrate my power over the natural and supernatural world. You, Pwyll have made me a God, your God, and I am an angry and

unforgiving God. And now Pwyll I shall return you to your deathbed."

Jim was suddenly aware that he was in his bed again. He was awake now; he could feel the sweat on his body. The room was still dark. He sat up and went to put the lamp on, but his hand didn't make it to the switch. There was a mephitic snarl, the glint of evil eyes in the dark and the flash of numerous sets of teeth. Fangs sank deeply into Jim's right wrist. Instinctively he moved to fight off the beast but another set of jaws grabbed his other arm. Jim's screams reverberated throughout the insulated house and he felt mouths close around his ankles. He was pinned down by snarling, slavering monsters that he could not see. The jaws on his wrist crushed down harder still and shook vigorously, like a dog playing with a rubber ring. Jim felt the duvet slide off his bare body and as his eyes became adjusted to the light, he saw a huge wolf, bigger by far than Drudwyn, pounce onto the bed. The wolf padded slowly towards him. Never losing eye contact, it stepped onto Jim's stomach and chest, put its snout to Jim's face, drooled into his mouth and urinated onto his body. It began to snarl. More saliva dripped into Jim's face. Then, something changed in the animal's controlled demeanour and it went wild. Jim saw it for a split second before it ripped his windpipe out.

Chapter 15

The next morning the police station was annoyingly vacant of worthwhile tasks. Because it was a murder enquiry, everything that needed doing was done immediately. Renshaw and the D.C.I. had the feeling that all they could do was to wait for another murder, or their only suspect to decide to confess. The only activity they could instigate was the taking of Lucy into care, but that didn't seem to be a reasonable line of action.

And so the morning passed and midday arrived, the time that Jim was scheduled to come on duty. It wasn't much, but other than lunch, it was all Renshaw and the D.C.I. could look forward to. Perhaps he'd come up with a way to solve the mystery.

The D.C.I. threw a paper plane at Renshaw it missed.

"We could do a house to house search," suggested Renshaw lamely.

"What are we searching for? We've done a house to house everywhere asking if anyone's got a large dog, and there isn't a Yorkshire terrier unaccounted for in twenty square miles. We've had more TV coverage than the Yorkshire Ripper."

"We could look for the occult related stuff, like the hooded tops Taliesin reckons he saw."

The D.C.I. scratched his chin. "That's not a bad idea. I guess there's a lot of hooded tops out there, but we might just find some that don't quite fit with someone's image." He paused and thought a little more. "Let's do it, organise it with Jim."

Renshaw looked at his watch.

The D.C.I. took the hint. "What time should he be here?"

"Half an hour ago and he's usually early."

"You'd better give him a ring then."

"Yes Sir."

The D.C.I. hung over Renshaw as he dialled the number. The phone rang and carried on ringing.

"No answer, Sir."

"He must be on his way then."

"Do you want me to get on with organising the search warrants?"

"Err no. Thinking about it, I doubt we'll get the warrants and it'll just be something more for the press to speculate on. I'll have to talk to the boss about it. He can take some responsibility for a change."

Renshaw felt let down. For a while it had looked as though there might be work to do, but it had just fizzled out. He picked up a book on witchcraft that he'd found in the library.

"Load of bollocks," he muttered to himself when he put it down half an hour later. "All there is to this case is reading bloody books and being lectured by professors. Glad I never went to college."

The D.C.I. came back in the office with a bag full of sandwiches and a can of coke.

"No sign of Farrier yet then?"

"No Sir."

"Try his phone again."

Renshaw called again and again. There was no answer.

"You'd better pop down to the Taliesin's farm to see if Alice knows where he is."

Renshaw picked up his jacket, grabbed a uniformed constable, knocking into Inspector Wilks on his way out.

"And where do you think you're taking my constable?" asked Wilks.

"On a job. Have you got a problem with that?"

"No, not at all," replied Wilks, spotting the D.C.I. ear-wigging.

There was no love lost between Wilks and Renshaw. Renshaw disliked officers like Wilks who seemed to get on in life and up the promotional ladder by the use of funny handshakes and a lack of common sense. Wilks didn't like Renshaw because he knew what Renshaw thought.

Renshaw headed off towards Kerry's farm, wondering what strange sight would greet his eyes this time and was thankful for the line of thought to disturb his stagnant mind.

When Renshaw arrived at the farm, Drudwyn was dozing on the front door step whilst Lucy had a goat tied to a drainpipe trying to milk it. Renshaw got out of the car and walked towards her.

"Hello," he said.

Lucy knew the car was there and was going to ignore it, but then she couldn't think of a good reason for doing so. She stood up and turned to Renshaw. "Do you know how to milk a goat?" she asked.

"I thought you just squeezed and pulled. Is Alice about?"

"Oh, we've given up all pretence have we? Heaven help us if she's the best undercover agent you've got. She's in the house."

Lucy smiled wickedly to herself and went back to milking, taking up a position from which she could view Renshaw.

Renshaw walked towards the front door. Drudwyn lifted his head. Renshaw drew closer. Drudwyn climbed onto the doorstep and sat down, calmly looking at Renshaw who bravely stood quite close and spoke in the fashion reserved for harmless babies and fierce dogs. "Good boy."

Drudwyn was unmoved. Renshaw tentatively put out a hand. No reaction from the dog. Renshaw chanced a pat on the head. It seemed well received so he risked a foot on the doorstep and was just quick enough to avoid losing a kneecap. Renshaw took a couple of steps back and called into the house.

"Alice!"

An upstairs window opened and Alice's head poked out.

"Oh hello. I'll be down in a minute."

When Alice came down, Renshaw explained the situation to her.

"No, I don't know why he wouldn't be at work. I've got a key hidden in the garden. We can go over now to check everything's alright."

There was no sign of serious concern in Alice's voice. She'd spent her years in uniform checking on people that had gone missing for a few hours and only one case in a hundred had unfortunate outcomes.

As Renshaw climbed back into his car, he glanced up at the house and saw Kerry looking mournfully out of the window down at him. He drove away, slightly spooked by Kerry's sombre appearance.

"Do you think it's worth staying here still?" Renshaw asked.

"It's hard to tell really. I mean, nothing much is happening. No one's paid the slightest interest in the horse, although I've done little else but ride him around the village."

"You've not got anywhere with Taliesin then?"

"No," Alice changed the subject. "How late is he?"

"Jim?"

"Yes."

Renshaw took a look at the dashboard clock.

"About two hours now."

Jim and Alice's house was about eighteen miles from the murder scenes. There was no reason to suspect any connection between Jim's absence and the enquiry, especially when they found Jim's car in the driveway. He kept a valuable sports car in the garage so the estate was always left on the drive.

"Well he's in," said Alice stepping out of the car.

Renshaw followed her round to the back door. It was locked. The constable walked around the house, peering in windows.

"Perhaps he's overslept. I'll get the spare key."

Alice went into the back garden and lifted a small rock to reveal a silver key on a bed of sandstone.

"Let's hope I don't find him with a mistress," joked Alice as she unlocked the door.

She stepped into the porch, followed by Renshaw and then the constable. Everything was neat and tidy as it should be.

"Jim," she called.

No reply.

She moved to the bottom of the stairs and called again. "Jim."

Nothing.

She ascended the stairs, Renshaw on her heels, a puzzled frown on her face. The constable remained downstairs, nosing around the house.

Alice went straight to her bedroom; the door was closed. For some reason she knocked, and received no reply. She opened the door and stepped into the room and there it was, the remains of her husband, a head and a spinal cord, blood mosaic on every wall, the carpet like the surface of Mars. Bits of bone were scattered around the room and the smell of urine and faeces choked the air like the concentrated scent of a car park elevator.

Alice was motionless, speechless. She couldn't take her eyes off the head. Renshaw took her by the waist and led her out of the room. Then reality hit her like a boxer's glove. She fell from Renshaw's grip to the floor screaming as she landed, writhing about, punching the ground, howling "no, no" between the tears.

The constable rushed upstairs and was bemused when he saw Renshaw standing over Alice, her holding onto his trouser leg.

Renshaw looked at him. "Take a look in there, then get on the radio."

The constable stepped over Alice's writhing form into the room. He instantly felt sick but held it in. He had to. Alice had staggered to the bathroom and began to retch and vomit. Renshaw stood over her. All he could think to do was stand there and put a comforting hand on her shoulder. No training could teach you the right way to deal with this situation. After a quarter of an hour, there was nothing left to bring up and no strength to stand.

"I'm so sorry Alice," said Renshaw.

"Why? Why?" Alice croaked. "Why?

Tears streamed down her face as she clasped her head in her hands, resting her elbows on the toilet seat. Renshaw moved to sit on the side of the bath. There was nothing else he could do.

The constable had informed his control room of the situation and within an hour the whole house was sealed off as a 'scene of crime'.

Alice didn't want to stay with neighbours and her parents were in Australia, so as most of her friends were police officers she was taken by one of them, Julie a WPC, to her police house in Becksworth where Julie did the best she could to comfort Alice.

The atmosphere at the murder scene was very sombre. Usually once any victims and relatives had left the scene, the police officers and forensic scientists would have a laugh and joke, anything to release the tension of being at a murder scene, but this time it was different. Almost everybody who attended the scene had known Jim as a colleague and friend, but that wasn't the only reason the mood was so serious. There was no point of entry and no point of exit. It was almost a confirmation that the murderer had supernatural powers, but no one said it.

Renshaw and the D.C.I. took heart in the fact that the forensic boys were taking a lot of samples from the room.

"I suppose," said the D.C.I., "that we must go on the assumption that the murderer thought Jim was onto something."

"I suppose so," replied Renshaw despondently.

The evening started to turn to night at Kerry's farm. No one there had been told about the day's events. All Kerry knew was that Alice had gone and not come back. A thought flashed across his mind; had she gone for good. A check of her room revealed her clothes still there. Kerry was further relieved to remember the horse, grazing in the ramshackle paddock at the back of the yard. But this left him with another dilemma, what to do with the horse. He didn't want to lose it and Alice had seemed to think that likely. Kerry went out of the house and harnessed the stallion.

"No one's going to run off with you tonight," he told it and then led it into the house.

It was a large horse, but the old house had a big door. There were no carpets in the house and the kitchen had a tiled floor, the best place thought Kerry from which to clean up horse droppings. He petted it a little. Lucy came down the stairs and took the scene in at a glance.

"You soft bastard," she said to Kerry.

"You don't mind do you?"

"It's your house. He's quiet for a lad with all his bits intact," said Lucy stroking his neck.

Emily came through to see what the fuss was. Kerry turned round to face her, looking more than a little sheepish, like a boy wanting his mother's okay to keep a stray dog.

"Perhaps she'll leave her husband," said Emily.

"Who?" Kerry replied, as if innocent of impure thoughts.

Emily shook her head at Kerry.

* * * *

At midnight Emily's bedroom door flew open. Emily's eyes shot open as something entered her room like a rush of wind. At first, it was just a part of the air but Emily felt it grow in one explosion into the entire room as though she had been dropped onto the sacrificial altar of a satanic cult. Her back froze against the bed sheets whilst her chest and face felt on fire. Emily knew what was in the room. It was Evil, so strong that she didn't have to be a witch to sense it, but as a witch she felt it all the more acutely. The intensity of the fear broke her bladder.

Imploding, the room relinquished the evil back into the air. Emily saw it as a black glow leave the room and instantaneously heard the bang as it shot through Kerry's bedroom door, this time leaving a large entry hole. Emily and Lucy were both quickly out of bed searching for the light switches, and each other.

"It's gone now," said Emily, meeting Lucy on the landing.

They both looked across at Kerry's open door and slowly walked to his room. He was standing naked, staring out of his now broken window. The complete fear that now possessed Emily was absent from his features. Lucy could only see the same expression that he had had when Alice had been driven away.

Emily attracted his attention. "Kerry."

He looked towards her, perhaps realising only then that he was naked.

Emily looked into Kerry's eyes, there was fear there, it just wasn't the type she expected and it was so very nearly hidden.

"You really ought to take evil seriously," she said.

"It'd only make it feel good," he replied. "The horse!" he exclaimed in panic, mocking his previous words.

He dashed passed Lucy and Emily heading down the stairs. The horse was still there, no longer calm but in one piece. Emily and Lucy followed him down the stairs.

Kerry turned to them. "What do you reckon?"

Lucy replied for them. "Very nice, but put this on." She flung her dressing gown at him, managing to lighten the situation a fraction.

"Emily?" said Lucy.

"Yes?"

"Do you think it's possible to sort of have an evil power in you and not know?"

Emily didn't really want this conversation. Her eyes crossed to Kerry who, although realising what Lucy was alluding to, was unperturbed.

"I doubt it," replied Emily. "Now we may as well get back to bed."

But before any of them had got up the stairs there was a loud knock at the door making all three of them jump. It came again. Kerry, Lucy and Emily glanced at one another. Midnight was not the time to expect visitors and the loudness of the knocks suggested the caller was expecting to awaken a household.

As Kerry walked to the door, it occurred to him that he was only wearing Lucy's nightgown. Undeterred he opened the door. It was two of the police officers that, prior to Alice's assignment to the case, had tried to dog Kerry's steps and, since Emily's conversation with Renshaw, been ordered to resume surveillance. They knew Kerry had been at home at the times when the murder of Jim could have been committed, but the D.C.I. had now decided to do a spot check on Kerry, just to make sure, one hundred percent sure. He was after all the only suspect and the D.C.I. wasn't going to let him go without a fight.

"Morning Sir," said the older of the two detectives.

Kerry looked at them blankly.

"Sorry to disturb you," continued the officer. "Can we come in? I'm D.C. Pollard and this is D.C. Read."

Kerry stepped back from the door to allow the detectives entry.

"Can I ask you, sir if you've been at home for some time?"

"Yes."

"When did you last leave the house?"

"Well, I've been gardening, and I went out for the horse."

On cue, the stallion neighed. The D.C.'s had thought that they'd seen Kerry bring the horse into the house, but they hadn't quite believed it.

"Other than that I mean, have you left the area?"

"The cortaulds," chipped in the younger officer.

"The what?" asked Lucy.

"Err, no," answered Kerry.

"Can you two vouch for that?" the D.C. asked.

Emily and Lucy nodded their answer.

"Thank you, that's all,"

The D.C.s turned to leave.

"Hold on a minute dear," said Emily. "Has there been another murder?"

There was a silence.

"Yes," was the older D.C's much contemplated answer.

"Who?" asked Kerry.

"A police officer," replied the D.C. before trying to leave again.

Kerry went pale. Emily could see he'd already jumped to a conclusion.

"Who?" demanded Emily.

"Inspector Farrier."

There was another silence. The detectives took their leave.

Thoughts raced around the three minds at Kerry's farm, never crashing together to form a sensible conclusion. Emily could think of only one person who had any reason for wanting Farrier out of the way. The three of them went back to bed, and although sleep would have brought a merciful release from the pain of the thoughts that fired from side to side of their heads, Kerry and Emily were denied the respite.

Gwawl grew angry. He felt that he had made too little of Pwyll's execution, in his haste to move on to the humiliation of Manawyddan and the impregnation of Rhiannon. But he had been angry for many years and could forgive himself for his eagerness. No matter how carefully he planned, a small detail always offered the possibility of adding years to his search for revenge. He had taken a rook but lost sight of the queen. Not a major draw back, he knew, for all life was cyclic and Rhiannon was sure to return. It was the fact that he needed to keep Manawyddan alive that infuriated him now, although bringing fear into his enemies life might at least push him into action, and breaking an old woman's bladder was always fun.

Chapter 16

The next day Renshaw felt that it was his moral obligation, if not his duty, to call and see Alice. He knocked on the door and Julie answered. She smiled compassionately as if they were co-conspirators and let him in.

"Alice is in the lounge, I'm just making us a drink. Would you like one?"

"Yes, thanks. Through here is it?"

"Yeh, that's the one."

Julie wandered into the kitchen and Renshaw into the lounge. Alice was sitting in a large armchair, watching morning television, with a waste paper basket full of tissues by her side. She looked up at Renshaw with dry, red eyes. What could he say? How are you would sound ridiculous. He gave Alice a part of the smile he had received from Julie's greeting.

"Hello," he said.

Alice sniffed. "Hi."

"Is there anything I can do?"

Alice shrugged her shoulders and the tears began to flow again. She tried to say sorry but her voice wasn't up to it. Renshaw knew nothing he could say would make the situation any worse, so he may as well talk whilst Alice couldn't.

"It wasn't Taliesin; he was at home all the time."

Alice looked at him over a tissue. She managed to stop the tears quickly this time. A professional attitude, or at least an attempt at one, Alice believed, was what was called for now.

"So he's not a suspect anymore," she said.

"No, but we still intend watching him; he could be the…" Renshaw wished he hadn't started down this road, but he wasn't going to make it worse by stopping mid sentence, "…next victim."

"I'll have to go and get my horse and things."

"Well apparently he took the horse indoors, for safe keeping I suppose."

Alice managed a smile at the image of a horse in Kerry's house. Then a thought crossed her mind, a thought that she felt was inappropriate. She was alone in the world now, and of the few people she knew, Kerry was the one she would like to stop the loneliness. She tried to chase the thought out of her head and wondered how wicked she would seem if someone could read her mind. But she couldn't banish Kerry from her thoughts. The harder she tried the more pointless the effort seemed.

"I'll take you over to collect your stuff if you like."

Alice didn't answer at first.

"Or, if you tell me what to get I could go over on my own."

Julie came into the room with a tray of drinks and put them down on the coffee table.

"No," said Alice. "I mean, where would I put them?"

"What's that?" asked Julie.

"My stuff that's at Kerry's."

"You could keep it here. I'd make space."

Again Alice was lost in thought. Where would she go? She had a house to sell. There was no way she could live there now and she couldn't move in with Julie, or any other friend, at such short notice. The sensible thing would be to go back to Kerry's and to carry on lodging there. Her stuff was there and now she knew that Kerry was not the murderer what better guardian could she have than Drudwyn? The farm had a therapeutic beauty and the horse could stay there too.

Alice again felt guilty at her thoughts, not because they were impure but because, surely, her every waking minute should be spent on weeping for the loss of a husband. But she had cried and thought of little else for twenty hours and now her mind was trying to find a relief from the grief. Should she open her mouth and say where she wanted to stay, what would they think? What did she think? Was it stupidity? She might not be welcome. And then she remembered something she had thought of hours previously.

"I could be next," she said.

"No," said Julie. "Jim must have just found something."

"We don't know that," said Alice starting to panic a little.

She was right and there was nothing worth saying but things have to be said.

"It'll be alright," said Renshaw comfortingly, doubting if things would ever be all right again. He was starting to fear for his own life now.

Alice continued to think about going back to Kerry's and when she put the thought of asking for a police house out of her mind she wondered if she was trying to deceive herself, that she really just wanted the chance to take another husband, but then again a police house meant living alone. Wherever she went it would mean being alone.

There were so many next likely victims, that Alice doubted if any of them would qualify for any form of police protection. No, whether she had an ulterior motive or not, Kerry's place had proved safe so far.

"I want to go back to Mr. Taliesin's now that I know he's not the murderer. It's probably the safest place for me."

Renshaw and Julie looked at her, gobsmacked.

"Why?" asked Julie.

Alice explained herself without hinting at any ulterior motives.

"At least stay here a few days," pleaded Julie.

"Thank you but I have my horse to look after."

"What, you mean you want to go now?" asked Renshaw.

Alice nodded.

"I've got to keep on the move, doing things you know, keep my mind occupied. There's a lot of fixing up that could be done over there"

Renshaw didn't want to aid Alice's move to the farm, but he knew if he didn't she'd do it herself anyway.

"I'll take you over and wait. It may be that he won't want you back."

"Thank you," Alice replied as she stood up, still clutching a man-size box of tissues. "Do you mind if I take these Julie?"

"No, please, take them and you know if there's anything you want or anything I can do, let me know. If you can't cope over there you can always come back here."

Alice smiled gratefully at Julie. "Come on then, no time like the present," she said to Renshaw and taking him firmly by the arm started to lead him to the door.

The journey from Julie's house to Kerry's took half an hour and Alice sobbed all the way. Her eyes had become painful to wipe a long time ago and now she just let the tears roll down her cheeks as she watched the scenery go by.

Renshaw pulled up outside the farm, he looked up at the house. Kerry was peering out of the same window that he had been at when Renshaw had left with Alice the previous day. The possibility that the man had been motionless at the now broken window, waiting for Alice to re-enter his life, sent a shiver down Renshaw's back. He comforted himself with the thought that Kerry was no more than an oddball and not a murderer.

"Would you mind checking that it's alright?" Alice asked Renshaw.

Renshaw smiled and nodded; it beat talking to Alice. He got out of the car. Drudwyn was not about. He knocked at the door. Kerry came towards the entrance from the staircase.

"How is she?" he asked.

"She's bearing up quite well now. I don't know if you know but she found the body, so she'll be weird for a while."

"Does she want her stuff?"

"Err no, not exactly. You see, she's decided, that if you'd have her back then she'd like to stay on here as a lodger."

Kerry looked at Renshaw with a mild expression of bemusement on his face.

"But why? I thought I was in the clear. Doesn't she get time off or something?"

"Well yes, she does, but she's got her stuff here and it was good for her horse and what with you being off the suspect list, she figures it must be relatively safe here."

"Well, who am I to turn a grieving woman away? I suppose she was only doing her job before."

Kerry followed Renshaw back out to his car and opened Alice's door. The sight of her crying tugged at his emotions. Alice's red and glazed eyes looked up at him and Kerry was taken by a sentiment that knew none of Renshaw's uneasiness with the situation of having to comfort a widow. Kerry bent his knees slightly and helped Alice out of the car. She stood erect, close to him and then took hold of Kerry with both arms and buried her gushing eyes in his chest. He held her tight, one large hand resting upon her head and resisting stroking her.

Renshaw felt enraged but he could still think of nothing to say. Kerry's comforting actions looked genuine, but Renshaw couldn't help thinking it was wrong. All he could do was drive away. At least he thought, she's wired up still. If anything sparked his suspicions about Kerry, he could get the tapes rolling again. Kerry waited until Alice's current wave of tears had dried up before he spoke to her, still holding her around the waist.

"You know, I think we cry for selfish reasons when we mourn someone's death."

Alice looked up at him. How dare he call her selfish.

"It's a little like a boyfriend going away for a long time to university or a relative going abroad for a better life. We know we should be happy for them but we cry because we'll miss them."

Kerry had studied death in his own way and he was not a believer in it being a taboo subject. He thought direct talk was the only way to comfort. Of course, he knew he could be wrong, but he didn't think he was.

"No matter what religion you follow, death should be a time for celebrating, a sort of coming of age party, when someone manages to break free from the grind of their life, to achieve a higher plane of living. It's a time to be happy for loved ones, be a little jealous of him perhaps, but not sad. If you truly love someone you shouldn't begrudge them shuffling off this mortal coil."

Alice heard the words and took them in. They made more sense than anyone else had in the last twenty-four hours. Kerry had said what he thought, nothing had sounded forced, though it had not made her feel any better.

"I made the right decision coming back here," she said.

Alice could now see Kerry as a totally different person. He wasn't the murder suspect anymore. He was warm and inviting, and not exciting because of the chilling thoughts and deeds that lay hidden behind his eyes. Alice could feel the pain leaving her body; it was almost a physical experience. She could only liken it to hugging her father when she had grazed her knee as a little girl. She missed her father now. Why had he had to go to Australia? That thought brought the truth of Kerry's words home to her. The feeling she had when her father left was not greatly removed from the way she felt about her husband's death and she knew that the stud farm her father had built up in Australia had made him a rich and happy man.

She didn't want to let go of Kerry now, she felt bound to him by magic. Even without words he seemed to be making everything better. Jim would have pulled away by now; he wasn't one for long embraces. Alice had, until a few minutes previously, presumed that her life, or at least the happiness in it, had ended with the discovery of Jim's body, but now she could feel a narrow beam of hope cutting through the darkness that surrounded her. Although one of the aspects of herself that that beam had lit was her sanity, she worried that this desperate grip on Kerry was some sort of tragic rebound. Was she a bunny boiler unable to cope without feeling loved? She felt not, but only time would tell.

The weather seemed to conspire with Kerry to work for Alice's happiness. It was autumn; the day was sharp but not chilly. The sun warmed it up and a light breeze occasionally blew vitalising air into Alice's lungs. Alice wanted to hold Kerry until she felt that all the sorrows would go away but still she shifted a little in his arms, to let him know if he wanted to let go he could. Kerry loosened his grip.

"Come on then, I'll make you a drink."

And with an arm around Alice's shoulder, he led her into the house and kept her with him whilst he made a pot of tea.

"Where are Emily and Lucy?" Alice asked.

"They've gone off for a few days, to talk to friends and other members of their venerable profession. A witch is like a scientist, they can't stand to be baffled by anything."

"Are they really witches?"

"It's hard to know. I mean, it's every human's nature to want to believe that magic is possible, except of course for scientific fundamentalists who can't think of a mathematical or chemical formula to explain magic, so rubbish it as psychological or impossible. If one thing in three that a practitioner of magic does appears not to work then they ignore the other two. Like the scientist whose experiments don't always give the results they should. They just ignore the results that go wrong and blame some extra factor that wasn't registered, chaos. The scientists don't always get it right. So it's not surprising that witches with their pinch of this and incantation of that don't always get it right either."

"Yes or no would have sufficed." It was weird hearing Kerry talk so openly with this flowing manner. The grumpy, brooding Kerry was nowhere to be seen now that she was there on honest terms.

"I think they have the ability to use powers that aren't often used by others."

"Was that a yes?"

"I think so."

"This is good," said Alice. "I can interrogate you now without you worrying."

Kerry handed her a mug of tea.

"I still reserve the right to silence," he said.

The rest of the day passed with Alice and Kerry just chatting, Alice occasionally shedding a tear and Kerry generally saying the right thing to comfort her. But as night closed in it became harder to keep Alice calm. The occasional tear was replaced by the occasional fear. Kerry hadn't wanted to talk specifics about the deaths but Alice wanted reassurance and she felt sure that whatever she asked or said, Kerry would be able to cope with it. "What do you think is doing it?"

It wasn't that Kerry had to come up with a snap answer; he'd been asked the question before and had plenty of replies. It was just a matter of finding the right one for the occasion without hesitating to think and thus blowing the pretence that he knew what he was saying was correct.

"Somebody cowardly," he answered. "It only attacks individuals and that to my mind means it's not something, it's somebody and that somebody can be hurt, otherwise he wouldn't be so cowardly."

"It killed my husband," Alice's voice faltered a little.

"It killed your husband in his sleep. He probably didn't notice until he got to heaven."

Kerry was sure that wasn't quite the right thing to say, but better to speak than say nothing.

"Aren't you scared that it might come for you?" The tears began again, both for Jim and the imagined loss of Kerry.

"I'm shitting myself, but if it was coming here it would have come a long time ago when I was here on my own." He thought about the previous nights visitation but kept it to himself.

"Perhaps it's doing things in an order."

"Now," said Kerry, "you're just trying to scare yourself."

It was eleven p.m. now. Alice and Kerry were sitting in the makeshift lounge, the room with a sofa, midi system and log fire. A breeze blew through the curtain that Kerry had hung over the broken window. Alice was putting off going to bed because although Kerry was good at comforting her in her loss of a husband, he hadn't worked such miracles on her fear. She knew what she was going to ask Kerry to do, but she was putting that off also.

Kerry on the other hand was waiting for Alice to go to bed. He certainly wasn't going to leave her up on her own. He was getting tired; a whole day of healing had taken a lot out of him. Why didn't she go to bed? Midnight crept closer. Was she going to spend the night on that chair?

"Kerry?"

"Yes."

"I know I shouldn't be scared but I am and I just don't think I can go to bed alone tonight."

She waited for the reaction. Kerry avoided an expression of shock and tried to treat the request as if it were an everyday happening.

"You could have Drudwyn in with you. Nobody with the slightest yellow streak in them would come near you with him by your side."

No, she hadn't thought of that. Should she accept or press harder?

"I didn't mean anything…" Alice shifted around in her seat uncomfortably, Kerry watched her. "…anything…" she forced the word out, "sexual. Just be there."

Kerry didn't want to go against Alice's wishes whilst she was feeling so vulnerable, but he didn't trust himself to sleep next to such a beautiful woman without laying a finger on her.

"I'll put a chair in your room and sleep in that."

That was good enough for Alice.

"Shall we?" said Kerry who had now been awake for twenty-four hours.

"Yes, I'll get changed first though, before you come up. In fact, if you don't mind, you can wait on the other side of the door."

"Okay, take Drudwyn up with you."

Alice stood up, patted the side of her leg and called Drudwyn to follow her, which he did. That still amazed Kerry. Perhaps, he thought, my dog has the same taste in women as I do. Kerry followed Alice and Drudwyn up the stairs, carrying an armchair. He put it down in Alice's room and then left to get a sleeping bag to sit in.

As Kerry re-entered the room Alice noticed the Massai mask had returned to the wall again. She felt a survival instinct to watch the mask. "Why do you keep putting that in here?" she asked of Kerry.

"What?"

"That mask."

A puzzled look crossed Kerry's face and seemed to Alice to be quickly suppressed.

"I didn't know where to put it," replied Kerry as he removed it from the wall.

Alice kept her eyes upon the mask as Kerry carried it to the open door and flung it into the darkness of the landing. He closed the door on the mask and Kerry and Alice settled down for the night.

Chapter 17

Over a hundred miles away from Becksworth and its troubles, Emily slept restlessly. She and Lucy had visited an old friend of hers in the hope that she might be able to shed light on the killer. Emily had also wanted to get Lucy out of the farmhouse. Lucy may have been a tough little nut but Emily felt as protective of her as if she were her own daughter.

Emily's idea was to do a sort of tour of the country, visiting friends and colleagues until she found something to stop the evil or until a down to earth culprit was arrested. The last straw had been Jim's death. The morning after receiving that news, Emily had packed her and Lucy's bags and left Kerry, much to Lucy's dismay.

Emily may have been a white witch but she was no saint and had no desire to hang around fighting something unseen until it made her a martyr or took Lucy away. Kerry, in Emily's opinion, could take care of himself better if he didn't have a schoolgirl and a plump, middle-aged woman to keep an eye out for. He had Drudwyn after all, an exocet missile amongst dogs, although an exorcist missile might have been more helpful.

Emily, in the bed next to Lucy's, was dreaming she was someone else, somewhere else. Lucy was restless and put the light on to read, waking Emily as she did so. Emily looked out from the quilt pulled high around her face with the slightly bewildered expression young children have when waking up in an unusual place.

"Oh sorry, didn't mean to wake you," whispered Lucy.

Emily's eyes widened and she hoisted her frame to an upright position.

"What is it?" asked Lucy angrily.

Emily was wide-awake now and obviously panicked by something.

"If we didn't know where Kerry was when that policeman was killed, who would you say killed him?"

Lucy looked at Emily as though she had said something extremely stupid.

"You mean Kerry?"

Emily nodded.

"But he's no witch; or do you think he's been having us on, using us as alibis? I mean you don't need to leave the house for a spell to work on someone miles away. It's all faith in your religion, faith, practise and knowledge. He could have all them without us knowing."

"I hadn't thought it that far through," replied Emily. "But it's possible. I mean, if we didn't know him, we would say it could have been down to him somehow. And if he has been misleading us, if he really is evil, then we don't know him."

"But is your faith so strong that you think someone could actually kill someone else, ripping them to pieces with just magic?"

Emily frowned. Lucy had never questioned the reality of her power since the day they had met, but it was true. Occasionally Emily did wonder if her successful spells we're just coincidence and that her failures merely lack of coincidence. But she soon brought to mind all the things that she had heard and seen in her life and the faith came rushing back.

"Yes, someone could do it. They could do it without raising a finger, by spells or astral projection, or something we've never heard of. I can't believe we've misread him though."

"What if he's possessed?" asked Lucy. "He may not even know he's doing it. What if something's controlling his subconscious while he's asleep?"

* * * *

Kerry's head began to nod as he watched over Alice.

All things would come to Gwawl, who manipulated and waited.

* * * *

"Alice!" squealed Lucy.

Emily didn't know if Alice had gone back to the farm and they had no reason to presume the police had decided not to bother with surveillance. Emily sprung out of bed and ran to the telephone. Lucy threw on a nightgown and followed her. Emily dialled, the phone rang and rang and rang and then someone answered.

"Hello, Becksworth Police Station. P.C. Bailey speaking."

"Inspector Renshaw please," said Emily.

"I'm sorry," said the constable, "but he's not on duty until 9.00 a.m."

"Someone then; it's about the murders."

The constable sensed the urgency in Emily's voice. "I'll put you through to the Chief Inspector."

The D.C.I's phone rang three excruciating times before he picked it up.

"D.C.I. Smegvick," was all he said.

"Hello, this is Emily Marthson. I spoke to Inspector Renshaw about the murders." Emily's words were coming fast. "I'm an occult expert. I've just realised that Kerry Taliesin didn't need to leave home to kill that officer. He could have done it from where he was by astral projection." Emily knew the futility of trying to convince a sceptic in a few sentences but she had no option. "That's why there wasn't any point of entry; he just appeared in the room. You have to make sure that Alice is protected."

The D.C.I. hadn't got where he was today by believing in witches, but nor had he got there by taking chances with anything.

"Get yourself to a local police station. Alice is at Kerry's farm. I'm going there now."

The D.C.I. didn't wait for a reply. He put the phone down and scrambled the officers that were on duty in the area to converge on Kerry's farmhouse.

Kerry began his sleep.

Six minutes later two police cars arrived at Kerry's farm, closely followed by three more, one carrying the D.C.I. No time was given to planning. The officers just got out of the cars and ran into the house. Three officers were running up the stairs when they heard a scratching and banging noise coming from a room, Alice's room, at the top of the stairs.

Suddenly Drudwyn appeared around the door. He leapt from the landing flying ferociously at the intruding officers, sending them flying back down the stairs. He snapped wildly at anything that moved as he hit the floor via a constable. Kerry raced out of his room. He wasn't expecting police officers and didn't instantly recognise them as such. To him they were merely intruders in the dark and so he followed Drudwyn's example and leapt at them as they drew their truncheons. He attacked the officers with a vicious fury, which he found he had to maintain in self-defence, upon realising that the intruders were policemen.

A truncheon caught Kerry a vicious blow on the side of the head and he fell to the floor semi-conscious. Drudwyn was forced into the lounge and the door shut on him.

Alice appeared at the top of the stairs. The D.C.I. regained control of his men.

At first Alice thought there had been another murder. There was enough blood. Policemen lay nursing bites. One had an ear no longer completely attached to his head, another officer's nose was streaming with blood and two officers lay in agony where they had fallen at the bottom of the stairs.

Alice focused on Kerry, laying face down, blood coming from his head. She slowly descended the stairs in a state of shock, the noise of the officers blanked out, their faces not in vision. All there was, was Kerry. She knelt down by his side. He groaned and then, as Alice whispered his name, he raised himself up onto his forearms.

The D.C.I. turned to an uninjured officer.

"Call for an ambulance or two."

"Kerry," Alice said again, tears flooding her eyes. Kerry turned his head to look at her but couldn't. His right eye had shut from a powerful blow, but he wanted to see Alice so he forced himself to a kneeling position and faced her. His plaster cast was as shattered as the bone it was designed to support.

The noise flooded back into Alice's ears; the moaning officers, the noise of Drudwyn repeatedly throwing himself at the door behind which he had been shut, and the busy radio transmissions.

Kerry smiled at her and by doing so opened a cut on his lip. "I could have taken them but I saw they were your mates," he said jokingly.

"Alice," the D.C.I. was trying to talk to her.

Alice heard him for the first time. "What?" she snapped.

"Can I talk to you in the kitchen?"

The kitchen lead from the hallway; Alice didn't want to leave Kerry's side.

"No," she replied aggressively and then turned her attention to Drudwyn's prison.

"Drudwyn, it's alright, lie down,"

Drudwyn growled but stopped throwing himself at the door. He was probably glad of the rest. He had received boots to the ribs and a glancing truncheon blow on his snout.

"Alice," repeated the D.C.I.

"Talk to me here if you've got anything to say," she replied.

The D.C.I. had never seen Alice like this. She was bitter and angry and, worse still, she was disobeying him in public.

"Kerry, are you alright?" Alice put a hand to Kerry's face, feeling for bumps through the rough stubble and matting hair.

He nodded. "I took a worse kicking than this on the Bean Field."

"Alice."

Alice ignored the D.C.I.

"Alice, he could still be the killer,"

That obtained both Kerry and Alice's attention.

"Now," said the D.C.I., "come into the kitchen and I'll explain."

Alice looked back at Kerry sympathetically. She kissed his cheek and instantly wondered why. She got to her feet and followed the D.C.I. into the kitchen, taking up a position from where she could keep an eye on Kerry's condition.

The D.C.I. related Emily's phone call almost word for word and as quietly as he could. His officers, he felt, wouldn't understand. Alice was not swayed, she had made her decision and this was the seal on it. Kerry was not the killer and he was the one that she chose to trust and stand by in this adverse situation.

"He's not the killer and he never was, there's not an ounce of malice in him."

"Alice, you're talking like a bloody idiot. Look what he did to my men. He's a maniac."

Alice answered, "He's the maniac that cares enough for me to have a go at ten truncheon wielding thugs. He's the maniac that'd stay awake all night to make sure I can sleep. He's the maniac that comforts me more than any grievance counsellor ever could." Alice wiped a tear from her eye. "He's the maniac I..." Alice cut her sentence short and instead pulled off the necklace that the surveillance equipment was in and flung it at the D.C.I's chest.

The D.C.I's words had been quietly spoken but Alice had replied for all to hear and for that Kerry felt the beating had been worth it.

The D.C.I. was speechless and in his lull realised that no court would see his arrest of Kerry as legal, but the action of a gullible fool. This case could be his last. Alice left him in the kitchen and went back to the side of her companion. The constables and sergeants awaited orders. The D.C.I. awaited divine inspiration.

"Right then, listen up everybody." The D.C.I. could at least demonstrate control. "It appears that the tip-off we received cannot, at the present time be substantiated."

The other officers muttered dissatisfied comments.

"However," went on the D.C.I., "the information came from a reliable source and had to be acted upon. You have all done your duty and I have seen no evidence of anybody acting outside of their duty. Due to the circumstances, I don't believe it would be appropriate to prosecute Mr. Taliesin for assault or improper control of a guard dog. I therefore suggest that you organise yourselves so that uninjured officers can drive the injured officers to hospital, leaving the ambulance to attend the more seriously injured. From what I can see, that means Mr. Taliesin and the two officers at the stair base."

There, that should do it thought the D.C.I. The officers organised themselves, none of them paying Kerry or Alice the slightest attention.

"Call a vet," said Kerry to Alice.

Alice nodded.

"And if there isn't one, get the R.S.P.C.A. out. They may not prosecute me, but I'll have a bloody good go at having them done."

Alice just stared at him, scrutinising his injuries. His nose and head were bleeding, but it didn't look too bad. Some of the police officers started to leave the house. One dripped blood onto Kerry from a hand as he walked past him.

"Help me up," said Kerry.

Alice took hold of him around the ribs. He winced a little but got to his feet anyway. He walked to the door protecting Drudwyn and opened it a little.

"It's alright boy," Drudwyn stood up and wagged his tail. "Stay!" Kerry and Alice went into the room with Drudwyn.

"How are you boy," Kerry stroked Drudwyn gently.

The dog also had a little blood on his nose, but he wasn't complaining, he was making a fuss of Kerry. Kerry turned to Alice.

"He couldn't have one of those biscuits of yours could he?"

Alice smiled and laughed to herself. How ironic it was that those thugs who pertained to be police officers thought that this compassionate man could kill anything.

Two ambulances arrived. The first carried the injured officers away whilst the crew of the second were directed into the lounge by the D.C.I. Two ambulance men came into the room. Drudwyn threatened to attack but was instantly calmed by Kerry.

"Crikey, you're a bit of a mess aren't you mate," said the slim bald headed man as he approached Kerry.

"Are you injured miss?" the other one said to Alice.

"No, I'm fine thanks." Alice wiped away another few tears.

"Right let's have a look then," said the bald man.

His approach was professional and his dialogue the standard, comforting but neutral speech Kerry had received from almost every medic who'd treated him in the past. Kerry had thought having one's own home might reduce the amount of patching up he needed, but apparently not.

The medic looked at Kerry's visible injuries. "You'd better come to the hospital with us," he said.

"I can't," said Kerry, realising for the first time that talking seemed to hurt an awful lot. "I have to wait for a vet."

"Well, I can't make you come, but promise me you'll get yourself to a hospital in the morning, and if that eye gets any worse, get yourself straight there. You don't want to lose your sight."

He then addressed Alice. "Keep an eye on him. He might have concussion, which means he could pass out at any time and whatever you do, don't let him drive."

"I won't," said Alice. "And he won't be going out of my sight for a very long time."

Kerry squeezed her soft, warm hand and felt better about the outlook.

The ambulance men left. The D.C.I. had stayed with one

constable, who although having received a punch, was relatively uninjured.

"I've got to talk to Mr. Taliesin now," said the D.C.I. to the young constable. "Just wait here for a while."

He left the constable in the kitchen and entered the lounge, closing the door after him. There were some interviews that no standards of ethical practise could persuade the D.C.I. to put on tape or even allow another officer to hear.

He strolled into the room and adopted a stance reminiscent of Columbo. Kerry looked up at him with his one good eye. Drudwyn didn't deign to even raise an eyebrow and Alice readied her tongue. Alice was sitting close into Kerry on the couch, holding his hand on her lap.

"Do you know why we came here tonight, Mr. Taliesin?" asked the D.C.I. removing a finger and thumb from his chin.

He received no answer.

"If you wanted to kill somebody, would you have to leave the house?" asked the D.C.I.

"You might find out if you stay here much longer," Kerry replied and decided that he would have to reduce his answers to nods and shakes of the head to avoid a painful jaw.

"I mean if a man wished to kill someone, could he do it himself without leaving his own home, and the intended victim was in another?"

Buggered if I know, was the answer that sprang to mind but that couldn't be put across with non-verbal communication. Kerry shrugged his shoulders. One of them ached a little too much to repeat the exercise and Kerry hoped he knew the answer to the next question.

"What do you know about astral projection?"

Kerry gave up; he'd have to speak. He opened his mouth a fraction to avoid aggravating a cut lip. "Out of body experience."

"Can you do it?"

"No."

"Have you ever tried?"

"Yes."

"And?"

"Nothing."

"Nothing?"

"Not a flicker of leaving my body."

"Do you believe it's possible?"

Kerry thoughtlessly shrugged his shoulders. The bad one hurt more than before. He winced. That action caused an involuntary 'ow' which opened up the cut again.

"How would you catch a man killing by astral projection?" asked the D.C.I, deliberately ignoring Kerry's predicament, but Kerry had had enough and stuck a finger up at the D.C.I. He immediately felt quite juvenile.

"Just answer the question," said the D.C.I. aggressively.

Drudwyn raised an eyebrow at the change of tone.

"I believe," said Alice, "that he's exercising his right to silence."

"Now you listen to me," the D.C.I. shouted impatiently at Alice.

Drudwyn's head lifted off the ground. It was an openly aggressive action in itself, but having just seen what the dog could do, the D.C.I. took his cue and decided that retreat might be the intelligent move. He had asked his questions and there seemed little else to keep him there.

"Look after yourself Alice," he said, apparently forgiving her of her disobedience, then left.

When the D.C.I. arrived back at the police station, a message was waiting for him to call a station in Huddersfield and ask for P.C. Warren.

"P.C. Warren please," said the D.C.I., hoping that this would be some new incriminating evidence related to the details that he had had sent around the country.

"P.C. Warren speaking."

"D.C.I. Smegvick. I've had a message to call you," said the D.C.I.

"Err, yes Sir. It's to do with a lady who's come into the station tonight. Emily Marthson. Do you know her?"

"Yes, can I speak to her?"

"Is there anything we should know about her?" asked P.C. Warren.

"No, she's harmless."

"I'll just get her to a phone. Hold on a sec."

A few seconds later, Emily's voice came down the phone. "Hello?"

"Yes, Mrs. Marthson."

"Oh, hello deary. What's happened?"

"Well everybody was alright and Alice won't leave him."

"Ah," said Emily, touched by the sentimentality of Alice.

"Ah!" repeated the D.C.I. angrily. "Is that all you can say? I've got officers in hospital after bursting into that house uninvited. You seemed convinced when you called earlier and now I might end up on charges myself!"

"Oh no, I wasn't convinced. It was just that it was still possible that Kerry had killed that policeman."

"He nearly killed a few more tonight."

"You still ought to keep an eye on him." Emily was not reacting at all to the D.C.I's anger and maintained a matter-of-fact attitude. "Lucy has this theory that he could be the killer and not know about it."

"Look Miss Marthson, I've had enough of this bloody black magic crap. Now don't interfere unless you know something more solid than a long-distance, sleepwalking murder."

He slammed the receiver down and instantly regretted it. She might be a stupid old bag or she might have been the only person that could ever work out what was going on at Kirk Eaton. Well, perhaps a more down-to-earth look at the situation was all that was called for.

The D.C.I. looked up from his desk to the wall in front of him where pictures of the victims were stuck to a white board, with brief details, times and dates and the suchlike written in removable marker underneath them. Was there a link?

Muriel Beck, possible occult involvement, did strange things with chickens, aged seventeen, local, killed in Kirk Eaton. Christopher Hanney, aged nine, local, killed in Kirk Eaton. Jane Fast, singer, one-time local, killed in Kirk Eaton. Jim Farrier, police inspector, killed in Hopton.

The D.C.I. stared at the photos. It was hard to concentrate. Only Kerry connected them, but was he victim or offender? Logically, thought the D.C.I., Kerry is the victim. He's been set-up by someone who didn't know we'd be watching him. That would mean someone stupid, but the killer clearly didn't fit that description. Perhaps he no longer had a need for a scapegoat; perhaps he was becoming careless, but that thought was no help, and it didn't point any fingers. He knew some serial killers did it to show their superiority to the police and revel in frustrating them.

A new line of thought came into the D.C.I.'s head. What was the result of Muriel Beck's death? A murder investigation. No, there was no mileage in that either. The murders were too random for somebody to be manipulating pawns in a game. But the more he tried to deny the feeling that he too was a mere chess piece, the more that feeling hinted at reality. There was another thought. Who had tipped off Ian Fast about the various theories about the murder? Could it have been Jim, and now he had had his pay-off. No, that was a ridiculous thought, but the only lines of thought available were ones, which would, if spoken, be ridiculed.

There could only be one reason, mused Smegvick, for a leak to Ian Fast: to publicise the murder, to get the Strange Days spin on the story. But all that would do was attract every type of new age, occult, charlatan in the country. Perhaps there was a lot more to this culture than met the eye. Individual egos might be at stake. There was certainly a lot of money to be made off the backs of the gullible.

Smegvick looked across his desk at a ringing telephone. After the call, Smegvick had yet another murder to connect with Kerry. Gloucestershire Police had found the body of a "New Age Traveller" over a year ago. He had bled to death from the wound created when his genitals had been ripped from his body. The victim had been known by the name Dog.

Chapter 18

The D.C.I. remained at his desk in a world of confusion and Gwawl waited.

Emily and Lucy had not gained any extra knowledge from the last friend they had visited and so were moving on. Travelling up the motorway the radio was playing one of "The Dog's Bollocks' records. Death had been a good career move for Jane.

"So who are we going to see today?" asked Lucy.

Emily twisted her lips giving the appearance that although the car was rolling, she wasn't entirely sure where to. Lucy awaited a reply.

"Janet Walkin," said Emily eventually.

Lucy brow furrowed, "That's a new one on me."

"Yes," replied Emily, hesitating over her words, "and I'm having second thoughts about it already."

"Why?"

"Well now I've mentioned her, you'll want to know about her and then when I ask you not to meet her you'll be stubborn and demand to, and I'll give in."

"Just tell me," said Lucy aggressively.

"She's a black witch. I met once and kept in touch with, out of curiosity."

Lucy's eyes begged for more information.

"She's not really out and out evil, she just performs for her own benefit and amusement."

"That is evil, isn't it?" said Lucy.

Emily shrugged her shoulders and said, "I just don't want you to be influenced by her. I'm sure you won't be. She's not the brightest of people and I think she just gets led down the occasional wrong path. Quite how she ratifies her actions with her religion I've never really understood."

"I won't," stated Lucy.

Emily had always been a little worried by Lucy's personality. She understood that it was a personality that had been formed by conditions that had led to suicides in others. Lucy always had a blanket up, through which Emily could never read her.

The two witches left the motorway and Lucy slept past the scenery, as the roads they travelled upon grew narrower. Eventually, Emily pulled into a short drive outside a modern looking bungalow on a small semi-rural housing estate. Not the place one expected to find a black witch.

"Does she know we're coming?" asked Lucy, rolling her shoulders to wake herself up.

"Never pre-arm a black witch," replied Emily as she switched off the engine.

Lucy waited for Emily to get out of the car before she did and then followed Emily around to the back door. When Emily rang the doorbell a tune played that Lucy recognised as having something to do with Adolf Hitler's weaponry. The door was answered by a slim, bleached blonde woman in her mid thirties with, in Lucy's opinion, far too much make-up, tacky jewellery and cleavage on show. Lucy wondered why Emily could possibly think that she was going to be influenced by someone who didn't know the meaning of moderation when it came to perfume. A white cat shot out of the door. She can't even get the colour of her cat right, thought Lucy.

"Emily," squealed Janet excitedly, her arms spread wide, showing off more of her speckled chest. "What a surprise."

Get a life, thought Lucy.

"Merry meet," said Emily, using the witches greeting. "How are you?"

"Fine, come in," replied Janet.

"This is Lucy, my, err, apprentice so to speak," said Emily putting an arm on Lucy's shoulder and ushering her into the house first.

"Well, pleased to meet you, Lucy,"

Lucy could tell that Janet wasn't very happy inviting a stranger as scruffy as herself into the house, but she hid it quite well.

"I'll put the kettle on," said Janet.

The house was neat and tidy. Typical housewife at home all day crap, thought Lucy. Expecting Janet to ask her to remove her boots at any moment, Lucy pre-empted her by taking them off anyway, not prepared to take orders off such trash.

"Do you both drink tea?"

A beer would have been nice, thought Lucy.

"Yes, one sugar each," replied Emily.

Janet poured the boiling water into a teapot. "So," she said, "what do you want?"

This is it, thought Lucy, the queen of tack getting down to some blunt black witch talk.

"Well it's about the black magic murders."

It was the title the press had started to give the case. Lucy had been right. An evil smile appeared on Janet's powdered face with an expression of wicked interest.

"Oh yes," she said as though commenting on a Freudian slip. "Yes."

Over the next half hour and two cups of tea, Emily explained the whole situation at Kirk Eaton to Janet who listened quietly, never losing her impish expression.

"Well, what do you think?" ended Emily.

Janet pursed her lips in obvious pretence of contemplation and then the evil smile returned. "Your Dr. McNatley knows more than you think, if I'm not mistaken."

Emily's face seemed to lose a little colour.

"You see Dr. McNatley is one of us."

"Do you know him?" asked Emily anxiously.

"I met him once. He had heard about me and visited me to do

some research for a paper he was writing."

"And?"

"And what Emily?" asked Janet.

"Is he powerful? Is he good, is he evil, what?"

The smile didn't leave Janet's face. "Who knows. He certainly didn't, because it was me who pointed his abilities out to him and I haven't seem him since."

"Did you give him any training?"

"Oh no. He was a dreary man. Kept asking questions once I told him, and I couldn't bear to have him around all the time. It was about ten years ago and other than that I can't think of any explanation for what's going on."

Emily put a few suggestions forward, but received non-committal responses. Eventually, after the exchange of some pleasantries, Emily thanked Janet for her help. "I wish we could hang around and chat some more but I feel we must get on now." Emily stood up, followed by Lucy.

Janet shook her head in mock disbelief. "What do you get out of all this rushing around?"

"It feels right," replied Emily.

"Does it feel good?" Janet set a primitive trap.

"It feels right," she reiterated.

There were a few polite goodbyes and soon Emily and Lucy were once again on the road.

"She was helpful," said Lucy, surprised at how quickly Emily had ended the visit.

"Did you think so? She was very reticent. Normally she would give out opinions just to have me deeper in her debt," replied Emily. " Perhaps she thinks McNatley is a big enough lead to warrant some pay back in the future."

"So do you think McNatley's involved?" asked Lucy.

"Do you?" returned Emily.

"I can't see how."

"Or why," said Emily.

Lucy leaned into the back of the car in search of a can of beer she'd hidden in her coat.

"I threw it out," said Emily, who didn't feel capable of direct confrontations with Lucy about her drinking and so resorted to disposing of her stashes whilst Lucy's attention was elsewhere.

Lucy was used to it and strangely never over reacted to Emily's actions. On this occasion she didn't react at all.

"If," said Emily, "he is involved, and there's no more reason for believing he is involved than for believing you are, then what he said about the white stallion might have been a deliberate lie."

"To what ends?" said Lucy.

Emily shrugged her shoulders. "Dunno,"

Lucy frowned as she started to realise where they were heading. "Where are we going?"

"We have to go back to see McNatley."

Lucy paused as she linked information in her mind together. "Isn't that, err, slightly dangerous?" McNatley was an obviously weak man and she found that sort the most worrying.

"Yep," said Emily. Janet always brought the best out in Emily. "As you're so keen on saying, better dead than smeg."

Lucy giggled to herself, the seriousness of the plan of action seeming not to be at all important, compared with the funny side of Emily's new courageous streak that came straight from a Hollywood movie.

"You're not leaving me at home this time," said Lucy.

"Not if you don't want."

"I don't want,"

Lucy laughed again as she imagined sweet, plump Emily dressed as Rambo, or perhaps just a bullet belt over her Laura Ashley dress.

"Hey," continued Lucy, tongue in cheek, "when the going gets tough the tough get going."

When Emily and Lucy arrived at the university where they

expected to find McNatley, they were psychologically pumped up and ready for action. Unfortunately, McNatley had moved universities and was now too far away to drive in that day. Emily and Lucy sat despondently in the car in the university car park.

"That's a bit of a bugger isn't it," said Lucy.

Emily sighed. "What now?"

Lucy had no reply.

"I suppose," said Emily, "we should try and convince the police that McNatley could be involved."

"I wouldn't bother," replied Lucy. "And where are we going to stay tonight?"

Emily tentatively suggested, "Kerry's?"

"It can't hurt," said Lucy. "Well it could," she corrected herself, "but I doubt it. I mean, Alice is still alive."

"How do you know?" asked Emily.

"It'd have been on the news." Lucy nodded towards the radio.

"Mm." Emily wasn't entirely convinced, but they didn't have to stay if they found bits of Alice scattered down the driveway. "Right then, first stop Becksworth."

Emily was back in control.

A short while later the D.C.I. had his head in his hands, having been informed that an Emily Marthson was at the front desk asking to speak to him. Emily chose to ignore Lucy's advice and although aware that she was pushing her credibility rating with the police, felt informing them was surely the good thing to do and something Janet wouldn't do. Aware that Lucy had a deep-seated dislike of police stations generated by her lack of control over her mouth when in the proximity of police officers, Emily suggested she walk around Becksworth whilst she did the business.

"Show her up," said the D.C.I. wearily to the constable.

"Yes Sir."

A minute later Emily was in the D.C.I.'s office. He was past being hospitable, and was quite obvious in his tiredness of life. He remained seated whilst Emily stood.

"What now, Mrs. Marthson?" he asked.

"Dr. McNatley is a witch." No point pussyfooting about thought Emily.

The D.C.I. looked up at Emily. "Surely you mean wizard or warlock," he said sarcastically.

"No."

"So?"

"That's it, I thought you ought to know everything I know, dear." At which point, Emily turned and walked out of the office.

She had hoped the D.C.I. would call her back and in fact he did consider it, but that would have been too much effort. Instead he called the front desk and had Emily stopped by a constable, under orders to take a statement with a straight face.

Emily was led through to an interview room where a uniformed officer took her statement. There really was no danger of him laughing. Spirits were low all round in the police station and everyone was a little nervous since they had lost one of their number.

As the young officer talked to Emily he began to wonder if dealing with paranormal situations was a regular part of the job and if in fact there was a whole network of people whose job it was to stop the public finding out the supernatural implications of many crimes. As Emily spoke to him, she could see the pressure the realisation that she might be telling the truth was putting on him. The constable wrote down, word for word, Emily's story as he had been trained to do, but by the time he had finished the worry of handing the statement to a senior officer began to give him doubts.

"Do you mind waiting here whilst I check this over with my inspector?" he asked.

"No. Take your time, I'm not in a rush," replied Emily

The constable showed Emily's statement to Inspector Wilks.

"Thank you, constable. I'll have a word with the witch myself now."

Emily was patiently awaiting the return of the constable when she felt the faint beginnings of what developed into a burning hot flush as the door handle moved and Wilks stepped into the small room. With her back to the wall, only a melamine table separated the two witches.

It was now Emily who felt agitated. There was something very disturbing about Wilks's attitude. He could have hidden his secret as Lucy did. Emily felt as though the criminal had removed his mask with all the significance that such an act held for her own life.

Wilks stared down at Emily. His lack of expression was as unnerving as his silent assessment of all that Emily was. Then, with a derisory snort, he left the room.

"Kick her out constable," he said as he passed his colleague.

Emily left as soon as asked, fearful now of what Wilks's next move would be, or Dr. McNatley's, or indeed any member of the coven that she now had no doubt existed.

As Emily exited the police station, she stepped on to the pavement of the main street to see Lucy running across the road towards her. Emily hid her recently heightened fear.

"I've been followed," said Lucy shakily. "They could see through my blanket. They're all around."

"Who?"

"Witches, fucking everywhere."

"How many?"

"Three or four. Look, let's just go and see Kerry, then get out of this fucking place."

Emily had never seen Lucy scared like this, but her own fear was now just as deep. These were the blackest of all witches.

Gwawl could see Emily moving closer to the truth. Letting his coven show their true colours would be an amusing distraction before he decided whether or not Emily was of any use alive.

Chapter 19

The sun was starting to set as Emily pulled up in Kerry's yard. Alice came out to welcome them home.

"Well that's settled, we're staying tonight," whispered Lucy to Emily as they entered the house.

"Where's Kerry?" Emily asked of Alice.

"He's resting upstairs. We didn't get much sleep last night."

"Oh iy," was Lucy's saucy reply, but it lacked any enthusiasm.

"He got beaten up last night."

"By your lot." It wasn't a question. Lucy could have guessed as much after Emily's telephone conversation with the D.C.I.

"I'm not sure if they are still my lot. I'm on bereavement leave and I'm not entirely sure they'll have me back at the end of it." Alice's reply seemed to indicate that she attached little importance to her job now.

"Can I go up and see him?" asked Lucy. She didn't wait for a reply but started to ascend the stairs.

"I was so sorry to hear about Jim. How are you?" Emily asked after Lucy had left the room. Alice clearly appeared very tired.

"Well I'm a bit knackered, but compared to the state he's in, I'm fine. How about you?"

"Scared," replied Emily.

"Mm, being at the centre of a murder enquiry does have that effect on you."

"Your Inspector Wilks is a witch."

"That's nice," replied Alice who didn't really think straight on five minutes sleep.

"Is it?" asked Emily.

"What?" replied Alice, vaguely aware that she didn't know what

Emily was talking about.

"I think, Alice, that I ought to make you a nice cup of herbal tea, something to help you relax."

"Oh, I don't need that," said Alice. "Now you're here I can go to sleep, that is if you promise not to let any policemen near Kerry."

"I think you'd be better off asking Lucy, she's much better equipped for fighting policemen. I'm afraid I just do whatever they ask."

Alice hadn't taken in Emily's words and headed off to her room, zombie-like, before Emily finished her sentence.

Lucy, meanwhile, had found Kerry asleep and peaceful. She stood over his bed, studying the blemishes on his face, a place that now looked as though a small battle had been fought upon it. It would soon look worse she felt. She gave a one-fingered gesture to his closed eyes before quietly leaving the room.

Lucy found Emily making tea in the kitchen.

"I don't think he'll be terrorising anybody tonight."

"Who?" asked Emily.

"Kerry. He's had a real battering; still looks good though."

Emily shook her head. "Pity," she said. "I think we could really do with him awake and fit. If you've spotted all these witches and they are involved in the murders, I'm sure they won't want us around to tell anybody. And they know where we are."

The air took on the deadly seriousness of the situation. Lucy felt compelled to comment on Emily's stiff upper lip. "You're a brave old bint Emily."

It was the wrong thing to say. Emily's resolve broke at hearing what she knew to be an untruth and tears began to roll down her cheeks as her chin rippled into quivering flesh. She sat down at the table and sobbed into her hands.

"Get a grip. Nothing's happened yet and I'm more of a match than a dozen covens if all the witches are as wimpy as the ones I've met today," said Lucy.

Later, after night had fallen, Emily and Lucy were in the living room, a fire burning in the hearth to scare away demons hiding in the dark and cold. They had left Drudwyn upstairs with access to Kerry and Alice's rooms and had decided to try and stay awake until morning, when Kerry or Alice could watch over them.

To pass the time they were playing scrabble. Some homemade wine hadn't helped their alertness but it seemed to scare away the demons that the fire hadn't. Or at least it did, until about four o'clock in the morning when Lucy's concentration on getting a Q out was disturbed by a noise from elsewhere in the house.

Emily and Lucy looked up at the closed door. Steps could be heard and the door slowly creaked open to reveal Kerry in his underwear. He looked at Emily and Lucy with concern forcing its way through sleep.

"What are you two doing up?"

They explained about the witches.

"Oh," said Kerry before returning to bed, without a flicker of concern crossing his face, or any acknowledgement of his friends' return.

A few moments later Lucy followed him out. "I need a piss."

As the door shut behind them, Emily noticed the massai mask hanging upon the door. Kerry had asked her about the mask before but she had not seen it until now. She rose to her feet and approached the door. Seizing the mask in both hands, she lifted it from the door. The furrows on her brow deepened as she noticed that there was no hook on the door. She turned the mask over looking for its method of suspension, praying to her Goddess that she would find one. Her prayer was not answered.

Emily had sensed evil emanating from the mask and seeing its power to defy gravity, committed herself to its destruction. She turned and took a few steps towards the fireplace, then tossed the mask towards the exterminating flames. But the mask never reached the burning logs. Before it even got close, stubby black wings sprouted out of the mask's sides, acting as an instantaneous brake. A flap of the wings and the evil creature tuned itself to face Emily. Two more wing-beats and the mask metamorphosed into a magpie, which came to rest on top of the mantlepiece.

Emily screamed the loudest noise that her lungs could manage. The magpie regarded her. It tilted its head to one side, like a dog puzzled by a whistle, and then it grinned, it's beak curled up a the edges and opened, revealing jagged black and white teeth.

She stared back at the thing, petrified; like a rabbit caught in headlamps, she awaited the impact. Seconds passed, the grin only widening on the aberration's face as it revelled in the fear it was causing.

Gwawl wanted Emily out of the picture, but he could wait until she became more entertaining prey. Right now, he had an old friend to reacquaint himself with.

The magpie vanished, no puff, no pop, just suddenly it wasn't there. Emily could now only wonder where it had gone.

Alice opened her eyes; she was in the room Jim had found himself in only days previously. She could feel the cold tiles on her bare feet. She was dressed, as she had gone to bed, in just a nightshirt. An eclectic mix of people milled about, some dressed like circus performers.

She heard a sudden intake of breath and saw a woman mutilating her face with a dagger. Blood oozed from a cut about her cheek. Alice looked away to the other side of the hall. Two hooded, cloaked figures had their backs to her. She heard a baby cry from the direction of their hands. She watched them until, like a yolk falling from an egg, blood and organs splattered on the floor at their feet. They stepped apart incanting something that grated on the subconscious like chalk on a blackboard.

A voice laughed from somewhere in front of Alice. She looked ahead to where the rusting steel ball was hanging by a chain from the ceiling. Inside it was the corpse of a woman. Beyond and below the ball Alice could see white marble steps and fresh blood flowing from a higher point than Alice could see.

It was easy for Alice to imagine a throne at the top of the steps, or an altar perhaps. It seemed to take an almost central place in the windowless hall.

Smoke filled the air mixing with a putrid smell that made Alice feel physically sick. A deeply evil voice spoke.

"Do you like the smell of smoked human, Rhiannon?"

Alice knew that she was being addressed.

"Who are you?"

"Or perhaps you like them tender and hung like pheasants for a few days," came the voice. **"Time for the maggots to refine the meat a little."**

A large sweaty man in what could only be classed as leather bondage gear, including mask, pulled a chain and the hanging body of a tramp came speeding into sight and swayed sickeningly above Alice's head where it stopped, the occasional droplet of liquid seeping from it. Alice stepped back from the leachate.

The voice laughed a rich deep laugh. **"You see, Rhiannon, I've become awfully bored since I was sent here and I've had to come up with new ways of enjoying myself."**

"You've got me mistaken for someone else," replied Alice.

It was slowly dawning on her that this dream had become a form of reality.

"Whore!" boomed the voice with the venom of all the world's snakes. **"You are the cheapest form of life in this pitiful world. I have waited almost a thousand years to have you and when I do, I'm going to make you scream. And when you're carrying my seed I shall see to it that you can never be unfaithful again and that no man would ever want to bed you."**

Alice could almost see the bitter spittle flying from the clenched teeth.

"I am Gwawl," roared the voice like a lion declaring its dominance over its domain, **"and I want more than I have, and I shall have it. And I will start with you."**

Alice felt people moving behind her. Two crones placed a bench behind her, like a low gymnastics box, although this one had manacles attached to it.

"You see my despised, Rhiannon, you will have the child I stole from you, the child sired by Pwyll. But I shall beget it and return to my own kingdom in my world. I hate you above all things. You are the bitch that was to be mine and so I'm going to make you suffer. When I have your body here, I shall also have your new love, Manawyddan, here. The pleasure of knowing he is watching, helpless, will almost equal the pleasure I shall experience when I hear you beg for mercy as your sides split open."

"I don't understand," yelled Alice.

"No, you wouldn't, but when you awake you can tell your friends, the witches of nowhere, and they will tell you what I mean. While you're doing that, tell Lucy I look forward to getting to know her young body. I shall see you later."

Everything went black. Alice opened her eyes. She was still at the farmhouse though the smell of putrid flesh hung in her nostrils. She screamed out loud.

"Kerry!"

Lucy and Emily were first into Alice's room.

"Where's Kerry?" she screamed hysterically.

"Lucy, go and wake Kerry," said Emily. "What happened, Alice?"

"A dream. They came for me. Gwawl spoke to me. He called me Rhiannon."

"It's alright," said Emily taking a position on Alice's bed. "He can't get you while your friends are here."

Kerry hobbled into the room

"What's up?"

"Gwawl came to her in a dream."

"Yeah?" said Kerry excitedly. "What did he look like?"

"I didn't see his face," Alice replied.

Kerry saw her distressed state and went to her side. "Are you okay?" he asked.

"No," Alice began to cry. "He's coming for me, to rape me."

"He'll die first," replied Kerry. "He's starting to show his hand. We know it's him now." Kerry was clearly excited and didn't try to hide it.

Alice began to recount Gwawl's words, but stopped herself mid track.

"You do believe it wasn't a dream, don't you?"

Alice looked at all three companions.

"If you believe it wasn't a dream, I believe it wasn't a dream," said Kerry and meant it.

Emily managed to speak, failing in her attempt to hide the gravity of what she had just heard.

"If you know how to do it, it's possible to enter people's dreams with practise."

Two thousand years, thought Emily, would be plenty long enough to practise.

Alice continued to recount her dream, reassured that it was significant.

"I've waited long enough now," said Kerry. "We must have options other than just waiting for this Gwawl's next move."

Silence greeted the statement. The group stared at each other, each sure in some way that another member of the group would have an answer.

Emily eventually broke the silence. "Well, when I was talking to that nice detective Renshaw, he told me about a lad called Ian Fast who ran some stories on the murders that would have required insider information. Perhaps he got that from Wilks. They must have a connection with what's going on."

Kerry nodded agreement. "Whatever they know, we need to know."

"So, we all go out together and find this Ian Fast," stated Alice, still shaking and colourless.

Kerry looked at her. All he wanted to do was hug some life back into her face, but he resisted.

"Come on then. Everybody in the car in quarter of an hour," Alice continued as she removed her feet from the bed.

Kerry called Drudwyn to the room and leaving him in there, he and the two witches went to get ready.

Alice felt the cold, clamminess of her skin as she removed her nightshirt and shivered. Drudwyn sat by the window, his great head lifted the new tablecloth curtain to peer out and away from Alice's nakedness.

Alice pulled layer after layer over her flesh in a vain attempt to keep out the cold, which was already inside her.

She began to concentrate on a game plan, wondering how they would find Ian Fast and how best to get the information she wanted. Ideas were proving a little elusive but she knew she would pin them down. Clear thinking had always been her forte. Admittedly the death of her husband was giving her problems in this department, but her own will to live was greater than her bereavement, perhaps because Kerry was giving her something in the form of hope for the future.

Gwawl could not sit back and breath a sigh of relief in his current form, but could at least smile at the words and emotions he had unleashed upon Rhiannon after days of keeping his feelings hidden from her.

Chapter 20

It was 9.00 am by the time the group was assembled by the car. Alice addressed them.

"You three probably find accepting this whole supernatural thing a bit easier than I do, but as it's the only theory we have I'm willing to go with it. Now correct me if I'm wrong: Gwawl was banished from the other world for eating Rhiannon's baby and I'm Rhiannon." Alice paused. "I'm Rhiannon," she repeated firmly, trying to convince herself, "re-incarnated. Jim was Pwyll and Kerry's Manawyddan. So all we have to do is find Gwawl and either arrest him or kill him."

Kerry nodded agreement. Alice was wrong about one thing though. He wasn't finding this whole supernatural thing easy to accept and he certainly wasn't desperately keen on finding Gwawl, given that he felt Lucy could probably deck him in his current state. Still, how tough could a 2000 year old be?

"Okay," continued Alice, "we find Ian Fast first. My guess is that we'll find he's a witch as well and if we can't get the information out of him, we go to Wilks. I can easily get him alone."

"Of course," said Emily, "we should be aware that Gwawl might be listening to us right now and if he's sure of who we are, he's probably just about to make his move."

When the group arrived in Becksworth, Lucy was sent into the paper shop and was out in a few seconds carrying a copy of 'Something Strange'.

The others huddled around her at the side of the newsagent's doorway, scanning the now unfolded paper for an address.

"There," pointed out Alice. "Floor 2, 14 South Street."

"That's handy," said Kerry.

"Why?" enquired Emily.

Kerry pointed across the road to number 14 and then along to the street name further down the road.

"Right," said Alice, "we've got to try and scare this one more than Renshaw did."

They crossed the road, Kerry taking the lead.

Next to the glossy, black door by the hairdressers, a few feet above the 18th century boot scraper was a 21st century intercom. The word 'Strange' was printed to one side of the buttons.

"You should feel at home here then, Kerry," Alice said in the nervous and light-hearted way that some people talk when about to face their own fears.

Kerry smiled supportively at her and pressed the button.

A female voice replied.

"Hello."

"D.I. Renshaw to see Ian Fast," said Kerry.

The door buzzed and the group traipsed into the hallway. A little sign with an arrow and the name of the paper pointed them up a flight of stairs and again up a second flight. The stairs seemed new, as did the décor and the occasional original piece of artwork. The group eventually arrived at a grey door with 'Something Strange' emblazoned upon a plaque attached to it.

Kerry walked straight in, followed by the others and found himself in an office comprising of a few computer laden desks and the smell of recently unwrapped furniture. A woman sat at one desk by the door and looked at Kerry with a growing expression of bewilderment. The only other person in the office was Ian Fast, sitting much as Renshaw had found him, feet on the table and a lighted cigarette dangling from his mouth.

Kerry's attention was soon on Ian and all it took was the start of an intense stare to dislodge Ian's feet and bring him, with a jolt, to a rigid position, as if he had been discover taking an unauthorised break from work by a tyrannical boss.

"Can I help you?" asked the woman, a business-like lady of a similar age to Alice.

Emily answered her. "No thank you dear. We've come for a chat with that nice young man over there."

Ian rose to his feet as Kerry began to cross the room towards him, but the confrontational stance had little effect.

Kerry had a way of holding his tensed frame that, even when injured, could make most men feel like prey. Ian looked straight at Kerry, but it was an obvious attempt at bravado. There was no courage in his expression, just nervous anxiety.

Alice found it hard not to smile and suddenly felt guilty, as though she was the school bullies' sidekick. Whether or not Ian really could turn himself into a wolf seemed irrelevant to all in the room, for Kerry was certainly a link above him in the food chain.

Kerry gave Ian his best Jack Nicholson stare. "I know who and what you are, and I still know I can rip your head off and shit down your neck, but that would leave you brain dead at the end, so save yourself the trouble and tell me where I can find Gwawl and anyone else who is in this pathetic excuse for a real coven."

Ian kept his eyes on Kerry, even as they started to glisten with fearful tears that took away all of his cockiness. Ian's body began to shake with adrenaline, telling him to run not fight. His dilemma held him speechless. He knew what Gwawl could do whilst this man in front of him presented a visible danger. Ian was not entirely stupid and had occasionally wondered just what the man Gwawl was so keen to destroy was capable of.

"I don't know about any covens and I certainly don't know what the fuck Gwawl is."

Ian was not an actor. Kerry could see the anticipation on his face, waiting to find out if his story had been believed.

Ian knew a lot about the coven and as much about Gwawl as he wanted to. He did as Gwawl said and, in return, received power - in work and in the craft. That was all he wanted. Kerry stared hard into Ian's eyes and almost into his thoughts, trying to wrench out the truth by imparting even more fear onto his neurones. But Ian was not forthcoming and with each passing and silent nanosecond his expression was shifting to one a little more sure that Kerry held very few cards up his sleeve.

Kerry cut the silence that could only have lasted long enough for one intake of breath as a memory of Ian's face dropped into place.

"Are you scared of Smith-Kurr?" he asked having found a lone card up that sleeve.

An uneasy expression flashed across Ian's face and disappeared.

"You could kill him, he isn't immortal," continued Kerry, but this time it was his turn to look shocked.

HA!

Kerry stared at Ian in disbelief now. He had heard Ian or someone at least, 'Ha' but no one's lips had moved. It had been a dismissive sound, suggesting that Kerry had just shown his ignorance.

All eyes were on the now silent Kerry whose turn it was to feel the adrenaline shaking his body. He had been worked up before, but this was a fear he had never encountered.

"You're very wrong if you think I can't kill him," resumed Kerry acting better than Ian had managed under less pressure. "Now, I'm not offering you riches. I'm giving you the chance to live."

Kerry had managed to still sound threatening even though it was he who had no answers and a set of morals that wouldn't allow him to carry out a single threat.

Ian was still non-compliant. Kerry was at a loss. He wanted to look around to his friends for advice but felt that that would weaken his position. He knew them well enough by now to know if any of them had a suggestion as to how to loosen Ian's tongue, they would make it known.

"Because he can't beat me and he knows it."

Still there was no sign of crumbling from Ian but Kerry felt he had seen enough in his face to point the finger at Smith-Kurr.

"It really will be your funeral," he said before turning and exiting the room followed by the others.

"Well, that didn't get us very far," said Alice a little scornfully as they reached the street.

She had hoped for a little more information to be forthcoming from Ian and had not clearly seen his facial expression or read as much into them as had Kerry.

Emily, having sensed something unnatural had occurred in the office they had just left and knowing instinctively that it had had a deeply distressing effect upon Kerry, was about to speak in his defence but Lucy tugged her arm, unseen by the others and Emily remained silent, puzzled but apparently happy to trust her protégé.

"I know," replied Kerry, "but I couldn't think of anything else to say. He just wasn't going to say any more, but I'm sure from the way he reacted that Lord Smith-Kurr's got a lot o do with this, even if he's not Gwawl. Fast was in the hunt on my land, so was Wilks and McNatley."

"Come on then," said Alice heading in the direction of the car.

"What?"

"Well, no point wasting time. We'd better get to his place before it's dark."

"Why?" asked Emily.

"Because, I'm scared of the dark," she replied.

There was no arguing with that sentiment. They were all scared of the dark, even Kerry whose fear had only just manifested itself.

There was nodded agreement and the party continued towards the car park. Kerry retook the lead in front of Emily and Lucy. It wasn't an arrangement Alice was entirely happy with, but a little quickening of her step, an outstretched arm between the two witches, a tug on his sleeve and Kerry received her message, and was soon at the rear by her side.

"What?" asked Kerry in a poorly acted innocence.

Alice took his hand in hers.

"Nothing," she replied giving Kerry a little worried smile that helped take 'HA' off his mind.

Gwawl had not been stupid. He was prepared for every eventuality and a telephone tree had been designed. Ian only had to contact one other coven member and within ten minutes the entire coven could be ready to act. Ian made his call and left the office hurriedly.

Kerry and the others were walking back to the car past the brick wall of a supermarket. They were silent. It was unnecessary to discuss the fear that each of them knew. Kerry recalled how he had told Alice that he had made it a part of his life never to be in fear of anything. That was before he had heard the wroth of the thing. He knew now that there was no escape from it. He looked down at Drudwyn, his source of courage in hard times. At least the dog had been spared the fear that the rest of the party knew.

Alice was as dazed as the others, but had the advantage of ignorance. She had never had much interest in the supernatural and until recently had given the subject little thought. Even now she could not make witchcraft a part of her personal reality and so subconsciously ignored it.

Emily was about to leave the pavement to cross the car park when the scales of blameless ignorance fell from Alice's eyes in an event that none of the witnesses on the car park would ever forget.

A dozen wolves leapt from the solid brick wall and in perfect synchronisation, grabbed Emily with their jaws, their bodies seeming to by-pass laws of physics and interweave with each other to allow each extended, gaping jaw to place its fangs upon Emily's innocent flesh. The animals leapt together and in one huge bound had carried Emily's screams a hundred yards from her friends.

Drudwyn ran to fight the abominations but before he had taken two leaps, Kerry saw the wolves rip Emily open and disappear in another huge pounce, leaving behind the tattered remains of the only person he had ever trusted.

Drudwyn had reached Emily too late and was left not to fight but to shake, as if in a fit, above the body in incomprehension. Kerry ran to the spot repeatedly screaming Emily's name. He fell to the floor into a steadily growing pool of blood, his legs incapable of supporting him. Lucy began to cry quietly, making little more than a choking noise before turning away from the body with its missing windpipe.

Drudwyn began to whimper, triggering Alice's tears. Kerry recited his views on death in his head – not a terror but a mystery so deep that we would be foolish to wish to avoid it – but Emily's body mocked his thoughts and he knew it. He would rather have died himself than see this.

Alice felt guilty to be joining in the grief with Emily's closest friends, but Emily had been so endearing that in the short time that Alice had known her, she had made a place within Alice's conscious, reserved for loved ones.

The small number of people that had been in the car park were motionless, staring in their shock, unable to comprehend what had happened. Each of them felt a wave of relief as a police car entered the car park, taking away any need of the onlookers to involve themselves. The car had not engaged its siren and Kerry's group were the last to see it as it drew to a halt, metres from where they were transfixed.

Kerry looked up as the two officers alighted from the car. The policemen were responding to the D.C.I's request to question the public and had not expected to find a beast attack in broad daylight, exactly where they had intended to begin their enquiries. They recognised Kerry and Alice along with the genuine sorrow and incomprehension in their faces.

Kerry was thinking quickly within whilst he still allowed the outside to weep for his loss. He gazed at the officers as they came towards him.

"Alice, " he said just loud enough for her to hear, and without looking at her, "put Drudwyn in the car."

Alice required no explanation for the request. Everything she needed to know for now was in the tone of Kerry's voice. He had a plan and there was no time for questions.

One of the constables knelt down as if to check Emily for life signs. It seemed a pointless exercise but in some way, it gave Alice and Kerry the strength to stand up.

"What happened?" asked the other officer, compassionately, whilst looking into Kerry's eyes.

Alice had surreptitiously taken hold of Drudwyn and began to walk away.

Kerry had not answered immediately and the policeman repeated his question. Alice had just put Drudwyn into her car when a second police car arrived, this one with its siren blaring and lights flashing.

Kerry and Lucy saw Wilks in the car. Lucy knew they would leave Emily now intuitively guessing and approving of Kerry's next move. The plan changed in Kerry's head as the temptation to revenge Emily's death on Wilks closed his fists and locked his jaw. Kerry recognised the emotions as his own internal animal. He had broken it in many years ago and wasn't about to unleash it on the monkey – not with so much more at stake and the organ grinder's name on his lips.

Kerry gave the officer in front of him a sudden unexpected shove, sending him toppling over his companion and Emily's body. Kerry and Lucy bolted for the car shouting at Alice to start it.

Before any of the police at the scene had time to react, Alice had left the car park and was accelerating down the hill that led out of the town. Wilks was soon in pursuit and gaining on Alice until she reached the windier country road out of the town where she began to screw the car around the tight country lanes.

"Shit," swore Alice. "I bet there's no way off this road."

"Don't know," commented Kerry.

"Oh well, straight to Gwawl's place then," said Alice.

The police chased her for miles, never managing to overtake her as she swung into their paths. She led the chase to Lord Smith-Kurr's estate, taking a diagonal line across a verge to hit the wrought iron gates of his driveway with the front nearside of her car. The bolt shattered, and half of the gate swung open, allowing the car to career on into a statue of Pan, which it practically mounted, before coming to rest.

Alice, Lucy and Kerry leapt out of the car and began the long run up the drive to the manor house. Every jolt was agony to Kerry, but he was determined to reach the house with the others. Drudwyn bounded on ahead of them all. None of them were sure what they were doing or why. Emily's death and Wilks's sudden appearance had taken away any composure the group had left.

The police cars swung into the driveway and drove up to Kerry. The officers disembarked and gave chase on foot. One of the officers was gaining on Kerry swiftly. Kerry stopped dead in his tracks, turned and cracked the constable on the jaw with his plastered fist, and ran on as the officer fell backwards.

Alice reached the house with Lucy and was amazed to find the front door ajar. Too pumped full of adrenalin to consider the pitfalls an open door suggested, Kerry and Drudwyn dived in after them and bolted the door behind them.

Wilks stopped running and smiled. He had delivered the package, a little overweight, but safely where it should be. He didn't think Gwawl would mind about the dog.

They were in the huge entrance hall, with doors to all sides and a sweeping white marble staircase ahead. The officers with Wilks started banging at the door. The three witch hunters quickly took stock of the scene and wished they hadn't.

"I think," said Lucy nervously, "that this is the part at which someone suggests splitting up to find Gwawl."

"No chance," replied Alice.

It may have been daylight outside but it hadn't banished the demons that had stolen Emily's life. There was no safety now.

"Pussy," replied Lucy, showing signs of excessive adrenalin.

"Perhaps Drudwyn could sniff Gwawl out," carried on Alice.

"Maybe," said Kerry, and then: "Fetch," to Drudwyn. Drudwyn merely looked up at his master with an expression that begged the question "where's the stick?"

"Or maybe not," said Alice.

"I might be able to," said Lucy, "but I can't promise anything. Just follow me."

Lucy led them to a door on their right and opened it. The expected creak did not manifest itself. They stepped through the doorway into a large lounge area. There was none of the expected evil appearance to the room. Expensive red leather armchairs rested on deep crimson shag pile. A snooker table stood two thirds of the way into the room. The open fire glowed softly. There was a television screen that would have been measured in feet and not in inches and a scattering of paper racks. The whole room was well lit by the daylight that entered unhindered through vast windows and the occasional uninteresting oil painting hung on the walls.

"Can you feel it?" asked Lucy.

Alice looked at her. 'What' was the question in her eyes.

"A feeling that someone's telling you off for entering somewhere where you've no place to be."

Alice took a moment before answering. "I think so."

"Did you expect the welcome mat?" asked Kerry, as he bolted the door behind them.

"Come on," said Lucy, marching swiftly to the far end of the room.

They followed her.

"Can you sense something?" Alice asked of Lucy.

"Just a pain that grows worse as I presume we get nearer to Gwawl."

"A pain?" asked Alice.

"More a feeling of suffocation actually," clarified Lucy.

"I think I do feel that now," said Alice. "What about you Kerry?" she continued turning to look at him.

Kerry's appearance seemed to be changing, to Alice's mind. He was more like the dark brooding man she had found when she first called at his house, although he was still walking with the careful manner of one in pain. He seemed to have straightened out, perhaps even grown. He bore the face of the deadly serious and to Alice it was an almost deadly excitement. She could feel that everything that made Kerry so unique was now rising to the occasion.

"I feel ready," he answered quietly.

Alice looked into his eyes and something in the cold blue told her not to ask – for what? Did he know more than he was letting on she wondered?

Lucy arrived at the far end of the room where a choice of three doors confronted her. Alice and Kerry awaited her decision. Lucy felt the handles on each door and decided upon the one that 'almost makes me vom'. She opened it quickly and viewed the room. A dance hall, like those ballerinas practise in, wooden floor, mirrored walls and a bar. Two doors were at the end of the room. They entered. A key was in the lock. Kerry locked the door behind them and followed Lucy and Alice to the far end of the room. The only sound was Drudwyn's claws tapping on the bare floor. Lucy stared at the doors.

"I think," she said, "that we have to accept that we've lost the element of surprise."

"Which door Lucy?" asked Kerry impatiently and then he suddenly lost his look of urgency. Alice viewed Kerry as he stared at the glass in the walls. It was strange in some way that Kerry could not immediately put his finger on. The glass didn't seem to reflect as much light as it should. It was like looking at the reflection he had seen of himself when he had taken money to appear in a police line up in front of one-way glass.

Lucy picked a door. It led into a short, tiled corridor with two doors on the right hand side. She picked another and they found themselves in a shower room, up to a hundred showers surrounded a large sunken bath, full of steaming water. The only sound was that of a dripping tap, that echoed around the room and ran shivers up Alice's spine. On the far side of the bath and past the row of showers was the only other door. To reach it Lucy had to walk beneath showers on the three foot wide tiled floor between the wall and the bath. When she reached the door Kerry and Alice started to follow, but half way to her, the showers suddenly came to life firing powerful jets of steaming water at the couple. The shock made them both jump but Kerry jumped the wrong way and stumbling over Drudwyn fell into the bath.

"Kerry," shrieked Alice instantly recognising that a plastered arm wasn't a good swimming aid. The water was at least three feet below the side of the bath and so Alice, forgetting all life saving skills, jumped into the water to rescue him.

Before Alice's head hit the water, she heard a shriek but could not react to it. Alice grabbed Kerry and swimming him to the side pushed him up out of the water enough to allow him to swing his own body out of the pool and then he in turn helped Alice out.

Kerry took in Alice's washed beauty for a second.

"Lucy!" squealed Alice recalling the scream.

They looked around but Lucy was not there. Drudwyn however was, scratching at the door by which they thought they had entered. Alice and Kerry exchanged a puzzled look, ran back to the door and opened it into the tiled corridor. Drudwyn ran to the door that led into the dance hall. Alice opened it but the dance hall was not there. In its place was what appeared to be a film studio with a myriad of equipment focused on three makeshift sets, a bedroom, a bathroom and the rear half of a car.

Drudwyn was uninterested and ran on to another door. Kerry

and Alice exchanged further bemused looks.

"The rooms, the rooms, they're not right," moaned Alice.

"No," said Kerry, "all we can do is follow Drudwyn. He may not have been able to sniff Gwawl out," continued Kerry, "but he can certainly follow Lucy's scent."

"Are you sure that's what he's following? He's a wolfhound isn't he? And where the hell's the room we came through?"

Kerry shrugged his shoulders.

"He must have moved the walls or something," said Alice trying to answer her own question.

Kerry opened the next door and they found themselves in another corridor. Small, low-powered lamps lit the walls. Drudwyn went straight to the opposite door. They entered and this time found themselves in a small dark room, a number of empty chairs either side of a projector faced a flickering movie screen. Drudwyn was already scratching at a door at the rear end of the room but Alice and Kerry had been caught by images on the screen. A blue movie was rolling. Alice recognised the scene as the car set they had just seen in the previous room. Kerry lost interest and went over to Drudwyn, but as his back turned the groaning and panting from the scene stopped. Kerry looked back. He saw that the reel of film had come to an end but instead of silence, a voice came from behind him. There was still an image on the screen.

"And now for any paedophiles out there."

The voice was deep, smooth, cultured and, above all, evil. The image was a swirling wheel, nothing else, until the wheel started to slow. Kerry's eyes widened with rage. On the screen was a wheel with Lucy clamped to it in a figure X, as though in a circus knife-throwing act. She didn't look conscious.

"But those with more human morals shouldn't worry. You can stop this pretty little girl from coming to any harm," said the voice.

Kerry saw Lucy with her eyes closed, as a scared young child, not the battle scarred tramp she usually gave the appearance of being.

"How? I hear you ask," said the voice. "Well, it's in your hands, Alice"

The voice had now affected a game show host style of talking, the sound sending Drudwyn's hackles up. He curled back his lips revealing vicious fangs.

"Yes Alice, just leave Manawyddan and the dog behind and I shall set Lucy free."

Alice stared at the screen. There were no clues. Lucy was on a white circular board, apparently vertical in a dark red room

"He's lying," said Kerry. "He'll just take both of you."

"I know," snapped Alice. "But there's no choice."

"They'll hurt her anyway, but if we're quick we can find her together. He must be scared of us if he wants you away from me."

There was an evil laugh from the screen, mocking Kerry's words. Alice wavered on uncertainty. Kerry watched her, eyeing the door they had entered by.

"Alice!" cried Lucy, "help me."

Alice looked up to see a large fat man, naked but for a leather mask and G-string, appear in front of Lucy. He ripped off Lucy's tie-died blouse, revealing the small bra that protected her young breasts. Putting his head level with Lucy's hipbone, he licked her with a stubby tongue from midriff to armpit.

Rage took hold of Alice's senses and she bolted from the room. Kerry grabbed for her but was too slow. The door swung shut behind Alice with a force that had not been imparted by Alice's hand. A second later, when Kerry, still calling Alice's name, attempted to reopen the door, it would not budge.

Whilst Gwawl had been talking on the screen, Drudwyn had not ceased from behaving as if he was about to be placed in a fighting pit, but now he simply barked at Kerry as though he was ready for his walk. Reluctantly, having searched the room for a weapon or tool to open the door with, Kerry returned to following his dog.

As soon as Alice had left Kerry, her rage began to subside and the enormity of her action began to become apparent. She had run through the film set room and then taken another door and, without looking back for Kerry, who she had presumed was following her, entered a corridor. It was unlike any other room they had seen, part of the original house, untouched by the money.

The stone floor was well worn and barely visible by the candlelight that flickered through the eyeholes of the skulls that rested bodiless in tiny alcoves, apparently made for the purpose. Long canine teeth distinguished the bones from human skulls, but what they were Alice could only guess. The faint noise of clinking chains was all the sound available in the room.

Alice had reached the vein to the hidden heart of Gwawl's kingdom, but she wasn't foolish enough to think that she had just stumbled through the right door. She had been scared before, but nothing compared with the fear that gripped her as she stared along the corridor, unable to make out where its end was. Her imagination, proving too hard to control, was giving the skulls a past.

The Lord's Prayer was all that Alice could think of to stiffen her upper lip. Over and over again she repeated the final line 'and deliver us from evil'. A wind blew up the corridor, extinguishing all the candles on its way to Alice's hair. It wasn't like the wind on the moors; it was unholy. She knew that that air had no place in her lungs, as if she could see the poison carried on it, but she could see nothing now.

"I've done what you asked," shouted Alice. "Now let Lucy go."

There was a deep rumbling, snarling, growl from ahead of her. Alice's heart pounded. The noise stopped, but something was left, a sound like that which Drudwyn had made walking across the hard dance floor. Two tiny red lights appeared at the far end of the corridor, not glowing brightly enough to illuminate anything. As Alice stared at them, she slowly began to realise that they were staring back.

Chapter 21

Neither Renshaw nor the D.C.I. had understood what was occurring on the car park as they listened to radio messages referring to beast attacks.

"It'll just be a body and someone will have jumped to the wrong conclusion," commented Renshaw.

"Well, if it was a beast attack then we're going to have a lot of answers as soon as we get there," replied the D.C.I. "Have you noticed that there's been no radio contact from Wilks."

"Yes sir." Renshaw felt prompted to say a little more than he wished and erred on the side of caution. "Perhaps he's just being a little unprofessional, you know, trying to get some of the glory."

"I hope so."

The D.C.I.'s contemplative expression suggested that what he hoped and what he believed were at opposite ends of a scale.

The two of them were crossing the car park now, heading towards the morbidly fascinated crowd and other officers gathered near Emily's body.

"All of our little group of suspects seemed to take an instant dislike to Wilks didn't they?" commented the D.C.I.

Renshaw wished that his boss would just say what he thought, rather than prompting him into saying it.

"They didn't seem like the type that made friends with police officers on a regular basis."

The pair pushed their way to the body. The D.C.I. took a slow, deep breath as he looked down.

"This one did."

A uniformed sergeant stood uneasily by the side of the D.C.I. waiting for him to raise his head and listen to the details that he had gathered from witnesses.

The D.C.I. seemed lost in his thoughts for a moment and as Renshaw was impatient to know what had happened he called the sergeant over to one side. Appearing a little dazed, the D.C.I. followed the sergeant to Renshaw.

"What do they say happened, sergeant?"

This was the moment the sergeant had been dreading. He repeated the story. Some witnesses had described the incident exactly as it had happened, others adjusted the story a little to sound more believable.

When the sergeant had finished, the D.C.I. lifted his head.

"Why do you think they ran away when Wilks turned up?"

It wasn't the question the sergeant had expected. He stuttered a little and was unable to produce an answer.

"So who radioed in to say where the chase ended?" asked Renshaw giving in to his own suspicions about Wilks.

"The second car there."

"Not Wilks?" interjected the D.C.I, now out of his moment of contemplation.

"No sir. He was in the other call sign and asked for radio silence immediately after that call."

"Sergeant, you stay here and deal with this situation: scenes of crimes, statements and all that. But send as many officers to Lord Smith-Kurr's place as you can, and get someone to try and contact Smith-Kurr by phone to see what's happening. Now come on, Renshaw, let's get over there," said Smegvick.

The pair grabbed a constable with a car and left for Smith-Kurr's.

Kerry's infuriation was growing as he tried room after room. Some he was sure he had been through multiple times. He had placed his hand on a door to exit a library when the voice that now vibrated with evil spoke to him from nowhere.

"I fear nothing, least of all a mortal like you, Manawyddan. I am a shape shifter. I can come for you day or night. I can have

what is yours from your liver to your lover. I could hound you wherever you roam or I could bring you to my jaws. I could be a book on the shelf or the carpet beneath your feet."

Kerry responded by reciting part of the 23rd psalm.

> "Yahweh is my shepherd,
> I lack nothing,
> Though I pass through a gloomy valley,
> I fear no harm,
> Beside me your rod and your staff
> are there to hearten me."

He opened the door and Drudwyn bounded out. He was back where he had begun, in the entrance hallway, but the situation was worse. Wilks and three other officers were waiting for him. Kerry stopped dead in his tracks, Drudwyn by his side.

"Arrest him," demanded Wilks, trying to think on his feet.

The officers were aware of their duty, but they were also aware that Kerry and Drudwyn were prone to sending officers to hospital.

The eldest of the other officers, a sergeant, spoke to Kerry in a firm voice. "Now then, son, are you going to come easily or are people going to get hurt?"

One of the constables winced, embarrassed at his sergeant's words. He watched Drudwyn leave Kerry's side and scratch at another door. The constable moved to the door, opened it allowing Drudwyn through, then closed it behind the dog.

"Good work, constable," said Wilks. "One down, one to go."

The sergeant walked over to Kerry who felt deflated at Drudwyn's exit. "Look," said Kerry, "Smith-Kurr's the killer."

"Arrest him sergeant," repeated Wilks.

"Wilks is one of them," continued Kerry, but he knew it was no use and with a surprisingly swift side-step, made it past the sergeant and headed to the door by which Drudwyn had exited. Only the young constable was in his way. A truncheon was rapidly drawn and swung at Kerry, catching his neck. Kerry fell towards the constable, managing at the last minute to find his feet capable of adding to his momentum, and delivered a weighty fist to the constable's solar plexus. The constable reeled backwards as Kerry bounced away from him. With a controlled thrust of the one foot in contact with the marble, Kerry threw his rag-like body against the door and was through it before the other officers, who had not seen the control in his action, could react. Drudwyn was not there and as Kerry ran past the snooker table, he had to make a choice of doors unaided by ESP or scent. He chose the closest one.

Kerry was passing the mirrored wall in the dance studio, heading for the next door when he caught sight of his pursuer's reflections. He couldn't believe that evasion was possible for much longer and as he pulled on the next door, all hope faded, as he realised that it was firmly locked. Kerry spun around to see the officers slowing down as they approached their trapped target. There seemed to be only one chance left and he wasn't optimistic about that. The door through which he had come was ajar. All he had to do was rush at the half dozen, truncheon wielding, professionals in his way.

Kerry dropped his shoulders and head in what he hoped to be a sign of surrender, but as he waited for some suggestion of relaxation on the part of the police, he heard a loud bang. The door he was aiming for had slammed shut. Kerry looked up to see Wilks's grin slowly widening. Wilks walked back to the door and checked it; it too was now immovable.

The other officers had stopped a few metres from Kerry and looked around at Wilks for guidance. Kerry could see that they at least weren't happy about being locked in the room.

"Cuff him," commanded Wilks.

One officer replaced his truncheon, produced his handcuffs and began to read Kerry his rights.

Kerry didn't listen. He looked around the room. The officer

seemed to have reasonably assumed that there was time to read rights before securing Kerry. Kerry's desperate eyes rested on his own reflection in the smoky, dark, mirrors. He knew he was probably wrong, but it was possible that they were two-way mirrors. He also knew that if he was wrong he'd look very stupid, and that if he were right he would probably hurt himself a lot more. He shrugged his shoulders and launched himself at the mirrors.

* * * *

Alice started to shake with fear. The eyes were closing on her and their owner had started snarling. She felt to the side for the wall and her hand touched what she knew to be one of the skulls. She recoiled suddenly from the warmth of the touch and then remembering the layout of the doors reached out again, picked up the skull and flung it at the eyes. There was a satisfying thud, which suggested her aim had been good. Alice quickly took a step backwards and felt for a door handle but instead someone took her hand in a rough hard grip.

Alice screamed aloud then, recovering her composure, threw a punch at where a face should have been. The punch connected, but not with a human face. There was a roar so close to her that she felt the breath in her face and the putrid smell in her nostrils. A door burst open and there was a sudden inlet of light. Alice saw something blurred in the sudden change of light, but it was gone in a flash. Drudwyn had been the cause of the door bursting open and Alice saw him as he chased something wolf-like down the stairs at the end of the corridor.

She followed, unable to shake that fraction of a second from her mind when she had stared at the abomination.

She ran down the steps, increasingly aware that the light was fading again and that she had lost sight of Drudwyn.

The steps ended. Corridors led off to the right and left, but ahead of her was a huge set of doors at least twenty feet high. They slowly started to open and Alice realised that she was looking into the room that Gwawl had taken her to in her dreams. She turned to flee but stopped herself. This was the room she had been trying to find; running now would achieve nothing.

She walked into the courtroom. The courtiers lined a path to the throne, Gwawl's subjects staring at her in an evil and knowing manner. The cage that had previously hidden Gwawl from her view was now hoisted higher. Gwawl could easily be seen, sitting in regal domination of all he surveyed. Alice walked to the foot of the raised throne.

Smith-Kurr looked down upon her, his massive frame, like that of a body builder, filled the huge, repulsive throne. Animal skins cushioned his form from the structure, which was crafted from human bones. Smith-Kurr's giant hands engulfed the two skulls set as ornamental ends to the arms of the throne.

He was not dressed as the modern day Lord now, but as the King he had once been. Like a holidaymaker preparing for the homeward journey, he was dressed in the attire of the land he would return to rule in a simple woven tunic, covered by a chain mail dressing. He wore a golden crown with tusks protruding from it at every angle. A broad sword, as tall as Alice, leaned against one of the skulls. On the other side of the throne rested a huge wooden and leather designed shield, his royal crest of three phoenix embossed upon it.

Gwawl began to laugh; the chain of engineered events had led Alice to him.

Alice had seen men that it would be wise to have some fear of before, but she had never seen anything like this. "Where is Lucy?" she demanded firmly.

Gwawl continued to laugh, deep and loudly, not at Alice but with the heady feeling of complete satisfaction.

"Let her go," ordered Alice.

"Do you see this?" asked Gwawl tapping his crown. "I am the king. I give the orders." He resumed his laughter.

"A crown doesn't make you a king," replied Alice.

"Now you sound more like Rhiannon than this peasant reincarnation," said Gwawl struggling to contain his pleasure.

"I am Alice Farrier," stated Alice proudly.

"You," said Gwawl, "are Rhiannon, once betrothed to me, but enticed into the mortal's world by Pwyll and Manawyddan.

Ride a cock horse to Banbury Cross,

to see a fine lady upon a white horse,

with rings on her fingers and bells on her toes,

she shall have music wherever she goes."

Alice looked at Gwawl puzzled.

"Do you recognise the rhyme? It was written of you."

"I take it then," replied Alice, "that no one ever bothered to write about you."

Gwawl's smile left his face momentarily. Alice was at a loss as to what to do or say. She could rush at Gwawl and attack him but he looked too confident for that to be an option and she couldn't see it achieving much, although she knew it was what Kerry would do.

"You, Rhiannon, are anonymously immortalised in prose. I am immortal in reality."

That's not right, thought Alice. Something in her subconscious told her that she'd heard he could be killed. Something Emily had said, but Alice couldn't recall it.

"Yes," said Alice, "you're obviously so immortal that you need armed guards on the door."

"I need nothing; I have everything. But you need me, my dear Rhiannon. Would you like to see me leave this world."?

"I'd like to see you dead," replied Alice.

"And I'd like to see you naked and I shall if you have any morals," said Gwawl. "You see, I only exist in this world because of you and Manawyddan. You could bring an end to all of my rape and pillaging because I can return to my other world kingdom if I give you a child. You must give yourself to me willingly and with passion, then you, and Lucy, and Manawyddan will be free. I shall be allowed home and this world will be a safer place to live." Gwawl smiled sarcastically.

Alice stared at Gwawl. What he was saying sounded similar to what Emily had said on the subject of the manuscript, but it was difficult to think clearly or remember precisely under the circumstances.

"Alice," said Gwawl, "I'm not of this world. I can't be expected to have your morals, but I have my own so I give you the choice. But you must give yourself unreservedly. Take your time," said Gwawl, "to decide whether a small sacrifice by you is worth the lives of hundreds."

She gulped back her feelings. Why her? thought Alice. If she really was the reincarnation of his old girlfriend, how had he found her? Perhaps it was all a joke and she could just say no.

"How did I find you?" said Gwawl smiling, at the fear on Alice's face. "What goes around comes around" is the modern expression. Of course, you have to wait a long time for three people to be incarnated at the same time, but I had forever to follow that dog. Then, when it found Manawyddan it was just a case of drawing people to him, hoping that you were alive. I'd tried before but never quite managed to find you before you had given birth."

"So will you give yourself to me, or do others have to die?" Gwawl gestured to one wall of the building where a projected film image of a naked and bound Lucy was focused.

"Yes," Alice said, hanging her head in disgust at her future.

Gwawl's face broke into an evil grin. The two crones from Alice's dream placed the box behind her whilst three young men appeared from around the throne, carrying filming equipment.

"A hobby that pays," explained Gwawl sarcastically. "I'd like to leave something for this world to know me by."

The camera focused upon Alice. She knew what she had agreed to do, but couldn't believe it would really happen. In her imagination it already was.

* * * *

The mirror shattered in the middle, allowing Kerry's body through but not without the unmoved jagged remains digging deeply into his flesh. The cuts went unnoticed. First he saw a small room with suspended railway-like tracks sweeping from one wall to another. He fell straight past this mechanism for what felt like hundreds of feet into blackness, but as Kerry came to his unexpectedly soft landing he realised that the drop must have been much less.

The policeman calling down to him could not be clearly distinguished from the shaft of light above that had once been a two-way mirror.

"Yuk!"

Kerry, becoming accustomed to the dingy light, found that his soft landing had been accomplished thanks to a pile of dead farm animals. The sound of flies filled his ears. As he looked around a little light was cutting through what turned out to be a sliding door. Kerry clambered over the carcasses and into the yard of the hunt kennels. He blinked at the light and was grateful for the fresher air.

Kerry wished that he could stay out in the open but the thought was only secondary to finding a way back into the house. The dogs barked constantly as he looked over the out buildings. They were of a different structure to the rest of the house. Around the back and hidden from sight, they looked as if they had seen no renovation since having been installed. If it hadn't have been for the fact that Kerry had arrived there via the main building he would have thought that the two were unconnected.

Stone steps led up to a small, old, wooden door. It seemed the only way into the out buildings and perhaps the house.

As Kerry entered the room, a Jack Russell of a kennel hand jumped up, spilling his coffee at the unexpected arrival of a stranger. He said nothing as Kerry stared at him, perhaps unsure of his place in the situation.

Kerry warily cast an eye around the room, spotting another door and a shotgun propped up in the corner.

The kennel hand broke his silence. "Who are you?"

"Sorry mate," replied Kerry, "just need to borrow the gun a second."

He turned hoping that he had bluffed the hand, but the turned back was all the invitation the kennel hand needed. Kerry was just quick enough to protect his head from a shillelagh. With what remained of his plastered arm, his free fist punched out, sinking into the hand's neck. The hand dropped to the floor and Kerry grabbed the gun. He had time now to search for cartridges as the man lay rasping on the floor.

Kerry found a cartridge box on the floor, feet away from the gun. He loaded it, without taking his eyes off the man on the floor. Kerry's own actions were disturbing him now, as he headed through the next door, a deadly weapon in his hands.

That door led to a small room that looked as though it might be used for very rough and ready social occasions, but the very next door brought him into a room that was definitely part of the main house. It was a plush drinking lounge, empty of people save for a short, uniformed bartender, who didn't express any surprise at Kerry's sudden appearance. Many strange people had entered the bar and from the beginning of his employment he had learnt to just accept the situation.

"Evening sir," said the bartender. "What can I get you?"

Kerry made a play of looking at the sparkling bar and huge selection of drinks, whilst trying to work out the scenario.

"Could I just have an orange juice please."

"Certainly sir."

The man opened a bottle, filled a glass and handed it to Kerry. The barman desperately wanted to offer some first aid to Kerry, if only to stop him from getting blood on the carpet, but that would not be on.

"Thank you," said Kerry. "This is a quiet job for you," he said conversationally, trying to lead up to some more pertinent questions.

"Yes sir."

Kerry was about to swallow his drink when the television screen mounted in a corner above the bar flickered into life with an image of Alice.

Alice was backed up against the box. Ten cloaked figures sat around the box, chanting. Gwawl came into sight, semi-naked, proud and grinning.

Kerry gritted his teeth, he could see fear and a tear on Alice's expression. But why wasn't she fighting or running?

"Take off your clothes," commanded Gwawl.

Alice began to unbutton her blouse.

Kerry looked away from the screen to the barman. The barman was used to the perks of his job, but was intently watching as Alice placed her blouse behind her on the box, removed her shoes and then her jeans. Kerry had returned his attention to the screen. He could see Alice was procrastinating over her strip. He presumed in the hope that some rescue would come, but there was only him and he had no idea how to find her.

"Is that live?" Kerry asked, without a hint of panic in his voice.

"I've absolutely no idea," replied the barman.

"Only I'm supposed to be having a business lunch with him."

The man tore his eyes away from the T.V.

Kerry could see that the barman was contemplating how to find Smith-Kurr for his guest.

"How do I get to that room?"

"I'm sorry, I don't know. I don't even know if it's in the house."

Gwawl had removed his chain mail and having grabbed Alice's arms from behind had her pinned to the box.

"Do you want me?" asked Gwawl.

"Yes," lied Alice.

Gwawl cut her bra strap with a knife that was then thrown out of reach.

Kerry could watch from afar no longer and raised the shotgun to the barman.

Gwawl's hands moved down and into Alice's last garment.

The barman's face changed.

"That room is in this house. Now tell me how to get there or you die."

"I don't know. I think it's in the basement." The bar man's attention was focused now, and although not panicking, he was clearly taking the situation seriously.

The barman's wording troubled Kerry. He couldn't see such a large room being in a basement. He stared intently at the man, weighing his fear up. He looked incapable of lying in his current predicament but that meant little; fear could be a regular part of the life of anyone embroiled in this horror show. "How do I get there?"

The barman could see the uncontrolled anxiety in Kerry and wanted to have an answer but did not. Kerry tried to calm his thoughts, took a few steps away from the bar and dragged his eyes from the screen where Gwawl had removed Alice's knickers. Kerry's eyes looked at the floor whilst his mind focused on a route into the room. He realised that Gwawl had control whilst he was in the house. He looked at the screen again as Gwawl spoke to Alice.

"Do you love me?"

Kerry could see a brazier smouldering in the background, the smoke from it slowly rising. He strapped the gun to his back and left the building as he had entered.

Outside Kerry could visualise the room he was looking for in comparison to the whole Ivy bound building with wisps of smoke emanating from its roof. In the back of his head was a small thought of his injuries, but he had no option as he began to climb up the ivy, which here at the bottom of the building was tree-like in girth.

Gwawl now stood behind Alice, her body completely bare save for the chains that manacled her to the box. Her fists and teeth were clenched at the thought of her fate.

"Now!" boomed Gwawl. "If we can't take the goddess to the altar we shall bring the altar to us."

The coven members assembled around the box in a circle emanating from Gwawl and began to chant with their arms spread out, fingertip to fingertip. Alice could tell the language was Welsh but no more than that.

A sudden jerk on her arm and ankles stretched her prone body into a star shape. The cold granite of the altar from Hafgan's Ring replaced the soft suede of the box, and the stone circle now stood where the coven had been.

"I hope you're ready, Rhiannon."

Alice looked to her arms now cast in the granite rather than chained to it and raised herself enough to look down the length of her body to see a part of Gwawl's metamorphosis into the creature she had encountered in the hallway. A huge red, dog-like penis unsheathed itself from the fur. Alice began yelling and frantically tried to twist free to no avail.

Kerry clambered over the ornamental castellation and was on to the flat roof, but now what? He looked around for a way in. Another police car arriving in the driveway briefly distracted him. Directly in the centre of the roof was a large chimney. Kerry moved as quickly as he could to it and peered down. There was a draft of stale smelling air upwards, but only a little smoke in the air and it did not appear to have a fire at the bottom. Kerry tried it out for size. It was a tight fit, he might get stuck in there forever, but alternatively he might make it down.

Kerry climbed into the chimney, using his legs to push against the walls of the chimney and so keep his weight from plummeting him to his death. There was a definite breeze upwards and as Kerry's feet displaced dust, he felt it in his face, taking a lot of it into his lungs. He slowly let himself slip down the chimney controlling the pressure his legs exerted and occasionally glancing down between them. Suddenly the chimney widened, Kerry lost his grip. He looked down and saw himself plummeting towards the whirling blades of the extractor fan that was at the end of the chimney.

Kerry brought his legs together and crashed feet first on the hub of the fan. The fan immediately gave way in a flash of electric sparks and flew into the crowd of courtiers even faster than Kerry fell onto them, receiving his second soft landing of the day.

The fan, followed by Kerry's landing, did their fair share of damage, reducing at least six of Gwawl's lackeys to the role of casualties. Kerry got to his feet. The armed guards from the door, which was only feet away, rushed over to Kerry pointing their guns at him, awaiting calm and Gwawl's order. They were professionals and had been prepared for this intrusion. Unfortunately for them they didn't notice Kerry had fallen clutching a shotgun.

Kerry fired at one and then the other. To his surprise they both fell, clutching their stomachs. Kerry saw the guns immediately and tried to persuade his body to recover from its fall faster than it was prepared to. The stones around Alice turned into wolves and leapt towards Kerry before he could get to the guns. One wolf leapt into his face, furiously snapping as Kerry's hand grabbed around its throat whilst two of its companions sank sharp teeth deep into each of his thighs. Kerry toppled forward, putting all of his effort into crushing the skull of the wolf in his hands on the marble floor.

Two of Gwawl's courtiers had seen enough for one day and after picking up the guns opened a smaller door within the great door in an effort to leave the scene. Drudwyn looked up at them before battering his way between them, pounding towards the wolf that was crunching its teeth on the bone of Kerry's leg. Drudwyn grabbed the wolf by the throat and ripped the life from it as he had ripped a hare from the undergrowth a week earlier.

The coven members weren't used to anything or anyone fighting back. They hadn't been brought up in the dog-eat-dog world that Gwawl had and his expectations of his staff proved too high as they began to flee. Drudwyn left another for dead before pursuing the last of the wolves out of the room.

A nervous looking courtier closed and bolted the door as soon as Drudwyn had gone, and then stepped away from the door, resuming a more skulking position with the small group of drugies, prostitutes and musicians that had remained and now viewed Kerry as he struggled to his feet.

The pain hadn't really set in yet; adrenaline was still pumping. Barely a patch of Kerry's clothing had remained dry of blood and he was as surprised as his onlookers when his legs held him erect. He looked over at the remaining courtiers; they appeared to be of little threat. With the disappearance of the standing stones, the altar had also reformed into the box. Kerry walked over to Alice, glancing from side to side, wondering where Gwawl had gone. He picked up a dagger as he got to the box.

Alice looked up at him as he began to prise the manacle anchors in the wood away from the box. They knew the lull could only be temporary.

"Are you okay?" he asked.

"Yes, but I've not seen Lucy."

"Where's Smith-Kurr?"

"On my throne," he bellowed.

Kerry looked towards the seated Gwawl, now in the image of Smith-Kurr, wearing his ancient battle clothing, the shield in one arm and the sword in the other hand.

"Did you get scared whilst your friends were running out on

you?" asked Kerry sarcastically.

Gwawl smiled back. **"We both know who's scared here."**

Kerry left Alice the knife to free herself whilst he, almost on autopilot, moved to the closest wall and removed a shield from it. Kerry then pulled at a sword but as it came free from the wall, its weight pulled his arm downwards with such unexpected force that Kerry feared momentarily that he might have dislocated a shoulder.

"Not much strength left, Manawyddan?"

Alice could see Gwawl was right. As he stood up from his throne and tossed his sword in his hand, Smith-Kurr's body seemed huge. Perhaps it had been bench-pressing for the last thousand years, just waiting for now. Kerry's body was barely intact and as for his mental state, Alice had no way of telling.

"I've really enjoyed toying with the two of you for the past few weeks. A little like foreplay really, but at the end of it all, one of you will be dead and the other pregnant."

"Let him go, Gwawl and you can have me as often as you like," said Alice.

"Is that the word of Rhiannon?"

"Yes," replied Alice.

A smug grin spread over Gwawl's face again.

"Pity I don't give a shit about what you want then. Manawyddan must die anyway."

Alice could see that Gwawl was going to kill Kerry now. She had freed her second hand and looked over to him. Kerry had steadied the sword in his hands but the punch drunk expression was still visible.

"Kerry!" she yelled, "Kerry!" The second shout got his attention. "Emily said you could kill him. Now fuck him up for her and Lucy."

Kerry looked over at Alice, the unintentional humour having brought his thought pattern back on track. He had to win because there was no way that bastard was going to touch Alice.

As Gwawl grew closer, Kerry raised his head from it's typical lupine position and, eyes on fire with hatred, stared into Smith-Kurr's own.

Gwawl was almost upon him now and then, with a lithe movement, he was right by Kerry. Kerry moved his sword to defend the oncoming blow from Gwawl, but the power by which Gwawl brought his sword around, sent Kerry's own weapon flying from his hands, simultaneously ripping his injured hand from its socket, leaving it rigid and dislocated. Kerry grunted in pain and ran away down the hall, but Gwawl bounded after him with a terrifying fleetness of foot and was in front of Kerry before he had covered six feet.

Gwawl was in no rush to despatch Kerry; he could play with him a little now that he was unarmed.

"If you're going to run away, Manawyddan, perhaps you ought to, and wherever you run to in this hall you can watch me fulfil my destiny and your wife."

Kerry wanted to fight but a sacrifice would not save Alice.

"You cannot kill me," said Gwawl. **"I am greater than life."**

"If I can't kill you," spat Kerry through gritted teeth, "why are you so afraid of me?"

Gwawl swung back with his sword and this time Kerry managed to jump out of the way of the swing. But then he stumbled backwards over the bodies that had given him his soft landing, and fell onto his own back.

"I'm not afraid of you. I merely need to kill you to return home. I who have fought vampires for amusement and to the death, have, unfortunately for you and me, no knowledge of fear."

Chapter 22

Renshaw and the D.C.I. were following the same course for Lord Smith-Kurr's house as Alice had taken. The D.C.I. took hold of the radio handset and called to the sergeant who had pursued Alice with Wilks.

"Sierra, Alpha, One. Is Inspector Wilks with you? Over."

"No sir. Over," came the reply.

"Please pass an update of the situation. Over," said the D.C.I.

"We are in Lord Smith-Kurr's house, carrying out a search for the suspects. Over."

"What are they suspected of? Over."

"I'm sorry sir, I'm acting on Inspector Wilks's instructions. I presume they are murder suspects. Over."

"Where is Wilks? Over."

"He instructed myself and the other officers to disperse in our search. Over."

The D.C.I.'s face contorted. He didn't want to have this conversation over the airways, but he was so suspicious that he felt radio procedure was superseded by urgency.

"Has Wilks done anything unusual? Over."

The sergeant felt as uncomfortable as the D.C.I. but could only respond subserviently.

"No sir. Could you expand. Over."

"Have you had contact with your suspects since entering the building? Over."

"Yes sir, we have seen Kerry Taliesin. Over."

"What happened? Over."

"We're here, sir," interrupted Renshaw as the car swung into the gravel driveway to the mansion house.

"He accused the Inspector of involvement, assaulted a constable and escaped. Over."

* * * *

Kerry pushed against the floor with his dislocated wrist. The pain was immense and brought home the reality of his impending fate. He thought he saw Alice moving behind Gwawl but would not allow himself to give her away with a glance.

Gwawl gently shook his head.

"You're so predictable, expecting her to save you as if something always saves you."

He waited for the attempted shot or flailing sword to prove his power.

Alice had freed herself but it was obvious to her that she had been allowed to; whatever she did next would have to be unexpected. She tiptoed towards Gwawl's back, knowing that he knew, fearing what he could do. His tree trunk legs were wide apart for balance amongst the fallen bodies and fan debris.

"Drudwyn, Kill!" she blurted before diving between the spread legs as Gwawl swivelled to see where the dog that he had thought out of the room was. Alice tossed the knife to Kerry who pounced from the ground up to Gwawl who, realising the dog was not present, lost another vital second glancing down at Alice.

Kerry thrust himself into Gwawl's chest and threw his arms around his neck, hoping that he would be too close now for Gwawl to use his sword. Kerry drove the dagger into Gwawl's neck. As Kerry pulled it out, Gwawl plucked him away from his body as if removing a ferret and threw him across the room with a strength that could not have been merely from natural sources. Kerry hit a wall fifteen feet away and softly fell to the floor; the fight was over for him.

Gwawl turned to face Alice. She could see no sign of concern on his face over the blood that trickled down his back. There was only an expression of evil lust. She ran, but with a graceful fleetness of foot, Gwawl was in front of her at every moment, laughing at his prey's ineptitude. Eventually he appeared to grow tired of the game and grabbed Alice with one great hand around her neck. He yanked her around to face away from him. Alice struggled but she was no more than a toy in the presence of such strength. He dragged her back to the box and forcing both her arms together behind her back, almost dislocating them, prepared to finish his plan.

Alice felt dampness on her back. Amidst her panic, she wondered if Gwawl had fallen foul of a premature problem. The liquid continued to spatter onto her back: blood from the wound Gwawl had sustained from Kerry. He could see it and his grip on Alice began to weaken until he released her.

She turned to see him walk away from her and to the unconscious body of Kerry, but before he reached him Gwawl's legs began to buckle and he dropped to the floor, like a runner who had given more than his all only to finish fourth, Alice prayed silently behind him that he would not get up again.

Eventually her prayers were answered and Gwawl collapsed into a foetal position, feet away from Kerry. Alice cautiously walked around Gwawl. She could still see his torso moving with his breathing. As she passed him, he stared up at her with expressionless eyes. She knelt down by Kerry's face, still able to keep an eye on Gwawl.

"Kerry," she said whilst taking his wrist to check for a pulse. There were none of the signs of life that Gwawl portrayed. Desperately she readjusted her grip making it lighter to detect the faintest of beats. It was there; he was alive.

"Kerry," she repeated.

She bent over him putting her cheek to his nose and mouth, hoping to feel his breath on her skin. The lightest warm movement of air brushed her face. She shook him gently and was repaid with a groan.

Kerry opened his eyes to see Alice's face. He stared at the soft lips that smiled down at him. They began to move but he could hear nothing for the first few words as his hearing slowly came back.

"….you get up? He's not dead yet."

Kerry turned his head and found himself looking into Gwawl's eyes. It was strangely the weirdest sensation Kerry had had in this whole affair. His nemesis lay bleeding and apparently incapable of any more fight but so did he. Only Alice separated them now. Kerry turned his attention to himself. Could he stand up he wondered. His leg was clearly in a bad way, as were both his arms. He raised the dislocated hand to Alice; the angle at which it stuck out was almost too revolting to look at.

"Pull it," he croaked.

Alice took hold of the hand and pulled, Kerry gave out a yelp and his hand was back in its rightful place.

"Manawyddan."

It was Gwawl, and the knowledge that he still had speech chilled Kerry. Alice looked around for a sword, as Kerry struggled to his feet, one eye on Gwawl, another on the streams of blood both dried and flowing that covered his own body.

"Save me from this pain, Manawyddan."

Kerry was on his feet now and Gwawl's words calmed him a little. The giant was dying but Kerry knew he could not leave that hall with the slightest chance of Gwawl being alive. He took a sword from Alice, unwilling to let her do what he was not sure he was morally capable of. He moved to Gwawl, hesitating by his body.

Gwawl groaned in agony, but still Kerry felt unable to kill the man.

"I will tell you where Lucy is if you promise to kill me now."

"I promise," replied Kerry.

"She's in the lounge that you came through when you first

entered the house. She hasn't been harmed. I only wanted her to get to you. You stole my wife and made me lose my Kingdom."

Kerry plunged the sword deep into Gwawl's heart. There were no last minute death throes, just silence and a surprisingly content look on his face.

Alice was redressing as Kerry stared down at what he had done. He was shaking as the adrenaline in his system became surplus to requirements. He was still standing there when Alice took hold of his hand. It shook him free of his guilt for it was the most welcome touch he had ever had. The warmth and softness had a soothing quality that he felt he could swim in all day.

"Come on," she said calmly. "We've got to get out of here and get help."

Kerry still could not allow his feelings to rush out and a smile was the only hint that Alice was given to the comfort and pleasure that he felt from her being there with him.

"I saw Renshaw pull up when I was on the roof. He should have found Lucy by now."

"Well, it's time to get out of here and face the music."

Alice tugged on the huge doors and they began to open. Drudwyn greeted them excitedly on the other side. The couple held each others' shaking hands as they headed back to the lounge room. This time nothing hindered them.

Alice could feel the congealing blood in Kerry's palm as he felt the back of his head and neck with his other, surprised that the two were still attached to his body. The pain that he knew was to come was still momentarily masked by the adrenaline that rattled around his body.

The two glanced at each other before opening the door to what they hoped was the lounge. Please God, thought Kerry, let me find Lucy alive.

The room was as it had been left, save for the presence of the motionless, bound body of Lucy. Alice ran to Lucy's horizontal form on one of the leather sofas, while Kerry hobbled after her. Alice shook Lucy gently, like a mother waking her child. Lucy's eyes opened slowly at first. They looked blearily at Alice's face then shot wide open as her lips let out a loud, short scream.

"It's alright," said Alice soothingly. "It's all over."

There was a relieved expression on Lucy's face as Alice undid the ropes that bound her feet and hands.

Chapter 23

Kerry knew the main threat had gone, but was uncertain of what would happen once the police got hold of him. "The immediate problem is that on the other side of that door there is going to be a lot of coppers wanting a lot of answers, but we may as well face them now. We can talk about what's happened between ourselves later."

Alice gave Lucy's hand a squeeze as she helped her stand and led her into the entrance hall where they were greeted by the sight of dozens of police officers, some armed, and most of Gwawl's courtiers in handcuffs, including Inspector Wilks.

Wilks's expression, along with McNatley's, Fast's and the other coven members, was amazing. They instantly stopped arguing over their arrests and stared in disbelief. Wilks began to cry as he came to terms with the loss of his master and guiding light, to which the living presence of Kerry and Alice bore witness.

Renshaw approached Alice, Kerry and Lucy with one eye on Drudwyn, who in turn had one eye on one of the police Alsatians.

"I'm sorry," said Renshaw, motioning a group of less occupied officers to his side, "but I'm afraid we're going to have to take you all into custody until we can resolve this matter into a believable file for the crown prosecution service." Renshaw waited for a reaction.

Kerry shrugged his shoulders in resignation to the fact that Renshaw had, after all, played his part in the whole drama perfectly and it seemed a reasonable explanation for their arrest.

Scores of police vehicles ferried officers and prisoners away to various interview rooms and remand centres across the county. Alice and Lucy were placed in one cell of Beckworth police station. Kerry, after some medical treatment, was put in the only other cell.

As Kerry sat in the cell, he contemplated how glad he was that he didn't have to make sense of the whole case. He felt guilty too. After all, he'd killed at least two people and a thing, and that was two people and a thing more than he'd ever killed before. He wondered about their mothers, wives perhaps. Had it been fair just to kill those two, armed men? It was instinct he told himself, before Renshaw, entering the cell with a constable carrying a tape recorder, interrupted his thoughts.

"I'm afraid," said Renshaw, "that we'll have to interview you in here. The interview rooms are being used."

"That's okay," replied Kerry deciding to take it easy on Renshaw, as he must have seen the body of Gwawl by now.

Renshaw began the interview with a legally required spiel and opened with the question. "Now tell me everything that's happened today."

Kerry gave the details in full, missing only the part of the story that was totally unbelievable: Lord Smith-Kurr's transformation into so hideous a monster.

"Is that it?" asked Renshaw as Kerry finished with his arrest.

"Yes," replied Kerry, expectant now of some reference to Gwawl's body.

"Right, well our search of the house and the courtroom as you described it bear out what you've told us. We also found a drugs factory along with a forgery press and illegally pornographic material. Smith-Kurr is evidently a very rich man from the profits of crime. But the only part of your story I don't understand is you say you killed him."

Here we go thought Kerry.

"But there's no body."

Kerry looked puzzled.

"What about an animal?" He was not going to be the first to mention werewolves on tape.

"What animal?" retorted Renshaw, afraid that this was a new twist to an already tangled mess of a case. He had seized some videotapes and they had given him an insight into Smith-Kurr's life. They had turned his stomach and illuminated some of the darker corners of the whole affair, in particular the activities of the coven.

Kerry looked at Renshaw who could clearly read the shock on Kerry's face.

Kerry did not speak; dreadful thoughts were rushing through his brain.

"What animal?" repeated Renshaw.

"I thought I saw a wolf," replied Kerry who had now lost much colour from his face. "Didn't you find anything…furry?"

Fear began to show itself in Kerry's body language and some of it was starting to rub off on to Renshaw.

"No," replied Renshaw. "Is it possible that you didn't kill Smith-Kurr and he somehow escaped? After all, the two armed men are only wounded. They're not dead either. In fact, the only dead are two that seem to have got mangled in the falling fan."

Renshaw had never seen Kerry look flustered but now he was watching a man who was frantically nervous.   There   was silence as Renshaw awaited some speech from Kerry.

Renshaw and Kerry stared at each other, both desperately wanting to know the truth whilst at the same time fearing what the truth could be.

Suddenly the cell door swung wide open and in the doorway, impeccably dressed in a suit, and scar free, stood Lord Smith-Kurr. Renshaw leapt up to effect an arrest but Smith-Kurr merely raised a hand and, as calmly as if he had been fetching a handkerchief out of his pocket, fired a silenced pistol at Renshaw. A second shot and the constable by Renshaw's side was dead.

Kerry was already on his feet without a clue as to what to do.

"You look puzzled, Manawyddan. You want to know why I'm

still alive. Well my dear enemy, it is because you are so great an impetuous fool that you didn't bother to see how you could kill me."

Smith-Kurr's voice was calm and level but then changed to that of a violent teacher abusing his pupil as he quoted from the Mabinogion. "Pwyll had to fight Hafgan, giving him but a single blow, but you didn't did you, you fool. I am Hafgan and I am Gwawl, and now you can never kill me. You are no more than the least of things in my sight now. You are a maggot and this time I shall use you to recapture Rhiannon. You see, I want her to come to me without my using force on her because I want you to feel responsible. She will come just to rescue you and it's you fault, your fault for presuming that you could show mercy upon me by putting me out of my misery. Misery is not an emotion I suffer."

Kerry swung at the gun in Gwawl's hand. Gwawl opened the hand, virtually giving Kerry the gun. Kerry fired and Gwawl smiled.

"You can't kill me, idiot." With an almighty blow from a clenched fist, he knocked Kerry to the floor. As his head hit the concrete, Kerry felt only a second of pain before he fell into unconsciousness.

When Renshaw was found he was barely alive and was rushed to hospital. There was no hope for the constable.

Kerry awoke in a dark, dank, circular, stone room not wide enough to stretch out both arms. He could see nothing and could only hear the babbling of water outside the structure.

"Are you awake Manawyddan?" called Gwawl.

His voice; the very sound of which was now so synonymous with fear in Kerry's mind that his blood froze. The voice seemed to come from overhead but there was only darkness there.

"I know you are and what I have to say will bring great pleasure to me. You see, Rhiannon, having been reincarnated from the other world could cause me some problems, if she were ever to use some of those powers entrusted to her by her previous incarnation. So, I shall arrange for Rhiannon's powers to be taken from her. I always knew she had the power and knowing that was fun. It amused me; the thought of her with the power to slay all forms of demons and yet have no knowledge of it and, as you say, knowledge is power. But I think she may be a little closer to that knowledge than is comfortable and that is why I killed Emily, for she certainly could have realised Alice's abilities.

And you see, Manawyddan, the only way to take away her power would be to kill her, but I can't impregnate her when she's dead. So, to be absolutely sure of no further inconveniences to myself I need Rhiannon dead and alive. Do you understand?"

Kerry did not and the disorientation that the darkness brought did not improve his concentration.

"You don't," read Gwawl. "Well, let me enlighten you. You have, I am sure, heard of vampires, if only from Dracula stories. You know some of the powers I possess, so it surely would be even less difficult for you to imagine that vampires exist and they, although normally of little interest to me, do possess one power that is not in my command. That power is the ability to create the undead. I have, in my thousand year life, become aware that compared to me, vampires are pathetic creatures to be pitied, but they will be of use to me by taking away your Rhiannon's power to influence the sight of…" Gwawl paused. "No, I shall not tell you. I must go now to prepare your Rhiannon for a life of darkness, decay and - the only good part – bloodsucking."

Silence and darkness were all that were left to Kerry following Gwawl's departure. It was an agonising lack of sensory information for Kerry. He could only worry for Alice and Lucy and wonder what influence it was that Alice could wield. If there was anything special about Alice it would have to do with her connection to the other world. If that was the case perhaps he too had whatever it was that he needed to influence the sight of whatever it was that bothered Gwawl.

The imponderable nature of the whole situation began to take its toll on Kerry's resolve and a sense of futility and depression began to set in.

* * * *

Alice had been released prior to Gwawl's appearance at the police station and was waiting at the farm for Kerry to be returned to her. He and Lucy had been detained because by their own accounts they had killed people, whereas Alice was victim through and through. But she expected the return of Lucy and Kerry as Renshaw had explained to her that everything that had befallen Lucy had been videoed and that every single coven member had been implicated on film with at least one of Gwawl's illegal schemes. Even Wilks had appeared in a pornographic film.

A car pulled up outside of the house and the woman, a small, sweet-faced lady in clothing much like Emily's, stepped out of the car and approached the door.

Alice opened the door and smiled before politely saying "hello" to the woman. Alice could not help but notice how strikingly honest the lady looked, which in itself, Alice decided, was a most strange instant assessment. She also seemed remarkably familiar.

"Hello," said the woman. "I'm afraid I have some bad news for you."

Alice doubted any news could be bad with Gwawl dead.

"You see, Gwawl's…"

The name opened Alice's eyes wide.

"…not dead," went on the woman. "He has Kerry and has told me because he has a hold on me, to tell you to go to Gloucester where he will direct you to him."

Alice began to shake.

"No," she said, "no, no, no."

"I'm sorry I had to tell you. He has lost all his power-seeking cronies and now has to get people like me, who he's trapped into serving him to carry out his little errands." And then the woman's face took on a graver look. "But I wont be a good slave. If he dies, I'm free. He thinks I don't know enough to be a threat, but he's wrong. You can make yourself as powerful as he is but you must promise if all goes wrong, to die before you tell him who told you." The woman was now shaking with nerves and appeared to be frightened for herself, making the sign of the cross upon her chest.

"I can tell you how to find him and defeat him before he can get you."

"How?" begged Alice.

"You may not wish to do it. I swear that by Almighty God no love would be so great for me that I would travel down the path which I am about to suggest to you," said the woman.

"How?" demanded Alice.

"You need immortality, but more importantly you need to be a vampire," again the woman crossed herself.

Alice nearly laughed, but caught herself. If Gwawl existed it was a small leap of the imagination to believe in vampires. It was a chilling thought.

"Why can't you just take me to him?" asked Alice.

"I do not know how to find him. He has taken Kerry to a secret place, but as a vampire you could find him. You would be led to him instinctively. Now, I can tell you where to find them and you must ask one to infect you. I know where they are as Gwawl, my jailer, avoids the place as though," the woman corrected herself, "as it is cursed. And then, poor lady, you have the free choice."

"Tell me," said Alice, "so that I have the choice."

"A place called Back Square in the city of Derby," replied the woman. She looked around and then, hurriedly and without another word, ran to her car and sped off. Alice called after her to stop, there was too much left unsaid, but the woman paid no heed.

There was one half-truth in what the woman had said. Gwawl

had now resorted to less trusted and motivated assistants since his disciples had been arrested or killed, but this messenger didn't fall into that category.

One phone call and the woman's words rang true. Kerry had gone missing from custody. After a short conversation, Alice was left in the nightmare world that she thought she had seen the last of. She had no choice. To see Kerry killed and herself raped, or to enter the unknown. How many times had she wished her life over in the last few days, only now to be confronted with accepting eternal life to save the one she loved. What would Kerry want? He had risked death to save Alice and Lucy, but now Alice must risk life to return the favour. What of the greater picture thought Alice? What of heaven and hell? Would I be outcast? Would I be evil for the rest of my days? The decision came to Alice. If I do this thing for Kerry, for love, then even God cannot judge what I do as wrong. I shall go to Derby.

The police had told Alice that an officer was bringing Lucy back to the farm and would be there soon. Alice stewed in her worries, hoping that Lucy would be able to advise her, but there was no comfort even in that ray of hope. How on earth could she take advice on such a matter from such an immature person?

Lucy walked into the lounge, startling Alice from her brooding.

"Where's Kerry?" she asked.

Alice told her all that she knew and without framing a question awaited Lucy's response.

Lucy slumped into a chair, a serious look of concentration upon her smooth and dirty face. Alice was at least given hope by the lack of a smart remark.

"It makes sense, the stuff about vampires. If Gwawl's shape shifting is that good that he can disappear in a near death state and reappear well enough to take Kerry from a police cell, you would have to have some extremely fine senses to know who or where he was. And of course it would help you find Kerry. If he's in Gloucester a quick run around the city might be all you need to pick up on his scent, if everything I know about vampires is to be believed, but then I never met one and tested his powers out."

"So do you think it's what I should do?" asked Alice.

"I wish I could give you an option, Alice, but I don't see any. It's not just Kerry you'd be saving either, it's us two, the rest of the world, and revenge for Emily and Jim."

Alice stared at Lucy. She could see that Lucy desperately wanted Alice to go down the route suggested by the strange visitor, but she would not give the outright advice that she should do it. It was like telling a child that you had no money for a Christmas meal but asking if they still want a present.

"I'll come with you to Derby," said Lucy. "I'll bring everything you need to fight vampires and if it all goes wrong, I'll sort it out."

Alice walked out of the room and into the farmyard as if some fresh air would give her the strength she needed. Drudwyn appeared from behind one of the outbuildings and padded up to her. He sat down beside her, his great head higher than her hips, looked up into Alice's eyes and whimpered, begging for his master as another dog would beg for food.

Alice looked away from Drudwyn to her watch and walked back into the house.

"Right," said Alice, "get your vampire fighting stuff together. We're going."

Lucy suppressed a smile. She knew the gravity of the situation but at least it was looking like an end might be insight. Alice had seen some wild garlic in the edges of the garden that Etta had maintained for vegetables and went to the front of the house to pick them, unsure what, exactly, she should do with them once picked.

Lucy gathered some bits and pieces together, including matches and a can of lighter fuel. She went around the house looking for Drudwyn and found him asleep on Kerry's bed. She woke him.

"Come on boy."

Drudwyn followed her out to the back of the house and to the stable where Alice kept her horse. She let Drudwyn into the stable. "You stay there out of the way."

Lucy placed her equipment in Alice's van and returned to the house where Alice was washing the soil from the garlic and her hands. Alice's every thought now was filled with what it would feel like to have the fangs pierce her skin and then sink deep into her jugular.

Alice put the garlic in the driver's door of her van and went to say what might be her last goodbye to the stallion. She saw Drudwyn in there and for a moment contemplated taking him with them.

Alice closed the back door of the van and called out for Lucy who came running a few seconds later.

Throughout the journey, Alice was amazed at Lucy's ability to just shut her eyes and attempt to sleep, but she wasn't going to allow that. She needed the constant conversation now.

Alice and Lucy arrived at Derby at eight p.m. The dark had already taken over the unlit corners of the city as they parked the car on the dull grey road that swept around the back of tall, dark, anonymous buildings and the front of the square.

Alice peered out from the car at the small lifeless paved square to her side. Boarded-up shops and a bench, kept company by an unhealthy tree, were all that she saw. For the moment, the car was a sanctuary and a place to have last minute doubts.

"This could all be a trap," Alice said, not for the first time.

"Well you don't have a choice do you?" replied Lucy. "Unless you want me to go out there."

Alice knew her only hope of coming out of this situation with her soul - something that until recently she had not even contemplated - in one piece was to do everything with the best of intentions, and as much as she wanted to send Lucy out she knew that this was a cup that she could not let pass by.

Gwawl was unsure of Alice's abilities. Rhiannon had been a magical woman with animals and he wasn't taking any more risks. He would destroy any chance she had of removing the scales from the eyes of his enemies before continuing what he should have finished in the mansion.

Without warning, Alice opened the door and stepped onto the pavement. The sudden rush of night air into the car made Lucy huddle up and cross her arms over her chest.

"Are you staying there?" Alice asked wanting Lucy to come with her, but sure that she shouldn't.

"I'm staying put," replied Lucy.

Chapter 24

Gwawl could have an apparently sleeping body in one place and one astral projection in another, but could not be active in more than one place at once. With no time to gather more disciples to him, that was a hindrance and he had had to leave Janet's house earlier that day, after having spoken to Kerry, to watch his plans bear fruit.

Janet was a distrustful type, not because a rough life like Kerry's had taught her caution, but because she had been born that way. She knew how selfishly she could scheme and was well aware that Gwawl had been plotting for more years than she herself had been alive. He must have known that she would double cross him if the result would bring her more power and so she had resisted looking too deeply into what he was up to. He had however told her about the vampires and that her reward for being Kerry's gaoler was to be the power and immortality of the vampires.

Janet had none of Alice's worries about eternal life. She feared death far more. With Gwawl away now and surely too involved in the completion of his plan to pay her any astral visits, Janet found herself for the first time in a position where she could consult the spirits. She didn't believe Gwawl would be back to pay his debt once he had accomplished his goal, but she did want to know how to get his powers; no one had ever been so masterful in the art of projection.

It was Halloween and her ouja board beckoned from its permanent position on a table in her pink setteed lounge. She had turned her back on the board to light a candle, not sure in herself whether she was actually going to take the plunge and double cross Gwawl, when she heard her small carving of a horned god moving around that board.

Janet had set no question for the spirits and spun around to see the carving that she used in place of an upturned tumbler, moving backwards and forwards over a very short distance, scratching at the board, demanding attention. She stared at it, fearful that Gwawl was on to her.

The carving began to move about the letters on the board GWAWL MUST BE STOPPED. SOMETHING FOLLOWED HIM INTO YOUR WORLD FROM THE OTHER WORLD. HE HIDES FROM IT. ALICE MUST LIFT THE CLOAK AND CALL ON THE WHELP.

Suddenly the figurine rose from the table and, as if thrown by an invisible hand, hurtled towards the wall where, upon contact, it exploded. Emily had repaid her debt.

Janet wasn't so sure. Now that she had an inkling of a secret, she was a threat to Gwawl and her experience had shown that that wasn't an enviable position.

She looked down at the powder that had been the stone of her carving. What had made it fly across the room with such force? If it was Gwawl, she wondered why she was still alive. She knew Gwawl had more important things upon his mind than her. Perhaps he had done just enough for now and would be back for her later.

Janet desperately wanted the secrets that Gwawl could reveal to her, but she wasn't prepared to risk all for the knowledge. She had begun her betrayal and now must follow it to its end. Janet grabbed her car keys and went out to the back of her garden. Herbs spaced out gaps between paving stones and led to a pretentious, ornate well. Snowy, her cat, sat mewing in the bucket, which lay on top of the padlocked, heavy, wooden doors that hid the well's contents from the rest of the world.

* * * *

Kerry knew that much time had passed since Gwawl had last spoken to him; whether it was a day or more he was unsure. He had risen above his depression and begun his imprisonment with attempts at escape, bracing himself against the cold wet wall that encircled him and climbing upwards until his head had hit the lid of his cell. He pushed up with his head but there was no give. He had tentatively tried to push up with a hand but there was not enough grip between himself and the stone and he plummeted back into the darkness of the pit. Unable to see the ground he landed awkwardly and screamed out in anger and pain. Like Robert the Bruce's spider, Kerry tried again, and again he fell painfully.

By about the tenth attempt, Kerry was able to judge when he would hit the floor, but by now there was no strength left in his ankles to allow a cat like landing and the pain bore into Kerry's mind. Tears began to flow, but for Alice he struggled up the well another ten times, and another ten times he fell into the dark.

The agony finally forced Kerry to stay on the ground in blackness where all he could do was think, and thinking was the worst thing of all.

He thought of Alice, of how he had failed her, of her in Gwawl's embrace, of how he loved her. He thought of Lucy's short life, so affected by evil and he thought about the loss of Emily. Until now there had been no time to think of Emily properly. The videotape of Kerry's mind played the murder of Emily over again. How could he have just run away from her body?

"Alice!" Kerry cried out. One more attempt; he owed them all one more attempt. Kerry stood to his feet, but they collapsed beneath him and he fell, cracking his head on the cold stone before coming to rest on the waterlogged floor.

Kerry was unconscious when Janet pulled back the wooden doors. Fresh night air filled the well as water once had. The movement of air and moonlight awoke Kerry and he managed to turn his head out of the muddy floor to look up at the starry sky. It hurt his eyes, but then why should they not have suffered like the rest of his body.

Kerry was aware of a change in circumstances but his thought pattern was too blurry to even know why he was in the well. All he did know was that he wanted to be out of it. Something hit his head; it was the bucket. Janet wasn't sure if it would take Kerry's weight or even if it did, whether she had the strength to pull him up with the simple handle.

"Hold on to the bucket," she shouted down.

The words made sense to the part of Kerry's brain that could operate on self-preservation autopilot and his bloody hands grasped the rope above the bucket. Janet had a death penalty hanging over her head and that was more than enough motivation for her adrenaline to lift 14 stone, 14 feet.

Kerry crawled over the side of the well and upon reaching full daylight collapsed into the herb bed. Janet pulled him to his feet, dragged him to her car and thrust him into the back seats. She had no time to decide whether he would live or die; they would both be dead as soon as Gwawl's attention was on them again.

Janet cast an eye over her shoulder every two minutes as she set off for Derby. On the eleventh occasion, bright blue eyes looked back at her in bewilderment.

"Can you hear me?" asked Janet.

"Who are you?" replied Kerry.

"Never mind that. We've got to kill Gwawl." Janet was not surprised at how easily she could contemplate killing Gwawl for most of her thought was now on self-abuse for being stupid enough to get involved with something like Gwawl in the first place

Kerry shut his eyes as if there might be some refuge there from the pain that filled every broken bone and dislocated joint in his now shaking and cold body. There was no respite, just thoughts of futility. He had had his chance at Gwawl and could never repeat it.

Janet had no time to allow Kerry to sleep.

"Look, as soon as he's finished with Alice, we're next."

Alice, yes Alice. He needed no more time for self-pity and managed to lift himself to a sitting position, his faculties drifting into focus.

"What is the whelp?" Janet asked.

Kerry managed to look even more puzzled.

"It's a dog."

"I know that, but what does it mean in connection with Gwawl?"

Kerry looked blank.

"Or the Mabinogion?"

Still no light of inspiration, but at least a reminder about his own dog.

"Can we go via my farm so I can pick Drudwyn up? Actually, where are we going?"

"Who's Drudwyn?"

"My dog."

"He couldn't be from the other world could he?" Janet asked clutching at straws.

"Where are we going?" Kerry demanded, now beginning to get some of his firm-handed personality back.

"Derby, to rescue Alice and kill Gwawl." Janet didn't actually care about the first item on that agenda but had been sharp enough to pick up the sobering effect the mention of Alice's name had had on him before. "But first we have to pick up your dog. Do you not know any way of stopping Gwawl?"

"I assumed you had a plan," Kerry said a little panicked, aware that a gung ho approach, even if he was match fit, wouldn't work.

Janet took brief directions from Kerry towards Becksworth and then began to explain what she thought Gwawl was up to in Derby, whilst getting everything she could out of Kerry. By the time they arrived at the Taliesin farm, Janet had a firm view of what the whelp was.

Janet parked at the front of the house. No lights were on,

confirming the absence of Alice and Lucy. Kerry opened the car door and called out for Drudwyn, who leapt over the half door of the stable in ecstasy at hearing his companion's voice. He bounded into the car, knocking Kerry back into a prone position. He licked Kerry's face once and then, standing astraddle Kerry with his head hung low to fit in the car, he stared at Janet, who stared back.

"Come on," said Kerry eager now to do what ever he could to try and rescue Alice. "Let's get going."

He tried to push the dog out of the way, but he held his ground as Janet stretched a hand out and placed it on the dog's head. She was sure now, not of the why but of the what, and allowed herself a smile at having found that which Emily had overlooked. She got out of the car and shut the rear passenger door before setting of again for Derby.

She was driving fast now and in a state of high tension, but still wanting to know more. It was nearly midnight, to her a special hour. She wondered if the same was true for vampires. "Why is he called Drudwyn?" she asked.

"I don't know. I dreamt it up. But now you mention it there is a dog called Drudwyn in the Mabinogion stories."

"That Dog," Janet stated.

Kerry, still groggy, looked puzzled.

"I think that Drudwyn is the whelp and Gwawl's scared of it for some reason."

Drudwyn was Kerry's friend. He had had him for years and wasn't about to believe he had come from the same place as Gwawl. "But Drudwyn was with us in Smith-Kurr's place. He did nothing towards him."

Janet looked disheartened at that piece of information and wished that she had just gone along unquestioningly with Gwawl.

They were on the outskirts of Derby when Janet saw another straw to reach out for. "When I met Gwawl he had a blanket up. Perhaps that hides his identity from Drudwyn."

Kerry felt sick as he saw the sign post "DERBY 5 Miles". This was going to be it. He new he was about to die and only hoped that he would be in time to save Alice from living.

"He did mention something about falling scales," Kerry said.

"Blankets!" replied Janet her suspicion finding firmer ground.

Kerry looked like he was trying at least to shake the bemusement from his head.

"It's Alice and you that he thinks are from his world. I'm sure you need to be involved in any spell to remove his cloak. Decloaking's normally just a matter of burning some body part of the subject, nails, teeth, hair or something bigger, with salt, garlic and a little incantation.

Kerry started to focus his mind on Janet's words.

Chapter 25

Alice took up a squatting position in one of the deep shop doorways, looking out onto the square; nothing was happening the knots in her stomach were excruciating.

Lucy remained in the car, watching the shadow that she knew concealed Alice.

Alice had been waiting hours, expecting that if anything was going to happen it would happen at midnight. But a distant church bell now struck one o' clock.

Harsh footsteps alerted Lucy to a couple approaching the square from behind the car. She tried to find them in the mirror. It was a man and a woman dressed -far too casually for vampires - in sweatshirts and jeans. Lucy snuggled into the jacket that she had brought, keeping an eye on the couple as their features came into focus. He had a skin only a shade off albino and short black hair, giving a very defined appearance. She looked healthier - bright red lipstick illuminating an elongated face.

They passed the car, glancing directly at Lucy. She thought for a moment that they were going to stop, but a slight movement in the eyes of one suggested that they had seen something to dissuade them and they turned right into the square. Lucy and Alice watched them approach the bench, swaying a little as if intoxicated, the woman seeming to support the man as she helped him sit.

The woman didn't sit, but stood erect like a guard meercat. Alice could not see what she was doing, but heard it. The long, deep intake of breath through the woman's nostrils and past her receptors. She said something to the man and his nose flared. His head turned quickly and his eyes stared into Alice's shop doorway, like the sights of a gun pointing directly at her.

With little reason to stay put, Alice stood up and walked out of the shadows and towards the bench.

The odd couple stared at Alice as she approached them. The worried look upon their faces made her doubt the old woman's story. Alice stopped in front of the bench, prepared to be her own executioner.

"I want to be a vampire," she said.

The man looked at her incredulously and with his companion rose to his feet.

"I think," he said, "you need help." With that, taking his companion's arm, he began to walk away towards the steps.

Lucy had closed her eyes. Gwawl was watching and cursed silently in disappointment at the vampire's reticence.

"I need to be undead," Alice called after them, "to defeat Gwawl."

The nosferatu stopped and turned around with startling speed, their faces suddenly coming to life, pulsing with anger, veins standing proud of the skin as if their bodies were in a rush to deliver blood to their brains.

The woman spoke to her companion, not in a feminine voice but a distorted, deep, manly voice. "Let's do it. Gwawl is the enemy of us all, and you need to feed."

"No," he replied, shaking his head. "Something's wrong. He's here." The man seemed to be panicking. "I'm sure he's here."

The woman put her hands out to calm him. "Okay," she said in a more human voice, "we'll eat elsewhere."

"No!" shouted Alice, "help me."

But the vampires just quickened their pace away from her.

Alice could see the last hope of seeing Kerry alive fading and her own fate worsening. "Please," she screamed.

The woman turned. "You can't defeat him as a vampire. Who told you that?"

Gwawl could wait no longer; he had to intervene.

"I did!" said Lucy, standing in the vampire's path.

Alice began to run towards the vampires, fearful of what they might do to Lucy, but Alice had not put two feet forward when Lucy shot out one arm to hold the vampiress by the neck, and lifted her off the floor. Without even looking at him, Lucy's free hand crushed through the skin and bone of the other creature's chest cavity, retrieved its heart and tore it in two with her teeth. They had cast him out in this small body as a final insult and so it was in this form that he would kill his enemies.

Alice stopped and began to turn, but Lucy ran after her, still clutching the female vampire by the neck. She caught Alice and threw her to the floor with a strength that would have been surprising even in the form of Smith-Kurr. She pinned Alice's arms to the floor, with her knees and brought the head of the surviving vampire towards Alice's neck.

Alice tried to struggle but the weight upon her arms and waist held her so tightly that movement was impossible. The vampire resisted Gwawl's demand until his other hand, smeared with her lover's blood pulled her hair back, forcing her mouth open in a scream, like a zoologist forcing a snake to give up its venom.

"Your grandfather is still a prisoner of mine and I haven't allowed him to eat for two hundred years. Now do as I say or live!"

The woman's gums drew back and fangs grew out of them, like claws from a cat's foot in an automatic response to the proximity of warm, pulsing blood.

The tyres of Janet's car squealed into the square. A rear door was flung open and Drudwyn leapt out, tearing toward Lucy and Alice. But he could only see one enemy and flew like a wolf at a moose into the vampire. Drudwyn's momentum rocked the vampire away from Alice's neck but Gwawl kept hold of the undead weapon and, grabbing Drudwyn by the scruff of the neck, flung him twenty feet away where he crashed with a whimper into the windscreen of Janet's car. Drudwyn's attack had given Alice a brief moment in which she had one free arm. Her hand clawed at Gwawl's face and grabbed at his hair to no avail.

Kerry had barely alighted from the car himself when he saw Gwawl look through Lucy's eyes at him. To see this little girl's body pushing a vampire towards Alice's neck with one hand whilst pinning her down and throwing a nine stone dog twenty feet was far more fearsome than Smith-Kurr had appeared. He saw Lucy look at him and then at Janet in the car, there was a brief moment when Kerry spied the suggestion of haste and indecision in the girlish face.

Kerry wavered with his own indecision and then instead of rushing towards Lucy he turned to Janet.

"Decloak her," he demanded quietly.

Janet was ahead of Kerry and had already extracted a saltcellar and a clove of garlic from her handbag and begun to arrange a pile of matches on the floor in front of her, but it would take more than such this-worldly things to affect Gwawl.

The vampire was beginning to resist Gwawl's attempts now that she could see a glimmer of hope of rescue. Gwawl looked up from his task as he heard the chanting. Grabbing Alice by the throat with his spare hand, he jumped up and ran towards where Kerry stood in front of Janet, the two bodies on either side of his tiny frame dancing in pain as they touched on asphyxia. Drudwyn looked on, barking in bewilderment as Kerry virtually stumbled into Gwawl's path with his fists not even clenched. His long, unplastered arm stretched out and grabbed at Gwawl's hair. Gwawl's raised foot kicked forward into Kerry's chest and sent him crashing to the floor centimetres away from Janet.

Janet stopped chanting a split second after Kerry landed by her side. Gwawl stopped dead in his tracks and looked straight at Janet, not now with rage or vicious intent but with the same expression Kerry had had when he realised that the girl he had looked after was Gwawl. It was a look of betrayal and of sadness for in front of the cross-legged figure of Janet was a small pile of matches, garlic, salt and in the fire, Kerry's open hand, burning as it delivered hair wrenched from Lucy's head, to the flames. Janet had imparted to Kerry the simple tools needed to remove a blanket.

There was a snarl from the side of Janet's car. Gwawl turned to face Drudwyn and Drudwyn looked upon Gwawl for the first time in 2,000 years. This had been his elusive quarry since his master, Manawyddan, had sent him into to this world in search of him. Gwawl dropped his two prisoners and metamorphosed back into Smith-Kurr, a huge sword and shield once more in his hands. As Drudwyn pounced he too changed, growing to reveal a terrifying hound, three times the size of his pet manifestation. Gwawl swung his sword at the dog as soon as it came into range but the hound moved so fast and was so large now that as it hit Gwawl his legs buckled and he fell to the floor. The sword did not swing again. Bone crushing teeth scythed through the soft neck muscle and Drudwyn emerged from the heap of body, shield and blood holding the dismembered head of Gwawl in his huge jaws.

He padded over to his master, his size waning and dropped the head now in the shape of Lucy at the feet of Kerry.

The end

Historical Note

The Mabinogion is a collection of Folklore from the British Isles, predominantly Welsh in origin. Sleeping Dog, was based on a number of stories from this collection. However certain details in Sleeping Dog, that refer to the Mabinogion have been changed and Sleeping Dog should not be viewed as an accurate description of any individual character from the myths.